No Rest
for the Wicked

A John and Sarah Jarad
Nantucket Mystery

MARTHA REED

NO REST FOR THE WICKED
A John and Sarah Jarad Nantucket Mystery
Copyright © 2017 by Martha Reed

ISBN-13: 978-0-9985648-0-7
ISBN-10: 099856480X

First Buccaneer/KMA Pittsburgh trade paperback print edition
Published February 2017
Cover art by Karen Phillips - www.KarenPhillipscovers.com
Printed in the United States of America

Available from Amazon.com, CreateSpace.com, other retail outlets, Kindle, and other devices.

DEDICATION

To my grandfather

Samuel Clarke Reed, Jr.
Gentleman and scholar

This one's for you, Pop.

**Books in the
John and Sarah Jarad Nantucket Mystery Series
by Martha Reed**

ACKNOWLEDGMENTS

With heartfelt thanks to:

Lori Rader-Day

Who first asked about "Invisible Book #3"

And to

Timons Esaias

Who kick-started the engine.

Thank you.

Additionally,

Sisters in Crime, Inc.

The Mary Roberts Rinehart Pittsburgh Chapter of Sisters in Crime, Inc.

Generous mentors and friends:

Annette Dashofy, Timons Esaias, Ramona DeFelice Long

Insightful editor: Ramona DeFelice Long

Graphic designer Karen Phillips for the amazing cover design.

Beta readers: Sue Em Davenport, Laura Seebacher, Holly Dynoske,

Alli Miller, Linda Banas-Reno, Carol Anne Sheppard,

Sandy Marciniak, and Betty Kubina.

With special appreciation to the members of The Mutinous Crew:

Stephanie Salo, Ginger Thomas, Nancy Holsinger,

Samuel C. Reed, III, Sarah Reed,

Joan Widdoes, Reed Widdoes, and Molly Widdoes.

The beatings will continue until morale improves.

* * * * *

Daisy, Daisy, give me your answer, do

I'm half crazy, all for the love of you.

It won't be a stylish marriage,

I can't afford a carriage,

But you'd look sweet, upon the seat

Of a bicycle built for two.

--Harry Dacre, *Daisy Bell*, 1892

CHAPTER ONE

Monday, May 30, 2011

I knew Sarah was gone the second I stepped inside our condo. Her closet was stripped bare. She'd left an untidy mess of hangers and shoeboxes piled in the middle of our bedroom floor. Picking a pillow up off of the bed, I inhaled her scent. I could still smell Sarah in the linen.

Strolling out onto the terrace, I studied the busy Pittsburgh cityscape spreading to the horizon beneath my feet. Sarah was out there now, somewhere, gone, but I am a patient man.

Stretching my arms to the sky, I filled my lungs with a promising new purpose. Dad used to say, "You need to always have something to look forward to, Mason, to add spice and focus to your life." As usual, he was correct.

I will find Sarah Hawthorne again, and soon. I am very much looking forward to this. Game on.

Chapter Two

Tuesday, June 5, 2012

John Jarad pulled to a stop before the landfill gate. The attendant was MIA, probably out back sneaking a quick smoke on county time. John gave the cruiser's horn a quick tap. He settled in to wait.

Old school Nantucketers were notorious for their thrift. They often had to be, since cash was scarce and everything on the island other than fish or sand needed to be imported. Make do, or do without, had been their timeworn motto. John recalled a childhood trip he had made once with his great-uncle, Ethan Jarad. Uncle Ethan claimed to have furnished his entire house with cast-off items he had culled from the dump.

"Folks these day are soft," Uncle Ethan had grumbled. "They've had it too easy. A flick of paint and some wood glue and these chairs will be good as new. You'll see. I recycled before it got fashionable."

That memory was almost twenty-five years old. *Time is a tricky thing. You take it day by day, until suddenly you look up, and a quarter of a century is gone.* Uncle Ethan wouldn't recognize the dump now. The landfill had gone upscale and commercial. John looked up as an attendant trotted around the gatehouse. He recognized Debbie Cooper, a 'Sconset neighbor. Deb put a hand up to shield her eyes from the mid-morning sun. She thumbed a button to release the gate, and she waved him in.

"Hey, Lieutenant Jarad. Nice to see you."

"It's detective now, Deb." John firmed his mouth. His demotion was fresh, and it still stung.

"That's right. Heard about that. Sorry." Deb uncomfortably shuffled her feet. "Talley's waiting by the chipper. Wouldn't tell me what it was about. Keeping it a secret."

"Thanks." John followed the asphalt lane past mounds of discarded appliances waiting to be cannibalized for parts. He turned right at the twenty-foot tall stack of bald tires and made a left at a gunmetal dumpster brimming with glass bottles and aluminum cans, part of a widely supported Boy Scout recycling campaign. He slowed the cruiser to a crawl as he passed a sixty-foot long flexible tube that processed bulk and soft discards into compost. "The Digester" terrified and fascinated John in equal measure. He knew that the compost produced was nothing but beneficial, and that it was distributed free to local gardeners who treasured the compost like black gold, but his imagination was random and slightly warped. He kept wondering how long it would take The Digester to process a corpse.

The cruiser bounced at the end of the asphalt lane. He began to follow an increasingly sodden and rutted track back to the older part of the dump, back to the cells.

Before Nantucket's population had mushroomed, public trash had been managed in a completely different manner. Earlier in the twentieth century, before the two great wars, dozens of enormous concrete cells had been built in the dump, one right after the other in one long row, like a honeycomb. Trash trucks had simply backed up to each cell and dumped everything in, moving on to the next cell once the first one was filled. The mixed trash in the cells was allowed to rot, often for decades, naturally composting until the need arose for a fresh empty cell. Then the landfill workers would excavate the oldest cells using a backhoe, emptying them out to be refilled in a never-ending trash cycle. The system had worked without a hitch until the Seventies, when the new recycling policy had swept the island, and the pre-sorting system came into play.

Talley was standing by the mustard colored commercial chipper. He stepped on his cigarette, opened the cruiser's passenger door, and lankily climbed in.

"We've got something bad, John. Big bad, I think."

John's internal alarm went off, because Talley was an old stoner hippie and the most laid-back person he knew, and Talley looked shaken. "What is it?"

"Head for the cells." Talley pointed his dirt-encrusted finger. "I'd rather show you." He straightened his neon orange safety vest, trying to regain his composure. "You know how these cells work, right? Fill 'em, and spill 'em?"

"Yes."

"We've been cleaning them out, same as usual, until last summer. Some UMASS grad student came by to shop the Madaket Mall. Took a look around at all of the crap and realized that the trash in each cell represented what he called 'a decade's worth of discarded cultural information.' Crap. Complete crap. Complicated my life, because the Commonwealth gave him permission to start excavating the older cells. Now, I don't really mind, because it's a stinking job no matter who does it, but still, I need to oversee things since the brainiac grad school boyo can't figure out how to operate the backhoe."

Talley patted his vest before remembering where he was. He slid his cigarette pack back into his pocket.

"I will say that sometimes what we find in the cells is interesting. That last one we dug out was WWI. Had to be pretty damn careful there.

4

Gave me the yips when we found live Naval ordinance in it." He coughed out a laugh. "The crew started excavating this new cell around the middle of May. Timeline looked about right, too. I'd say 1920 to 1930, between the war years. Thought it should be dull enough. Boy, was I ever wrong."

John pulled up in front of the stained concrete cells. Three of the older ones already stood empty. He parked in front of the half-empty fourth cell. A trim, middle-aged woman in a collapsible canvas sunhat, and a 30-something man wearing jeans and a denim shirt were waiting. Talley jumped out of the cruiser first. John followed as the landfill odor smothered his sinuses. No wonder Talley smoked like a chimney. You'd have to do something to counteract the acrid reeking stench.

"Detective Jarad? How d'you do? I'm Dr. Belinda Peabody. This is my assistant, Brad Lamott."

"Nice to meet you. What have we got?"

The state archaeologists were standing over a small, half-rotten steamer trunk. The trunk's convex lid was banded with heavy leather straps. It had protective brass corners and decorative tacks. Back in the day, the trunk had cost someone real money. A name was stenciled across one end in bold black letters: Mrs. Howard Greaves Spenser, Stuyvesant Square, New York.

"Late nineteenth century would be my best guess." Brad was so excited he was bouncing off his toes like a greyhound before a race. "Once I recognized the name, I suggested to Dr. Peabody that we should notify the police. If this trunk really belonged to Nell Spenser, it might contain important evidence."

"And I concurred." Dr. Peabody polished her glasses eagerly. "This trunk may have had something to do with the Baby Alice Spenser kidnapping."

The name hit John like a gong. Baby Alice Spenser was the most notorious cold case crime Nantucket had ever known. A ransom kidnapping from the Twenties, the toddler had never been recovered. Her kidnappers had never been identified, or brought to justice.

John noticed that Dr. Peabody and Brad were already wearing gloves. "Lift the lid," he said.

Brad grasped the corroded hasp and tugged. The trunk was swollen shut from the years of burial dampness. The lid resisted. Brad dug in his heels, grunting with effort. The lid sprang open, spilling a choking wave of mushroom mold into the air.

They leaned in. The trunk was filled with faded linen dresses and straw hats. Dr. Peabody removed three of the hats, placing them gently on the opened lid, revealing a layer of crumpled newspaper. She unfolded the newspaper carefully. Her shoulders slumped. She took one step back.

"Dear sweet Jesus."

Wrapped in a bundle were the mummified remains of a toddler wearing a lace dress and kid leather shoes. Her auburn hair had not decayed. John could still see her famous shoulder-length curls. The child lay on her right side, with her face turned to left. He noted her sunken, hollowed eye sockets. Her mouth gaped open in a silent and eternal scream.

Talley swallowed hard. "That ain't no doll now, is it?"

"No," John said, as his world exploded. "We just found Baby Alice Spenser."

CHAPTER THREE

"Chief Nunn is on her way." Detective CJ Allamand inspected her digital camera. "ETA twenty minutes. She wanted to download the Baby Alice case notes first."

John reached for the crime scene kit in the back of CJ's SUV. He wished CJ wouldn't keep her voice so carefully neutral when speaking about their new chief. John knew CJ was doing it to be kind, but in the end it only sounded awkward, and actually made things worse. "I'd do the same thing, in her shoes."

"I don't know how you stay so reasonable about this. If I got demoted, I'd still be pissed."

"Chief Nunn had nothing to do with my demotion, CJ. The Council unanimously sanctioned it." He straightened. "I had two choices in April, after Chief Brock retired: I could swallow my pride and accept the demotion, or I could quit. I'm not a quitter. Never will be."

"No one is saying that you are. We all hated the way the Council dropped it on us. Chief Brock is retiring, here, meet the new Deputy Chief, by the way, we're restructuring the force and removing the Lieutenancy to streamline command. What a complete load of bullshit. Council needed a scapegoat because of what happened to Toby Talbot, and they picked you. Bastards! They used our own Collective Bargaining Agreement against us.

I'll give you credit for holding your temper in the union hall that day. I would've walked."

"I did give the idea of hitting the door hard some serious thought."

"Half the force would've walked out with you." CJ took the CSI kit from his hand. "You should have seen Ted's face. I thought he was going to have a stroke. He wants to have "Fucked by Section 3.2" tattooed on his arm, as a reminder that the union steward caved. You didn't do anything wrong."

"Yes, CJ, I did." John crossed his arms. "I lost control of my service weapon. Because of that, Toby died. That's what the Council, and the public, can't forgive. I let them down. I need to own it."

"Toby was a cop. He died in the line of duty. He knew what he was getting into going in. What happened to you could've happened to any one of us. I'd bet money Mercy Talbot was behind that whisper campaign."

"She's his mother, can you blame her? Mercy may never forgive me. I know people are gossiping. I know they wonder why I didn't find a new commission somewhere else. My own mother suggested that it might be time to consider a career change."

"With George Robey dead, there's an opening for an island land developer."

"You do know that's not funny, right?"

"Sorry. Couldn't help myself. What does Sarah have to say about all of this?"

"We haven't really talked about it much."

"Really? Why not?"

"She's got enough to worry about with the twins, and preeclampsia, and all the rest of that medical shit, plus the new house. She knows that I'll deal with it." John rubbed his hands together. "Some folks call me stubborn, but I'm not leaving Nantucket just because things got tough. I know I made a mistake, had a lapse in judgment. Now I have to make up for it. In the end, my title doesn't matter. Lieutenant-Commander, Detective, what the hell. I don't care what I'm called. Taking care of this place, and doing the right work, is what really matters to me."

"Damn, John. I'm glad to hear you say that. Two years ago, you would've said fuck it all, and walked out."

"Thanks, CJ." Their boots crunched the gravel as they walked toward the half emptied cell. "I know I made the right choice. This Baby Alice case, it feels like what I was born to do."

"Are we certain about the ID?"

"As sure as we can be, right now, until the DNA test. The body fit the description, clothing and all."

"That happened so long ago it seems like a myth. What year was that?"

"1921. Don't give me that look. I'm not that smart. I Googled it on my iPhone. Wikipedia had a nice summary, too."

"Ha! Modern police methods." CJ snorted. "I can remember my grandparents discussing Baby Alice when they had cocktails on the porch." She scratched her head. "Holy hell. I'm not sure how accurate what I remember really is. A cold case from ninety some-odd years ago." CJ mashed wet newspaper into the mud as she stepped around a greasy puddle. "Good thing I wore gumboots. This ground is nasty. Who are those two?"

"State archaeologists from UMASS. They discovered the trunk and found the body."

He turned as an unmarked police cruiser pulled up next to the SUV. Officer Hank Viera was driving. Hank ducked his head. He wouldn't meet John's eyes. Deputy Police Chief Anetta Nunn was seated in the passenger side of the vehicle. She stepped from the car first. John saw that the new Chief was wearing sensible rubber Wellington boots. Grudgingly, he gave her credit for anticipating the damp conditions at the dump. His own boots were plastered with slime, and most likely permanently shot. He'd probably never get the smell off of them.

The Chief pointed between two tall stacks of retread tires. "Officer Viera, tape this area off. Keep the public out. That includes members of the press. No one gets through without my direct say-so." Chief Nunn was carrying her Samsung Galaxy tablet in one hand. Early on, she had impressed them with her technical savvy. She stepped around the front of the cruiser as Hank opened the trunk. "Detectives Jarad, Allamand? You told me the Film Festival would be our excitement this month. I hope we're not setting a precedent. What have we got?"

Once again John noted that Chief Nunn had more than a passing resemblance to a stockier version of First Lady Michelle Obama. The Chief was in her mid-forties, handsome rather than pretty. She seemed partial to tailored pinstriped pantsuits and sleeveless blouses that revealed her ripped arms. John already knew that the Chief rented a modest studio apartment mid-island, that she could be seen running on the moors every morning at dawn, and that she nursed a bum right knee.

"I believe we've found Baby Alice Spenser, sir." John still had some difficulty saying "sir" when looking at a woman, but Chief Nunn had directly ordered the entire force to do so. She had explained that it was easier to use one consistent term to express seniority, plus it had simply been too painful to watch Sergeant Ted Parsons repeatedly stumble whenever Ted had tried calling her "ma'am."

"Nothing like starting out of the gate with a bang." She flicked the tablet. "Baby Alice Spenser kidnapping, Nantucket, 1921. Nationwide manhunt. Ransom paid, child never recovered, kidnappers never identified." She looked up. "Think *Great Gatsby*. The Roaring Twenties was quite a time. We'll see a huge media response with this one." She turned for the trunk. "Are those the archaeologists? What have they got for us?"

"Dr. Belinda Peabody, sir. And her assistant, Brad Lamott."

The Chief strode ahead. "I'm Deputy Chief Nunn. You've made a discovery?"

"Yes." Dr. Peabody blinked repeatedly. "As you can see, Chief, we retrieved the trunk *in situ* from this cell. Nothing else around it has been touched. However, once Brad noticed the stenciled name, we called the police immediately."

"Thank you both for that. That was extremely responsive." Chief Nunn peered over the lid. "I can see what appears to be a child's body, and that it matches the description of Alice Spenser. Who has touched this trunk so far?"

"Just us two." Brad momentarily looked confused. He held up his hands. "Dr. Peabody and I. We wore gloves."

"Good." She raised her tablet and fired off a panoramic series of pictures. "I don't want anyone else touching this trunk, unless they're wearing a full Tyvek suit. I don't want anyone else even breathing on it. Brad, please put everything back in the way you found it, and close the lid. I want to avoid additional contamination. From this point forward, the trunk needs to be kept as pristine as possible." She pointed at the gritty cells. "Detective Allamand? We'll need a digital sweep of the entire crime scene. When you're done, I'll call the Coroner's office and have them collect the trunk. We'll continue the examination at the county morgue, under controlled conditions." She turned to the archaeologists. "Do you have any objections to us collecting DNA samples from you both, right now? A cotton swab on the inside of your cheek will do. Detective Allamand brought kits."

"If that's what you need, certainly," Dr. Peabody said.

"I don't have a problem with it," Brad agreed.

"Detective Allamand? Please proceed. Detective Jarad? One moment, please."

She pulled John to one side. "I want you to lead this investigation. Before we go any further, I need to know that you're comfortable taking on that role. This case will be extremely high profile. The Bureau will want to send a team." She shrugged. "Yes, this is our jurisdiction, but the FBI has a long memory on unsolved kidnappings. I can cover the Bureau angle, I still have some contacts there, but I need to know if you can handle serving as the local lead."

John touched his holster to make sure his replacement Glock G17 9mm was secure. He despised this new nervous tic, but he couldn't seem to stop doing it. "Yes, sir. This case is mine. I want it."

"Good. I thought so. Detective Allamand will serve as your CSI support." Her shoulders relaxed. "We'll need to notify the Spenser family, before news of this gets out. They deserve to be forewarned, so they can prepare for what's coming. Let's do that face to face. I'm not a big fan of cold calls, or text messaging." She folded her tablet, and tucked it under her arm. "Ready, Detective Jarad? Let's roll."

CHAPTER FOUR

The moorland along Milestone Road was alive with dancing blossom. Guidebooks suggested that October was the best month to see Nantucket's natural beauty, but early June had its moments, too. The hillocks sheltered pockets of daisies, and they protected the tough clusters of magenta beach rose and yellow Scotch broom. On the left, the landscape flattened into a meadow before the land dropped into the sea.

John noted their location. He started looking for the stump of the tree where Billy Bear had died. Back in February, a private landowner had called to complain that someone had illegally axed a tree on her property, without her knowledge or her consent. John suspected that Ozzie and some of his friends had chopped the tree down to eliminate the constant and painful reminder of his father's hit and run homicide. Technically, it was trespassing with intent, but once John had explained his suspicion to the landowner over a tepid cup of Earl Grey tea, she had immediately declined the offer of further investigation. She had ended the discussion by stating point blank that if the culprit was ever found that she would not be pressing charges.

John glanced at Chief Nunn. She was busily scrolling through her hybrid tablet, reviewing the Baby Alice Spenser case notes yet again. John gave her credit for tackling her new duties with both hands, but as he studied the receding tree stump in the rearview mirror he wondered if not being from Nantucket might prove to be a handicap. Life on Nantucket was multi-layered, and complex. Island history was alive, intertwined between the living and the dead. Past events still echoed into the present day. Chief Nunn might be able to come to grips with their new cases going forward, but would she ever comprehend the meaningful depths of their older ones?

She double tapped the screen with her index finger. "The Coroner wants to see the trunk *in situ*, first, before he sends the van. Is this normal? Is Dr. Jenkins usually so thorough?"

"Pretty much," John said. "Paul has a curious mind. He has professional caliber OCD."

She nodded, and looked ahead as he turned right on Archer Lane.

"I'm fond of that water tower," she said. "It's the only other black on this island." She cut her eyes to see how he took the remark. "That was meant to be a joke, Detective Jarad." She sat back. "Listen. I know our situation is awkward, but I'm counting on your support. You know Nantucket, and the Spenser family, better than I ever will, since you grew up with them."

Speaking her mind was another aspect of the new Chief that John admired. He knew she had drive. He had seen her impressive list of accomplishments with New Orleans Metro. He knew she was tough, because she had been awarded special commendations twice for her work during Hurricane Katrina. Even with all of this to like, John still found it difficult to work with the Chief directly. It wasn't her fault. It was his. His bruised ego continued to insist on making things as uncomfortable as possible. The hurdle was getting tiresome. John felt the need to push past all of that, and get on with the job. He cleared his throat.

"Not really. I mean, I didn't grow up with the Spensers. They only summer here. They're American royalty, like the Kennedys. Fly in on a private jet." Once again he was starting to sound negative and obstructive. John changed tack. "They're not snobs. I don't mean to say that. They're very active socially. You can always count on them for a donation at a charity fundraiser, but I wouldn't say that we mingle. The Spensers keep to themselves. They always have."

He turned right again onto private Spenser Way. The driveway topcoat was imported pea gravel and not the familiar crushed oyster shell. The driveway also stretched for a solid three quarters of a mile. John didn't want to calculate what that amount of pea gravel had cost. On an island where property was valued by the square foot, the Spenser's estate Moorhaven held sixteen acres. John overheard Howard Spenser IV once joke at a benefit that he regretted that Moorhaven was so puny; the family had to restrict themselves to using the private putting green since they didn't have enough land to build a proper nine-hole golf course.

John tapped the wheel. He felt at a loss for words. *How do I explain to the Chief that even the Spensers' summer home implied the family's unlimited wealth and power?*

"What can you tell me about them?" Chief Nunn asked.

"I've heard the scuttlebutt. Back in the day, Howard Spenser the First saw Eleanor Winthrop on the Broadway stage. That would have been around 1900. Nell was beautiful, and barely twenty. Her act was wearing a skin-tight flesh-toned bodysuit covered with strategic silk flowers, like an Eve. She sang popular songs as she rode a golden bicycle around the stage. Howard the First fell head over heels in love with Nell. He proposed marriage."

Chief Nunn settled in. "Nice story so far."

"The problem was that Howard was only a junior at Yale University in New Haven, and students couldn't get married. If he did get married, he'd be expelled. Besides, his Boston Brahmin family was appalled by Howard's choice. Actresses were no better than prostitutes, in their eyes. They carried Howard off to a minister, who advised Howard not to marry anyone, since his poor choice of a future wife indicated an obvious mental instability. The minister also said that if Howard did marry Nell that they shouldn't have any children, since those undesirable character traits could be inherited. The sins of the father, and so on."

"And?"

"Howard immediately dropped out of Yale to marry Nell. His family wrote him off because of the scandal."

"Good man! I like Howard already. But you said he was from Boston. How did they end up on Nantucket?"

"Howard and Nell never lived in Boston. They preferred New York. 'Sconset was the summer retreat for the New York acting set. Howard and Nell built Moorhaven as their summer home. Wait until you see it." John pointed a finger down the lane. "It's some house. Sixteen bedrooms, with matching tiled baths. The plumbing was considered cutting edge for its day. A walled garden with fruit trees. Tennis courts, a croquet lawn. They used to keep albino peacocks. Howard and Nell hosted blowout weekend parties. Male guests slept in the yard on cots under a big canvas tent. Local folks used to sneak up to the house and peek in the windows to watch the dancing. It was quite a scene. Their enemies called them Noward and Hell. They were legendary."

"Sounds like it. Where does Baby Alice fit into all of this?"

"Remember how the minister warned Howard and Nell not to have children? They had six." John reached up and massaged his temple. "Let me remember this right. Three in a row: Howard Junior, Franklin, and

Daisy. There was a skip, and then they had three more: Winston, Millicent, and Baby Alice."

He slowed to navigate a curve around a solitary spreading oak tree. Its trunk was lushly covered with a blanket of blue-green ivy. John was sorry to see that underneath the ivy, the tree was dead. The bark had sloughed off leaving ugly bare patches. Its skeletal branches clutched at the sky like ivory talons. John was enough of a Nantucketer to feel a momentary sorrow over the loss. Big trees were rare on the island.

He shook the grim feeling off. "All of the Spensers are extremely good-looking people, both the women, and the men. They all share ginger or auburn hair. From what I've heard, Daisy was the standout. They called Daisy the Spenser Rose. No one could touch her for looks. Daisy was the ideal flapper: slim, energetic, with golden-red hair. I've heard she was rebellious. She rolled her stockings down to her knees. She was seen smoking cigarettes in public."

"Daisy Spenser was a ho?" Chief Nunn laughed. "How times have changed. Howard and Nell were what, the current Howard Spenser's grandparents?"

"Great-grandparents. There's another generation in there. The current Howard Spenser is the Fourth. He has one son, Addison, who's around my age. Five generations of Spensers - wait a minute, six now, with Libby - have summered on Nantucket, for over a hundred years. They're one of the island's legacy families." John straightened the wheel as Moorhaven swung into view.

"Oh my." Chief Nunn sat up. "You weren't kidding."

"I warned you."

Moorhaven was a massive three-story shingle style home with a full-length porch. A row of sharply pointed dormer windows punctuated a roofline that ended in rounded turrets at both ends. The shingles were stained a soft pigeon gray, a rarity on Nantucket where most shingled homes were allowed to naturally fade as a concession to the constant and corrosive salt air. Moorhaven's windowsills and its double-hung front door were thickly painted a crisp white. The driveway spilled into a square gravel court surrounded by mounds of pale pink roses that matched a cascade of larger roses framing the front door. John pulled into the gravel court, and parked.

Chief Nunn picked up her tablet and stepped from the cruiser. She squared her shoulders. "I will not be intimidated. Gave that shit up years ago. Detective Jarad, I'll lead."

Knee high boxwood hedges, trimmed to perfection, lined the crisscrossed brick path. On either side of the walk, a formal English garden sprouted a riot of lavender, spotted foxglove, yellow iris, and Russian sage. In the center of the garden, a nude female statue was doing her very best to protect her modesty with her hands while perched on top of a three-tiered fountain that spilled into a shallow reflecting pool. John noticed sudden underwater flashes of bright orange and brilliant gold. The pool was pulsating with imported Japanese koi.

"Let's do this." Chief Nunn mashed the doorbell with her thumb. A stately eight note Winchester chime echoed through the house.

John looked up. He studied Moorhaven's original quarter board hanging above the door. It had been allowed to weather. He could barely make out the Spenser family's motto, *Nos Protegat Nostrum*, from the faded lettering under its coat of ancient shellac. Unfortunately, his pursuit of a law enforcement curriculum had precluded the study of romance languages, including Latin. John reached for his iPhone and quickly snapped a picture. He would have to look the meaning up later.

"You're paying attention to the wrong things, Detective Jarad," Chief Nunn said. "Don't get distracted."

"The Spensers have a butler," he warned.

"Get out. Who has a butler, on Nantucket?"

"They do."

The left half of the front door swung open to reveal a sallow man wearing a well-cut navy blue suit with a crisp tuxedo shirt and a butler's tie. The drooping bags under his eyes made him look like a basset hound. He expressed no obvious surprise at seeing members of the Nantucket force standing on the doorstep.

"May I help you?" He had a deep bass voice with an English accent.

"Deputy Chief Nunn, from the Nantucket force, with Detective Jarad. We need to speak to Howard Spenser, immediately."

"Mr. Spenser is on the court. He left orders not to be disturbed until his match is over."

Chief Nunn settled her stance. "Our information is of the gravest concern to his family. He will want to hear what we have to say, ASAP."

The butler appeared to consider their request. "Follow me."

John pocketed his Ray-Bans. The butler led them through a cavernous central hallway toward a glassed-in Victorian veranda in the back. Moorhaven's grand double staircase had two four-foot tall lighthouses, including glass lenses and working light bulbs, for newel posts. Lithesome mermaids riding seahorses and carrying tridents adorned the spindles on the bannisters that rose up either side of the hall to a shadowy second floor landing. Their footsteps echoed intermittently whenever they encountered one of the woven sea grass rugs scattered across the Spanish tile floor. Everything about Moorhaven spoke of an elegant and sophisticated sensibility. Antique Boston lowboys hugged the walls between sets of finely painted local seascapes. A large gilt-framed painting featured a cluster of children busily building a sandcastle near Brant Point. John recognized the artist's signature immediately. *Kurt Stockton*. He shivered, and firmly shook the feeling off.

The veranda was filled with leafy tropical palms and potted orchids. It opened onto a lush lawn with a shimmering rectangular swimming pool. A young man was standing in the shallow end of the water. He was holding a wiggling toddler high above his head. The family resemblance between the two was obvious. The man sported a well-trimmed red beard, and the child's damp auburn curls clung to her scalp. The bearded man suddenly dipped the child into the water. She screamed with delighted laughter.

"Again, Daddy! Again."

The sunlight dappling the water nearly blinded John to the vision of the stunningly beautiful brunette woman in a polka dot bikini raising a glass of iced tea to her lips. As John followed Chief Nunn outside, the family froze.

"Jamison?" the man in the pool asked. "What is it?"

"These officers have asked to speak with your father, Mr. Addison."

"Has something happened to Mother?" Addison Spenser clutched the toddler to his chest. He waded to the side of the pool, and handed her up. "Here, Julia. Take Libby." Placing both hands on the edge of the pool, Addison Spenser easily lifted himself out of the water. He reached for a towel. "Call Dad off the court, Jamison. Will you, please?"

There was no need. John overheard the bantering words of a friendly dispute, and Howard Spenser IV stepped into view. He was wearing tennis whites and matching black elastic knee support. He was arguing with a fit, extremely tanned woman with a stylishly cut magenta pageboy and pink plastic framed glasses. John recognized Howard's cousin, Camilla.

"It's no use arguing, Cam. That last serve was an absolute ace. It clearly hit the tape. You should have been wearing your cheaters." Seeing them clustered by the pool, Howard stopped in his tracks, blinking rapidly. "What's all this?" he rumbled.

Addison draped the towel around his neck. "We're not sure yet, Dad. They wanted to talk with you."

The Chief stepped forward. "Deputy Chief Nunn, sir. This is Detective Jarad. We have news that concerns your family."

"I don't believe we've met yet, Chief." Howard grasped her hand. "Detective Jarad. Seen you around. Don't keep us in suspense. Out with it. What have you got?"

"Sir." Chief Nunn cleared her throat. "We recovered a trunk from the Madaket landfill. It contains the body of a child, a young child, a girl. Our investigation is still preliminary, but we believe we've found Baby Alice Spenser."

"Good God." Howard IV fumbled for a chair. He sat down hard.

"Howard?" Camilla placed her hand on his shoulder. "Are you alright?"

"I don't believe it, Cam. After all these years! It's come back to haunt us again."

CHAPTER FIVE

Camilla Spenser was clearly used to taking charge of things. "Chief Nunn, you said? Detective Jarad? Please, take a seat. There's no need to stand on formality."

She reached for the pitcher with her long-fingered hands, and poured out a glass of iced tea, handing it to Howard before pouring out a second one for herself. John noticed that her hands were trembling.

"I hope you can sympathize with what your news means to us. The family was devastated when Alice was taken. Any reminder of that event is painful, even after all of these years."

Chief Nunn sat on the edge of her chair. "That's why we wanted to speak to you immediately. It was our first consideration."

"Thank you for that. Would you like some refreshment? Mango tea, Arnold Palmer? Some water?"

"Water is fine," Chief Nunn said politely.

"Frizzante, or still?"

"I'm sorry, what?"

Confusion clouded Chief Nunn's face. John realized that she didn't understand that she was being offered two different types of water.

"Still is fine," he said, reaching for the glass.

Howard plucked off his canvas tennis hat. He ran his hand over his bald, heavily freckled head. "I can't believe it. This seems like a dream. Who would've thought we'd be dealing with this now? It's been over ninety years!"

Camilla steepled her fingers. "You said you found Alice in a trunk. Are you sure it's her?"

"We're as certain as we can be, until we test for DNA." Chief Nunn powered her tablet. "We have some *in situ* photos, if you'd like to see them. I need to warn you, they're graphic."

Addison leaned in over Camilla's shoulder. He peered at the screen. "Is that the trunk you found?"

"Yes. This is the trunk we recovered from the Madaket landfill."

"I suppose it could be one of ours." Camilla adjusted her glasses. "Lord knows there are two dozen more just like it upstairs. Dusty, old things. You can't give them away."

Chief Nunn flicked the screen. "This one had the name 'Mrs. Howard Greaves Spenser' written on it."

"That would mean it was one of Nell's," Howard said promptly.

"Is there any way to confirm that this trunk was hers?" Chief Nunn asked.

"After a hundred years?" Camilla pulled her glasses off. "That was before my time. I can tell you that I never heard anyone say that a trunk was missing from the house. Howard? Did you ever hear anyone say that?"

"No." He rubbed his chin. "Not to my knowledge."

Julia moved closer, jogging Libby on her hip. Chief Nunn flicked the screen again. Julia gasped. "Is that her? Is that Alice?"

"Yes. These are the remains that were found in the trunk this morning."

"I can't look at that. It's too horrible." Julia quickly turned her back. Libby had fallen asleep in her mother's arms. She looked like a red-haired cherub. "It's too sad. Addison, I'm going to take Libby upstairs. When she wakes up, I'll get her changed, and give her some lunch."

"Sweetheart, do you want some help?"

"No, Addy. I've got it. You stay here. You can fill me in later on what I've missed."

Howard rested his forearms on the wrought iron table. "Could you turn the screen this way a bit? Oh my. Yes, that is grim, isn't it? It does look like Alice, though, from the pictures we have in the family albums." He sat back, and rubbed one ear. "Strange to see her in color."

"How did Alice die?" Addison swallowed. He pulled out a chair and sat. "Did she smother? In that trunk?"

"That still needs to be determined." Chief Nunn closed her tablet. "Dr. Jenkins, the coroner, will perform an autopsy as part of the investigation. Of course, we'll share any news with you, as soon as we can."

Camilla rapped her glasses against the table. "I suppose our next question is, what do you expect from us, from the family? What do we need to do?"

"That's a good question," Chief Nunn said. "At this point, we wanted to alert you to our investigation, and to what may be coming. I've seen similar high profile cases at New Orleans Metro. I have to warn you. The press will be all over this. Things will get ugly. You should anticipate a media frenzy. You'll need to prepare for it."

"Cam, remember Dad and Mimi's divorce?" Howard asked. "Paparazzi hiding in the hedges, and all those clacking tongues?"

Addison shifted in his chair. "That was back in the Seventies, Dad. There's social media now. Twitter, Facebook, Instagram, Snapchat. It's gotten worse."

"I don't even know what any of those names mean," Howard grumbled.

"He's right," Chief Nunn said. "To protect your family, we should map out an initial response strategy."

"Now you're talking! That's the ticket!" Howard clapped his hands together. The report sounded like a gunshot. John flinched. "Stewart Payne is already on retainer. We can ask Stu to speak for the family, right out of the gate. He'll manage the press, by God."

"You should also consider installing a security system, sir, if you haven't already. You may see an increase in walk-on trespassers on the property."

"Moorhaven is already covered by Safe Alert."

"Safe Alert?" John asked. "Isn't that a keypad entry system?"

"Yes," Howard said. "Only the family knows the combination."

"Some of the maintenance contractors do too, of course," Camilla added. "But they can be trusted. We've known them for years."

"It's a start." Chief Nunn hunched her shoulders. She folded her hands. "You might also want to hire additional private security. We can supply a list of companies who do that type of work, if you do decide to go that route."

"I'm not wild about have security guards and cameras everywhere I go," Addison stated. "We come to Nantucket to get away from that."

"Addison?" Camilla reached for the pitcher. She carefully refilled her glass. "Perhaps you and Julia should consider taking Libby and living in the London townhouse for the duration."

"I'd hate to feel like we were running away, Aunt Cam."

"It's not running away, dear. It's being prudent. If you do leave, you should go now, take the Gulfstream, tonight." She centered her glass on a sea grass coaster. "There's no need to give the press additional fodder.

They're going to think the worst of us as it is. They always do."

"I don't really think it's going to be as bad as all that, Aunt Cam, do you?"

"You've never been through anything like this before, dear. We have."

Camilla's gaze grew distant. Her angular face softened. John realized that she was lost in a memory in the very same instant that he recognized that Camilla Spenser must have been a beauty in her youth, before the decades of cigarettes, unfiltered sun, and salt wind had taken its toll. She gave her head a quick shake, and reached up to smooth her hair. John also realized that Camilla was wearing a wig.

"The practical response is to simply not engage any members of the press. I know that's going to be difficult, but it's completely necessary." She pointed a finger at Addison and stared over the top of it. "Trust me on this. This type of thing is the very last definition of fun."

"I've never suggested that any of this would be fun," Addison said quickly. "Jules and I will discuss."

"There! Sounds like we have our plan." Howard interlaced his hands. He rested them on his belly. "So, Chief? What's your next step?"

"Detective Jarad will be leading the investigation. He will serve as your primary contact."

John reached for his iPhone. "I'll need contact information, for the family."

"Use mine," Addison said. "Email or text works best. It's Spenser5, like the number, at gmail dot com. I'll send you the rest."

"Got it."

"And I'll liaise with the FBI," Chief Nunn continued. "They'll want to weigh in on this."

"Jesus! The FBI?" Howard's bushy eyebrows rose. "We've never had to work with them before. The family worked with the State Attorney General's Office and the Massachusetts State Police. Am I remembering that right, Cam?"

"Yes, I believe so." She pursed her lips. "There was also a gentleman from the Secret Service at the Treasury Department, because of the ransom money, since we asked for sequential bills." She shifted in her chair. "Not a dime of that money has ever showed up again."

"I'm sure that's right," Chief Nunn said smoothly. "Authority was still at the state level, in 1921. Federal authority wasn't enacted until President Hoover signed the Lindbergh Law in 1932." She smoothed her lapels. "I've worked with the FBI before, back in NOLA. A nonfamily child abduction out of Lafayette. I know the Bureau appreciates being notified about these high profile cases."

"How did that one go?" Camilla asked.

"It didn't end well." Chief Nunn looked uncomfortable. "Let's start with the players. What does the family remember?"

"Hold up a second." Addison checked his cell phone. "Dad, don't forget. We have that Cottage Hospital Board meeting at one."

"Cam, can you take over?" Howard pushed back his chair. He lumbered up. "You're better at remembering family history than I am, anyway. I still need to change. They'll be expecting a button down shirt and an old school tie."

"Of course." Camilla playfully waggled a finger. "Don't give all the money away."

CHAPTER SIX

"Alice was taken from us on June 6, 1921." Camilla resettled her glasses on her nose. "We'll certainly never forget that date. Alice was only two, the same age as our Libby is now. She had just started talking. Vanished from her crib in the middle of the night. Nanny went to check on her in the morning, and Alice was gone."

"Keep going." Chief Nunn flipped her tablet open. "I want to get this down."

"Personally," Camilla leaned forward, "I've always thought it was strange that whoever took Alice got past Rex, the dog, an English bulldog. That always seemed like a suspicious part of the kidnapping story to me."

John silently agreed.

"The family received a ransom note in the mail, two days later. The kidnappers demanded fifty thousand dollars cash, in twenty dollars bills, which was a lot of money back then. *A lot.*" Camilla tapped the table with her fingertips for emphasis. "We, of course, paid it. Followed their directions to a T. Stephens delivered the ransom, just as we were told to do. We never heard from the kidnappers again." She frowned sadly. "We never saw Alice again, either. Well, until now, if what you're saying is really true."

Chief Nunn glanced up. "Who was Stephens?"

"George Stephens, Winston's tutor. He was actually a suspect at the time." Camilla raised her glass in a mocking toast. "Stephens was a secret drinker. The police found his closet filled with empty gin bottles, stolen from the downstairs cabinet, when they searched his room. He was in love with Daisy. Wrote her love poems. Slipped them under her bedroom door. It caused quite a scandal." She sipped her tea and toyed with the plastic straw. "Shouldn't have come as any real surprise. Everyone was in love with Daisy."

Chief Nunn tapped her screen. "Who else was in Moorhaven at the time?"

"Whew! That was some production, back in the day." Camilla settled into the chair like a contented hen. "The family was here, of course. They had arrived for the summer. Back then we enjoyed Moorhaven for the entire season, from Memorial Day right through the Labor Day weekend. Nowadays, not so much. Everyone is so busy, off doing other things." She waved her hand and began to tick names off of her fingers. "Howard and Nell came up from the city with Daisy, Winnie, Millicent, Alice, and the staff. JR joined them straight from Yale. JR took the train, and met the ferry. Franklin, oh, this is so sad. Franklin was already dead. Such a promising young man. Franklin was only eighteen when he died. Insisted on taking flying lessons, like Amelia Earhart. Crashed his plane into Holm's field on his maiden flight." Camilla lowered her voice, as if his ghost was listening. "He should have known better. Franklin was too dreamy to be a good pilot. He never really learned to stay present, or to focus properly."

"What about the staff?" Chief Nunn asked. "Where any of them in Moorhaven that day?"

"Let me see. Who slept in?" Camilla tapped her fingertips together. "Howard brought old Tom Harvey, his private secretary. Tom took care of the business side of things. I suppose he was more like Howard's unofficial business partner. Howard also brought his valet, Jenkins. Jenkins was English. He was so sweet. Stayed loyal to Howard until the day Howard died. The two of them, Jenkins and Tom, shared a room at the back of the house, in the servant's quarters. Up the back staircase, over the kitchen." She pushed back her chair. "Would you like to see their rooms? And see Alice's nursery?"

Chief Nunn looked surprised. She quickly folded her tablet. "I'd love to do that. Moorhaven is fascinating."

"I'm glad you think so." Camilla rose. "We do love it here."

She led the way across the patio toward the veranda's side door. John stepped forward quickly. He unlatched the heavy glass door, and held it open.

"Why, thank you." Camilla pushed the overgrown palms aside. "Tiresome things! I don't know why the Trust insists that we keep them. Verisimilitude, I suppose." She stepped into the main hallway, adjusted her wig, and turned right. "Frances Dormont was Moorhaven's original housekeeper. She used to beat the sand out of the rugs using an old tennis racquet. She was a local woman. She and Mrs. Ketchem only came in for the day."

"Mrs. Ketchem?" Chief Nunn asked.

"The cook. Oh my, yes." Camilla laughed as she strolled down the middle of the hall. "We grew up hearing stories about the infamous Mrs. Ketchem! Nell had some trouble with her. She put a pound a butter in everything she served, even in the breakfast oatmeal, and in the chowder. Her mashed potatoes were notorious. They came to the table floating in a pool of melted butter. It drove Nell mad."

Camilla pushed though a swinging double door and entered the all white kitchen. It was a cavernous room, tiled floor to ceiling and as cold as a cave. After being pleasantly warmed by the sun sitting next to the pool, John felt the sudden chill.

Moorhaven's kitchen had been built facing due north. Its large double hung windows were fringed with hairy gray lichen and desiccated moss. Two electric stoves backed up against an interior painted brick wall. The linoleum floor was patched with different and contrasting patterns: pre-war plaid by the refrigerator and groovy Sixties paisley beneath the steel sink. The sink still had its original hot and cold toggle faucets.

"Nell was very particular about her food." Camilla clasped her hands. "She wouldn't eat anything white. No bread, no rice, and definitely no potatoes. Nell fought to stay slim, since Howard preferred that she keep a small waist."

Chief Nunn looked puzzled. "Must've been some chore after having six kids."

There was a child's sudden giggle. John jumped. He spotted Julia and Libby sitting at one end of an epic kitchen table. Libby was happily ensconced in a wooden highchair. She was wearing a plastic lobster bib and waving a spoon at her mother. When she saw John, Libby dropped the spoon, scattering Cheerios across her tray. Libby continued to study him with her wide solemn eyes, before sharing a charming gap-toothed and very gummy grin. She cooed.

Julia turned. She smiled warmly. "Of course, as soon as I put her down, Libs woke up."

Camilla took one step closer to the table. She studied the food on Libby's tray. "Surely we could have done better for her than a slice of processed cheese and a banana."

Julia froze. She slowly raised Libby's sippy cup. "She has her milk, and the cereal. It's what Libs likes to eat."

"I suppose you know best." Camilla shrugged. "You are her mother."

"Yes, I am." Julia returned her focus to her daughter. "Was there something here that you needed?"

Camilla straightened. She tugged her tennis sweater. "These officers were asking about Moorhaven's staff. I was giving them the tour."

Julia handed Libby a thick slice of banana. "Don't let us interrupt you."

Camilla placed her hand on a battered butcher's block and continued. "This kitchen was Mrs. Ketchem's domain. I can tell you that it took some effort. She served three meals a day, to over thirty people, not to mention catering Moorhaven's many remarkable special events."

"This place is insane." Chief Nunn rested her fists on her hips. "Looks like a train station. I assume the poor woman had help?"

"Yes, we hired the locals. It was quite an honor to serve at one of Moorhaven's famous dinner parties." Camilla brushed some crumbs to the floor. She daintily dusted her fingertips. "We've always hired townies whenever we could. We like supporting the local economy. That's been our practice for over one hundred years. It's a part of the Spenser legacy."

John bit back a retort. He felt irritated by the obvious pride in Camilla's tone when she talked about Moorhaven, a place the Spensers only temporarily lived in for three months out of the year. John knew he was being petty, but he chafed to mention that his family had pretty much settled Nantucket in 1659. What really galled him was Camilla's unspoken suggestion that somehow the Spensers were superior to the folks who made Nantucket their home all year long. It irritated him because John knew that the Spensers believed this was true.

Camilla crossed the kitchen toward a simple wooden staircase. The first step creaked as she started up. John fell in line as Chief Nunn followed.

"Mind the broken step." Camilla pointed. "Before we visit Alice's nursery on the third floor, I really should show you this." She turned left on a small landing, opened a paneled door, and stepped through. "This is the butler's pantry. It's the show stopper on a Moorhaven tour."

Chief Nunn stepped across the threshold. She stopped in shock. John had to pull up short to avoid bumping into her.

The Chief stared. "Wow. This house is something else. I wasn't exactly sure what a butler's pantry was. I didn't expect to see this."

"Isn't it amazing?" Camilla stood in the center of the room. She raised her arms. "Our handyman built this." She snapped her fingers repeatedly. "What was his name? Karl something. Dammit! The young German fellow, the Dutchman. Honestly, my brain has turned to mush. Karl Schlagel. Yes, that's it. This was his masterpiece."

John paused in pure and overpowering awe. The butler's pantry was approximately thirty by forty feet. Instead of simple plaster walls, he saw neatly fitted lockers and drawers of every shape and size. The craftsmanship was unbelievable. Even with all of the exposed wood, John couldn't see a single knothole or blemish.

Camilla gripped a nearby drawer pull. Even after a hundred years, the drawer effortlessly slid open. She glanced inside, and slid it back. "There are over sixty lockers in this pantry. Each one of them is unique. Some held the Spenser silver, some simply held our candles. The flatter ones stored the family linen. The man was a genius."

"Look at the pulls." Chief Nunn stepped closer. "Every one of them is slightly different."

"Schlagel hand carved the pulls." Camilla pointed. "You'll notice that some of them are shells, and there are stars, and flowers. I believe those are edelweiss." She opened and closed a second drawer. "Schlagel was a local man, but he wasn't seasonal. He worked at Moorhaven year-round, staining the shingles and repairing the gutters. What is it about gutters that makes them so troublesome?"

"Where does that door lead?" John pointed.

Camilla turned. "That door would take us out to the main landing above the double stairs, where the family's bedrooms are." Her footsteps echoed as she crossed the empty room. "We'll need to circle back to see Alice's nursery on the third floor."

She shut the door to the butler's pantry, crossed the landing, and continued up the wooden stairs. "Nell had a new ladies' maid that year. Gladys Samford. Nell's New York maid quit to get married. Ladies needed a personal maid back then to help them dress. I've heard Gladys was a genius at dressing Nell's hair. It was quite an art form."

At the top of the staircase, Camilla paused to catch her breath. She pushed a plain door open. "Gladys shared this room with Pauline Dalwhinney. Pauline was Daisy and Millicent's governess. Of course, Daisy didn't really need a governess anymore. She was eighteen, and ready to come out."

"Come out?" Chief Nunn leaned against the railing. "Daisy was gay?"

"Oh heavens, no! I meant that Daisy was ready to be presented to polite society."

Julia laughed. Her voice carried up the narrow staircase. "She meant that Daisy wanted to start going to the parties."

Camilla shot the unseen Julia a dark look.

John pushed the door open wider. He estimated the bedroom's size. Fifteen by twenty feet with two twin beds and a shared dresser, roughly 300 square feet. "Kind of small for two people."

Camilla looked affronted. "The women only slept here. The rest of the time they enjoyed the run of the house."

"Where was Alice's nursery?" Chief Nunn asked. "I'd like to see that."

"This way." Camilla passed a miniscule bathroom. Ducking her head, she pushed through a faded curtain into an even smaller alcove. "This was Nanny's room. It connects directly to Alice's nursery through that entryway. Nanny was the one who roused the house that morning by screaming: 'Mrs. Spenser? Miss Daisy? Did you take the baby?' "

"Horrifying." Chief Nunn momentarily closed her eyes. "I can't think of anything worse than losing a child."

"The nanny never heard anything the night of the kidnapping?" John asked.

"Not a thing. She said she slept 'without a care,' until she found the empty crib."

Chief Nunn looked up. "What was Nanny's real name?"

"Nanny's real name?" Camilla paused thoughtfully. "You know, I'm not sure. Let me think. Huff? Yes, that was it. Nancy Huff. She was quite a character in her own right. If you look closely, you'll see that the alcove windows were nailed shut. Nanny insisted on it. She was afraid that some strange man would climb into her room. It must have been sweltering in August, but Nanny insisted on protecting her reputation, with all of the single men in the house."

"Single men in the house?" John picked at a nail still firmly embedded in the windowsill. "Would that be Floyd Mulloy? I saw him listed as a Moorhaven employee."

"Floyd Mulloy? Oh, you mean the chauffeur." Camilla shook her head. "No, he slept over the garage, in the room we use for Ping-Pong. George Stephens also slept there on a camp cot. Those two men used the outdoor shower." Camilla crossed the alcove, lifted a second curtain, hung it neatly on a simple cup hook, and stepped through. "This was Alice's nursery."

She led them into a room that was six times the size of any of the other bedrooms they had seen so far. Alice's nursery had a coffered ceiling and faded rose-trellised wallpaper above bead board wainscoting. The spacious room faced southwest, angled to catch the best light. Four dormer windows overlooked the English garden below, and they offered a splendid distant view of the wild meadow. In the summer, these windows would have been thrown open to catch the cooling ocean breeze.

"Pretty nice setup for a single two-year old," Chief Nunn noted.

The nursery was empty. There was no sign of any crib. The two twin beds were dusty, their mattresses and pillows stripped and bare.

"Does Libby sleep up here?" John asked.

"No." Camilla walked over to one of the dormer windows. She pulled the simple cotton curtain aside. "Libby sleeps downstairs, in a bedroom next to her parents. We don't really use this nursery anymore, with just the five of us. It's too much space."

"Have we covered all of the staff?" Chief Nunn asked. "Did anyone work outside?"

"Outside of Moorhaven?" Camilla frowned. "There was Joe Bolton, the gardener, another local man. Joe kept the grounds. He planted the vegetable garden for the kitchen. The family loved homegrown tomatoes and fresh sweet corn. We still do."

There was a rising string of musical notes. Chief Nunn quickly pulled out her phone.

"Excuse me. I need to take this call." She hurriedly stepped back out to the alcove, and disappeared.

Camilla dropped the curtain. She sighed. "There's always work to be done on a house like this. You have to stay on top of things, or it quickly becomes a disaster. Thank God the Spenser Trust covers the maintenance expenses. And pays the insurance and property taxes. I don't know how else we'd manage it."

Chief Nunn returned. Her shadow bisected the dusty floor. "Detective Jarad? The Baby Alice trunk has been delivered to the morgue. Dr. Jenkins wants to examine it immediately. He's asked us to meet him there."

"Chief? One minute, please." Camilla held up a hand. "Would you kindly do me a favor, and please not refer to Alice that way? The family has never said 'Baby Alice.' She is simply Alice Spenser to us. Using that nickname removes her identity. 'Baby Alice' was something the press cooked up to sell newspapers."

"Of course." The Chief blinked. "I apologize if I was being insensitive."

"Thank you. Now, will you two see yourselves out? The back staircase through the kitchen is still the quickest way." Camilla suddenly looked sallow and fatigued. "I don't know where Jamison has got to."

"Not a problem." Chief Nunn gently shook Camilla's hand. "We'll be in touch."

"We're counting on it."

Chief Nunn turned. She strode toward the staircase. John quickly followed. Their shoes rapidly slapped the wooden steps and their footsteps echoed down the dim hall. The Chief waited until the front door had closed before she spoke again.

"Shit!" She opened the cruiser's passenger door and slid in. "I stepped in it that time. 'Please don't call her Baby Alice. It removes her identity.' Shit!"

"Don't let it get to you, Chief." John cranked the ignition. "The Spensers have that effect on people."

37

"I should've seen it coming. Lord knows I've run across WASP privilege before." The Chief reflexively buckled her seatbelt. She crossed her arms. "Was it my imagination, or was there some tension between Camilla and Julia back there?"

John pointed the cruiser down the gravel drive. "I've heard there's bad blood. Camilla didn't approve of Addison's marriage."

"Why not? That Julia seems nice enough. The baby girl is adorable."

"Camilla thought Addison married too young. They married right out of college. Eloped. Got married on a charter boat in Aruba. Rumor was that Julia pulled the goalie on him."

"I'm sorry? Pulled the goalie?" She turned. "What does that mean?"

"Julia stopped using birth control and didn't tell Addison. She was pregnant before she got married. If Libby is two, the timing fits."

"Got it." The Chief settled back. "Goes to show there's no such thing as a perfect family, no matter how much money you've got in the bank." She studied the moorland rushing by. "Speaking of money, it's interesting that the ransom was paid using sequential bills. They've never returned to circulation. Unless Dr. Jenkins finds that cash in the trunk, it's still out there somewhere."

"I don't buy the whole ransom idea." John swung left on Milestone Road. He picked up speed. "I'll need to dig into that more before I follow that line of this investigation."

"Really?" Chief Nunn narrowed her eyes. "What bothers you about it?"

John tapped the wheel. "I've always thought it would be too easy to point a kidnapping investigation in the wrong direction by faking a ransom note. Someone in that household could have faked that note to shift the blame."

"Interesting. What makes you think that's what happened here?"

"Because of Rex, the dog Camilla mentioned. No one has said that Rex was doped. Rex let some scumbag take Alice without raising a fuss." John pulled into the Cottage Hospital lot. He continued on to the morgue entrance at the rear of the building, and parked. "We found Alice's body in a trunk that we know belonged to the family. Everyone in Moorhaven had the means, and the opportunity. Now we need to dig out the motive."

Chief Nunn stepped from the cruiser, but she hung onto the door. "The only problem I have with that, Detective, is that if someone at Moorhaven killed Alice Spenser, then why would Howard and Nell have protected their child's killer?" She shook her head. "What parent would ever do that?"

"They would do that." John paused. "If they thought Alice's killer was another one of their kids."

"Another one of their kids," the Chief repeated slowly. "Like who?"

John met the Chief's eyes. "When she found the empty crib, why was Nanny Huff calling for Daisy?"

Chapter Seven

"Thank God the Hyannis Target sells jersey dresses and stretchy yoga pants." Sarah Jarad tugged on the fabric around her middle. "I've been living in them. Can't stand having anything snug around my waist. Or, what used to be my waist, since it's disappeared."

"I love Tar-zhay," her sister-in-law Mary Rose agreed. She quickly captured a drip on her strawberry ice cream cone. "How are your ankles holding up? That's what bothered me, the swelling there, when I carried both of my boys. Had a real problem with it."

Sarah laughed. "I'll let you know, as soon as I see them again." She felt lucky, filled with a steady bliss, and humbly grateful for her new life. Sarah had always wanted a large family to call her own. She had envied John for having his. Her own family back in Pittsburgh seemed to have evaporated after her mother's death last year. John had literally hundreds of Jarad cousins tucked into every nook and cranny on Nantucket. She was a part of that extended family now. Sarah placed her free hand on her expanding belly, and snorted. *Make sure you know what you want, you might get it.* Her belly felt as firm as a basketball, but then, that's what happened when you were six months in, and carrying twins. "Can we sit down a minute, Mary Rose? I'm feeling winded."

"Of course. How about that bench?"

"Perfect." Gripping her cone in her hand, Sarah lowered herself onto the unforgiving wooden slats. They had been strolling along the Easy Street boat basin, technically getting some exercise, but also knowing that the siren's call of the Sweet Treats shop would eventually lure them in. Sarah had lived on Nantucket for more than a year. She thought she'd gotten used to the insane island prices. She was wrong. It still shocked her to see that one ice cream cone could cost eight bucks, almost twenty for two cones. *How did regular people do it? What if you had kids?* Well, she and John were about to find out.

She finished the expensive nubbin and dusted the sugar crystals off her fingertips. Looking up, Sarah scanned the inner harbor. Her artist's eye never stopped searching for fresh subjects to paint. The Easy Street basin was a natural pick for her next project. John would love getting a painting as a gift for his birthday, but reflective water was tremendously difficult to portray. Could she capture all of that shifting, subtle color? There was even a streamlined yacht moored in deeper water to anchor the composition. It might work. The waterline was planted with a row of tiny tea rose bushes, blooming now with overloaded masses of magenta and shell pink blossoms. The sun had warmed the roses. Their powdery scent drifted on the breeze.

"This is the life." Sarah blinked as the sunlight gently dappled the lapping waves. "It's so peaceful. I love this."

"Yep." Mary Rose finished her cone, too. She rested her arms on the back of the bench. "How are Jennie and DJ doing? Are you holding up?"

Sarah rested her hands on her belly. "We're fine. Only, I think we're running out of room in there."

"You're in the home stretch now. Ha-ha. Pun intended." Mary Rose turned her broad face to catch the sun. "We're all set for the baby shower on Thursday, right?"

"Yep. Noon at your mom's house. Jenny has everything covered."

"I still can't believe how much John's life has changed, in so short a time. Sarah, you're a real blessing to him. Do you even realize that?"

"I wish I felt like a blessing." Sarah pulled at the jersey dress. "I feel fat."

"Knock it off. You don't look fat. You look fantastic." Mary Rose checked her phone. "I'm a little worried about John, though. He's had a rough winter. First, you know, getting over Toby's accident, and now the demotion. How's he taking it?"

Sarah picked at the cuticle on her thumb until it bled. "To be honest, Mary Rose, John hasn't said much. I've tried bringing it up a couple of times, but when I do, he veers off topic. He did joke once that at least as a detective he doesn't have to wear a uniform anymore. He saw that as a plus." Mary Rose had voiced Sarah's own concerns. She had wondered about asking John to share more of his feelings. Lately, she had been feeling a lack of intimacy, as if the forever feeling had faded. John was often home, and he still shared their bed, but sometimes it felt like they were in a holding pattern, puppets in a show, playing acting at life and not really living it. Sarah had put that new uncertainty down to a fault on her side, because of the hormones. "I figure he'll open up when he's ready."

"I don't know." Mary Rose leaned forward. "John's always been kind of quiet that way. Maybe you should push it a little, make him talk about it. Get things out in the open, like you said."

"Really? You think?"

"I do." She checked her phone again. "I'd be curious to know how that goes."

"Mary Rose, don't mind me asking, but is there somewhere else you need to be?"

"What makes you say that?"

"Because you keep checking your phone."

"Oops! Busted. You're quite a detective." She stood. "We need to get to the Arts Guild by 11:00. I have a surprise for you."

"A surprise?" Sarah felt skeptical. "What kind of surprise? A good surprise, or a bad one?"

Mary Rose reached down to help her up. "I'm not telling. You'll have to wait and see."

"You already know that I hate practical jokes, right?"

"Yes. John warned me. Sarah, I'm so excited about this! It's awesome. I've been sitting on the news for a week. It's been killing me, and it's no joke."

Mary Rose led the way. They hurried down a crushed shell alley toward the Arts Guild building on Old South Wharf. As they turned the corner, a vacant shingled two-story building slid into view. The building had a *For Lease/For Sale* listing realtor sign prominently taped up in every one of its darkened windows.

"Slow down a second, Mary Rose." Sarah leaned against a lamppost. "I can't keep up with you." She massaged a sudden stitch in her side.

"I can't believe this building is vacant again." Mary Rose raised both hands. She peered through the plate glass. "They can't keep a tenant. Do you suppose it's because it's haunted?"

"That's not even funny."

Mary Rose polished the streaky window with her cuff. "When you and John sell Uncle Ethan's property, this building would make a nice investment. You could open a gallery on the ground floor, and rent out the condo above. Be a real money maker for you two."

"Let me be clear about this. I am never setting foot inside that building again. Kurt Stockton is a part of my past, and he's going to stay there."

"I know, I shouldn't tease. I can't help myself." Mary Rose looked contrite. "Do you still think about Kurt? About what happened?"

"Only every day." Sarah turned her back on the studio. Grasping a handrail, she climbed the two short steps and started walking down the wooden dock. "I've picked some real winners in my life. It seems like marrying your brother was the only smart thing I've ever done."

Mary Rose laughed. "So far, my friend, so far. Give it time. You're young. You still have plenty of time to make more mistakes." She moved ahead, and guided Sarah toward the Arts Guild building. The front door was propped open by a colorfully chalked signboard that read: LOCAL PRODUCE: WE HAVE A WINNER!

"Local produce?" Sarah paused. "What is that? Their new exhibit?"

"Yes." Mary Rose entered the gallery. "It's work only by local Nantucket artists. You have to live on the island to enter. It has everything: painting, sculpture, jewelry. I thought you'd like to see it."

"I do want to see this." Sarah stepped over the threshold. She immediately felt like she was home. Art galleries tended to look the same, with their matte white walls, canister lights, and gleaming hardwood floors, but that snug, comfortable feeling never got old. Sarah settled in "Thank you, Mary Rose. This was very thoughtful of you. Art galleries are my happy place."

"I thought so." Mary Rose fist pumped a triumphant gesture. "She shoots, and scores!"

They strolled through the central gallery, stopping to admire a polished driftwood sculpture of a mermaid using a pearl to play catch with a seal. The sculpture was obviously one of the featured pieces, but the paintings on the walls drew Sarah in. Most of them were strictly amateur hour, but a couple showed a real eye for composition, with a natural exuberance paired with homegrown talent.

"Next year, you should enter one of your paintings, Sarah." Mary Rose waved a finger. "You paint better than most of these folks do."

"Thanks for the compliment." Sarah gave the suggestion some thought. It would be fun to have something to offer the Local Produce exhibition next year. That way, she'd feel like she was making real progress in becoming a more active member of the Nantucket arts community. It would be thrilling to hang one of her landscapes on these walls, and not simply be known for her anonymous commercial folk art hackwork, although those commissions were coming in steady enough to pay some of their household bills, and there was nothing wrong with that. Sarah was proud of her talent. She hungered to be recognized for the best part of her genuine gift. But then, her thoughts turns dark, as they so often did lately. She flinched as one of the twins kicked. Sarah put her hands under her belly to reassure them that all was well.

Sure, she could hang her paintings in public, but what was the point if she couldn't sign her real name to them? Sarah had never admitted her deepest secret fear to a living soul. She still lived with the bone shaking terror that somehow Mason, her psycho ex-fiancée from back in the 'Burgh would Google her name, track her down, and find her. Mason was the sole reason Sarah refused to put anything - anything! - on the Internet. No joining Facebook group pages, no Snapchat friends, no Instagram pictures. Nothing! Sarah wanted to puke at the mere thought of that kind of exposure and risk. And now, she had John and the twins to worry about, too.

Of course, she could always use her married name, and sign her paintings S.H. Jarad. Would that trim job be enough to throw Mason off her trail? Sarah doubted it. If Mason was looking for her, he would never give up the search. Mason would take too much pleasure in the hunt. Each artist's individual style was as identifiable to a trained eye as a fingerprint, and even unsigned, Mason would recognize her work. His focus was maniacal that way. Sarah felt the familiar sinking dread, and she shuddered. She hated the fact that even after more than a year, with all of the changes she had made in her life that she still needed to hide.

"Ready for your surprise?" Mary Rose asked brightly.

"Surprise? I thought this exhibit was it?"

"No way." Mary Rose grasped Sarah's elbow. She guided her toward a back room. "This took planning. I'm quite proud of myself. Follow me."

They circled a hip-high stucco half wall and stepped into a secluded, well-lit cubicle. The calm quiet space spotlighted a single landscape painting with a large blue rosette and long golden streamers hanging from its frame. A knobby brass easel standing next to the painting offered a pasteboard sign showcasing a photo of the winning artist, with her biography in bold type. Sarah's stomach contracted into a spasm. Her knees gave out. She had to lean against the wall for support. A candid shot of her own face stared out from the poster next to the words: LOCAL PRODUCE GRAND PRIZE WINNER: ALTAR ROCK by SARAH HAWTHORNE JARAD.

"Taa-daa!" Mary Rose splayed her arms like Vanna White. "Surprise! We have a grand prize winner in the family! And it's you!"

"No, Mary Rose! You can't do this!" Sarah gagged as bile scorched her throat. She blindly knocked the pasteboard sign to the floor, then bent down and struggled to pick it back up. The effort left her panting. "We need to take this down, and hide it, right now!"

"What are you doing?"

"You don't understand!" Sarah felt dizzy as her secret fear erupted. A shower of golden dots sparkled before her eyes. She was so upset that she felt almost blind. Hot tears spilled from her eyes. "This painting was meant to be a gift! I gave it to you for Christmas." Sarah choked, desperately trying to dry her eyes using her wrists and the back of her hands. "You were supposed to hang it in your house, keep it private! Not hang it up for everyone to see!"

"It won first prize! Why don't you want folks to see it?"

Sarah's mind reeled. She felt trapped by her many little white lies, by her multiple deceptions. Of course, John knew about her blackened past. She had shared that knowledge with him, as part of an investigation, before they were married. There were no secrets between them, and he had sworn to never tell another soul. Now her ghastly history threatened to spill over into common knowledge. Sarah burned with the shame of it. It was bad enough that everyone on Nantucket knew about her romantic stupidity over Kurt Stockton. How would she ever be able to live on the island once they learned that her stupidity went even further back? That it went even deeper, went even darker, than with Kurt? That it went all the way back to her pre-island life, back in Pittsburgh, with Mason? It was all such an ugly, sordid mess.

"Sarah? What is going on?"

Sarah felt heartsick over all of the lies. It was time for this to end. The dam had burst. Mary Rose deserved to hear the truth, for what it was worth. "I was proud of this one. I signed it with my real name. Mason might see it. If he does, he'll know where I am."

"Mason?" Mary Rose pulled back. "Who's Mason?"

"My ex from back home." Sarah choked. "If you thought Kurt was bad, Mason is worse." Sarah dug through her purse hoping to find a tissue. "I came to Nantucket to hide from him. Mason's evil. He's insane. I don't want him back in my life. He'll ruin everything! I can't go back to feeling that way, Mary Rose. I can't! I can't! I won't!"

"Sarah, take it easy." Mary Rose gripped Sarah's arms. "This can't be good for you."

"I know, I know! We just need to take this painting down. Forget it ever happened."

"What is going on over here?" A woman wearing silk trousers with a cashmere sweater set stepped around the corner. "What is all the ruckus?" Her jaw dropped when she saw the paper scraps littering the floor. "My God! What have you done to our signage?"

"I'm sorry." Sarah swallowed her tears. She raised her hand and pointed a trembling finger. "We need to take this painting down. I never gave permission to have it exhibited."

"I entered it without her knowing," Mary Rose rattled out. "Forged her signature on the entry form. She didn't know, really. It was meant to be a surprise. Could you help us take this down? We'll take it with us."

"Take it down? Take it with you?" The woman gaped. "That's impossible! We've already issued a press release about the award. It hit the wire first thing this morning."

"Press release?" Sarah felt faint. "Hit the wire?"

"Of course! *Altar Rock* is already featured on our website, and on our Facebook page. We've paid Yahoo to boost the promotion. The Twitter storm has started. It's going viral, as part of our marketing campaign. We can't stop things now. It's too late."

"Oh God." Sarah dug into her purse. She fumbled for her phone. "Where's John? I need to call John."

CHAPTER EIGHT

One day at a time, John calmly reminded himself. *We need to take all of this one day at a time.* He tightened his arms, and pressed Sarah to his chest. These last few difficult months had taught him a tough lesson about holding onto, and learning to let go of, regret. Now, evidently, it was Sarah's turn. John loved his wife, and he would stand by Sarah no matter what, but they both needed to work on learning to take life's hurdles one day at a time, especially with the twins due in September. Nothing about any of this was going to get easier.

"You know," he muttered, his voice muffled by her hair, "hugging you was a lot easier, before you got pregnant."

She sniffled wetly into his shirt. "I'll be sure to tell the twins' father that, the next time I see him, you jag off."

John laughed. When his pickup truck had come barreling down the lane to their new home site, and Sarah had struggled out of it, John had feared the worst; that Sarah had spoken with Dr. Diballa and something was wrong with the twins. Her news about Mary Rose's big surprise and her own art gallery exposure turned out to be equally devastating, but not nearly so grim. With her smartass retort and her use of that strange Pittsburgh slang, John recognized the return of Sarah's twisted sense of humor.

She dried her eyes on the neckline of her T-shirt. "I'm sorry. I know you already have a lot on your plate. This just came as such a shock. I don't know what to do."

John never doubted Sarah's courage, and he understood the compulsive trigger for her fears. In the past twelve months, she had faced down two direct assaults. "Sweetheart, it's okay. You've been through a lot. Take a deep breath. Give yourself some credit."

"I know this is going to sound whiney. All I wanted was a quiet life!"

"That's not going to happen." He chuckled, and pointed to the concrete block foundation shaping up their dream home. "We're in the middle of new construction, with twins due in three months. Honey? We're not going to see quiet happening for the next twenty years."

She laughed. "No, lie. Jesus, John! How can you stay so calm about things?"

John dug deep, and he admitted the truth. "Because I've got you. All the rest of this, we'll deal with, when it happens."

Sarah pulled back. "What about Mason? What if he finds me?"

"Then he'll find *us*." This exposure really had Sarah spooked. "Has Mason tried contacting you?"

"No." She shook her head. "Not yet. But he will. I know him. He'll never let go. Mason doesn't think like that. It's not his way."

"Are you willing to file a restraining order against him now?"

"No!" Sarah splayed her fingers. "Never! Then I know he'll find me. No, I won't do that."

"Then, honey, there's not much else we can do."

"I know that." Sarah clenched her fists. "I know that, I do. I just hate feeling so helpless, so exposed." How could she explain the rippling anxiety that constantly beat its feathered wings at the back of her mind, a coal black crow that warned her that she should look over her shoulder everywhere she went, to see if Mason was standing on the corner? The past should stay firmly in the past where it belonged, only now, in this modern world, it didn't. It used to be, when you cut someone loose and said goodbye, it meant goodbye *forever*. Now goodbye meant *see you later*. People popped back into your current life with a daily friend request or an iconic poke. Pre-history had vanished. The line drawn in the sand between the past and the present was gone. Life now was one long constant present day, with no hope of reprieve. Sarah knew that she needed to learn to forgive herself for her mistakes, and to face her fears, but it wasn't easy. *Was that the problem? Because getting over this took work?* In any case, there would be no more running away. Sarah screwed up her courage. She needed to be strong for John, and for the twins. There was simply no other way out. "I feel like such a fool."

John pulled her into another hug. Sarah was not alone in feeling foolish. He felt a wiggle of guilt from a cluster of his own recent mistakes. What did it take to erase that sickening feeling from your mind? Time? Distance? Or, did it take the finality of death to clean the slate? "Don't say that, honey. You're not a fool. We've both made mistakes. Can't be helped. But Sarah, remember this: whenever that feeling gets to you, I'm here. You're not alone. You've got me now. We're part of the same team."

"You have no idea how good that sounds." She sighed, and combed her fingers through her hair. "Thanks for reminding me. My hormones must be whacked out because of this pregnancy. You should have seen me this morning, with Mary Rose. I was a mess. The Guild is never going to invite us back." She smiled weakly. "You will stick with me, though, right? Until I sort things out?"

"Of course, I will. That's not even a question."

John looked up to see a Ford F150 King Cab 4X4 pickup truck rumbling down the lane. The truck had a steel ladder rack bolted over its cab, and what was locally called a two-toned paint job, which meant it had the original factory paint, and rust. The Ford slowly eased its way around the soft sandy construction site before rolling to a stop with squealing brakes. The driver side door shot open, and Gus Schlagel clambered out. Gus was a stout, barrel chested man with a full head of snowy white hair that rose to a crest on the very top of his head and which he kept strictly parted down the middle, in contrast with his signature roughly-cut sandy mustache. As usual, Gus was wearing brown construction coveralls and steel-toed boots. His son Bernhard climbed out of the passenger side, dressed identically in matching gear down to the black-framed glasses both men wore. John had gone all through grade school with Bernhard, who had made it known in the fourth grade that he preferred to be called Ben, and who had backed up his new nickname with his quick ham-like fists. Ben was a hefty fifty percent taller and wider version of his father, smoothly muscled all over, and although no one ever said it to Ben's face, privately his friends called him Thor. Ben quickly finished his sub in two tremendous snapping bites before balling the paper wrapper between his hands and tossing it into the back of the truck.

"Afternoon, John, Sarah," he shouted around his final chewy mouthful. Reaching into the truck bed, Ben hefted a loaded tool belt single-handedly, and strapped it on. "Congratulations! The footprint is in. Looks like we're building you two a new house."

"Oh my." Sarah giggled, and she whispered, "Hello, Alpha Male."

John playfully blew into her ear. "I'm going to pretend I didn't hear that."

"It's a good design." Gus marched over, swinging a ruler like a swagger stick. Settling his hands on his hips, he surveyed the concrete block outline. "Easy enough to lift it and shift it, if you ever need to, hoping, of course, that you never do." The cement blocks rang as he tapped them with the ruler. "Best to be prepared with these coastal home sites. Erosion gets bad, this side of the island."

"Dad's right." The tide was out. Ben pointed his chin at the wide sandy flat. "Quammock storms are tough to out guess. One big winter surge, or a November hurricane, and off you go visiting Africa."

"We've set this site back two hundred yards because of that," John said. "We're crossing our fingers it never happens."

Sarah felt sour worry ripple across her mind. Yes, they had discussed choosing their new home site in great detail, over many candle-lit meals. John had explained that because of its location on the seaward side of the island, Quammock was prey to the sudden dangers of coastal erosion, but Sarah could never reconcile herself to building their dream home on one of Uncle Ethan's mid-island Lost Forest parcels. Luckily, money hadn't been a deciding factor, since John held the title to both properties. She had been the one who nervously veered away from choosing the Lost Forest as their dream home site, since John's brother, Danny, had originally been buried there. Sarah had never mentioned it to John, but she often wondered how they could live within sight of Danny's unconsecrated grave, forced to think about his murder every morning while they were starting their day, and enjoying their coffee? What kind of life would that be, living with that grim memory in your backyard? Even with its tidal risks, Sarah felt convinced that Quammock was the right choice for their new home. So she had fibbed, and told John she wanted a house with an expansive ocean view. She would postpone the worry about the other risks until later.

"It's incredible to see this has come so far, so fast," Sarah said. "Up to now, it's been a dream."

"It's a solid dream." Gus strolled up the slight rise, tapping the ruler against his broad thigh. "Your architect knew what she was doing, digging the garage into this grade. The ground and the poured concrete will keep things cozy, come winter. Smart. No need to pay for extra electric, just to warm your car."

"We're doing our best to keep things green."

"Green, green. Yes, that's the latest thing. Everyone wants that now." Gus puffed out his lower lip. "In any case, you two are going to be proud of this house. I guarantee it. Going to be the last one I'll ever build. I've decided to retire, once this is done. Been building houses for fifty years. That's long enough. Time to give it up. Relax. Enjoy life a little. Maybe do some fishing."

John was surprised by the news. Gus was a famous Nantucket icon. "Will Ben be taking over the business?"

"Him? Dimwit? Hell, no." Gus spat into the sand, barely missing his boot. "He wants to be a competitive gamer, whatever the hell that means."

"I can hear you, you know." Ben strode up. He was holding a hammer in his right hand, and his handsome, ruddy face was mottled with anger. "I've told you before, Dad. I'm not spending my life framing houses. If I can get the money together, I'm entering the professional gaming competition at the International this year." He returned the hammer to a belt loop. "I'm already the secretary of the Esports DOTA2 community. Competitive multi-team gaming is the future."

"Bah! Building houses is the future. Dimwit, are you blind? Look around! Construction is booming." Gus pointed at the many golden, newly shingled rooftops dotting the shoreline. "And he wants to give that up! Building homes runs in our family. There's honor in putting a roof over someone's head, giving their families shelter, a safe place to live. That's real man's work, not sitting around in a bomb shelter playing video games. What kind of a man does that?"

"Bomb shelter?" Sarah asked, lightly. She sat down on the cinderblock wall.

"They don't want to hear us argue, Dad." Ben laughed it off. "Building runs in the family. I'll say it does. We're still dealing with a bomb shelter Grandpap Otto built back in the Sixties, during the Cuban missile crisis." Ben straightened his shoulders, and he cricked his neck. "I use it as a man cave, whenever I need to get away from this old geezer. He can't climb down the ladder anymore."

"It's my knees. Arthritis gives me trouble." Gus scowled. "He's down there half the damn night. The new neighbors are complaining about the shelter now, too." He looked to John for commiseration. "The sand has settled around the godforsaken thing. Got two big stack pipes sticking up outta this dip in the middle of the yard. Council sent me a letter about it, just last week. The neighbors are calling it an eyesore, damn their eyes! Want me to dig it up, or fill it in. Another mess I get to clean up. Seems like that's all I ever do. Spend my time cleaning up other people's messes."

"Schlagel and Sons needs to fix that before you retire, Dad. Don't forget. Don't leave it for me to do."

The instant Ben said the name "Schlagel and Sons," the words pinged John's brain. He had been so busy dealing with the day's whirlwind events that he hadn't had time to process any of it, to slow it down long enough to put two and two together. That morning, during the Spenser interview, Camilla Dechert had mentioned "that young German fellow," Moorhaven's year-round caretaker at the time of the Baby Alice kidnapping. John gave himself a mental thump. He should have guessed. He knew how Nantucket worked. It wasn't what you knew, it was who. On the island, good jobs, marketable skills, and family businesses were handed down from generation to generation. "Gus, was your grandfather Karl Schlagel?"

"He was." Gus gaped in surprise. "What of it?"

"He worked for the Spenser family, at Moorhaven, in 'Sconset?"

"Only his whole damn life. We still do a bit of work for the Spensers." Gus narrowed his eyes. "Why are you asking?"

"Hold up! I got this." Ben snapped his fingers. He pointed at John. "It's because you found Baby Alice Spenser in the Madaket dump this morning. In a trunk, right? That's why you're suddenly asking us about Grandpa Karl." He smiled brilliantly. "Did I guess it? Am I right?"

CHAPTER NINE

"This isn't a game, Ben," John said severely. "How did you hear about that already?"

"Are you kidding me? Island grapevine." Ben massaged his arm. "Deb Cooper volunteers at the Madaket recycling center. She's the biggest gossip Nantucket's got. I bet Deb burned out her phone this morning, shooting video. She posted it on Instagram."

Once again, John felt like he was way behind the curve with all the new technology. Chief Nunn's earlier dire warnings about exploding social media had seemed overblown, but now John wondered if maybe her advice hadn't been strong enough? He was used to dealing with instant text messaging and public eavesdroppers listening intently to police scanner transmissions on their phone apps. Civilians now carried digital quality video capability in their pockets or purse. Criminal and accidental events were immediately subject to intense public scrutiny and potential outcry, even before the first responders had sufficient time to react. Members of the force had discussed needing body cams to counteract this modern accessibility and focus. How did you actually settle in to do your job, when you were constantly being offered a tsunami of multiple fresh opinions while being second-guessed? John felt like the narrow margin of time between initiating an investigation and following up on any leads had evaporated. Ben was already offering him feedback on a preliminary investigation John was still mapping out. He felt like he was losing an uphill one-man race on a treadmill.

"Crissakes!" Gus sputtered. "You're not going to reopen that can of shit again, are you?"

John turned. "Reopen what?"

"That Spenser kidnapping, of course!" Gus sat down on the cinderblock wall next to Sarah. "What the hell did you think I was talking about?"

John was surprised to see Gus so upset. The Spensers had lost Alice, a daughter, and they were relatively calm about the kidnapping. The passage of ninety years had softened the horror of it for them. "Why are you so ruffled?"

"Because you cops tried to fry my grandfather over it, you dumb ass! You nearly hounded him to death." Gus's face had flushed bright red. "You try going up against the government some time, once they've set their mind against you. That's not something you ever forget."

"Dad's right. Grandpap used to tell me about it all the time."

"Grandpap?" John asked quickly.

"My dad," Gus interrupted. "Otto, Karl's son."

"Grandpa Karl was their main suspect." Ben pulled a screwdriver off of his belt. He tapped it against his palm. "The cops arrested him. Kept him in a jail cell for nearly two weeks. Beat the living crap out of Grandpa Karl. He almost lost an eye."

"And all of that was illegal! Karl was an American citizen!" Gus shook both fists. "They never charged him with anything. His only crime was being German." Reaching up, he smoothed his hair. "There was a lot of anti-German sentiment floating around after the war. The joke of it was, Schlagels aren't even German. We're from Bavaria!"

"Trust me." Ben snorted. He silently appealed to John and Sarah for sympathy. "I grew up listening to this at our dinner table. My mom hated this conversation. Called Grandpap a broken record. But that Spenser kidnapping was the biggest thing that ever happened to him, in his whole life. Grandpap was a kid in the yard when the cops tore through the house. They used crowbars to rip the floorboards up in the attic. Dug up the dirt floor of the garage. They even sliced open the upholstered seats on Grandpa Karl's rickety Ford Model A. Can you imagine being ten years old, and watching the cops treat your family like that? And when they were done, they still hadn't found a single thing to connect Grandpa Karl to that kidnapping."

"That's because Karl was innocent!"

"Maybe so." Ben shrugged. "The cops sure thought he did it. They said it had to be an inside job. Grandpa Karl barely escaped getting sent to the electric chair on suspicion."

"Jesus." Sarah shuddered. "That's barbaric."

"Karl never had it easy." Gus lifted his chin. He studied the line of surf moving into the shoreline while drumming his fingers on the wall. "Immigrated to America in 1913, just before the War. Came over on the *Oceana* with his wife, Frieda, and my dad, Otto. Dad was only two. Frieda died making the trip. They were in steerage. Couldn't afford better tickets. Packed into that hold like cattle. Never saw the light of day." Gus shifted, and he crossed his legs. "Frieda was too ill to walk on deck to get fresh air. Karl thought she was seasick. She had appendicitis. By the time he got Frieda to the ship's doctor, it was too late. Had to bury her at sea, dropped off the side sewn up in a canvas bag. Even at two, my dad never forgot it. He hated the sea until the day he died."

"Must've made it tough, living on an island," Sarah said.

"How did they end up at Moorhaven?" John asked.

"That was Howard Spenser, Junior. They called him JR." Gus puffed out his lips. Clasping his hands around one knee, he leaned back. "Still a student, but a really decent guy. JR found Karl and my dad living on the street in New Haven. It's funny. You think that shit can't happen anymore, people living on the street, but it does. You see it all the time. When JR discovered Karl was a carpenter, he brought them here. Ignored the prejudice. Gave them a fresh start, a new place to call home."

Gus leaned forward. He massaged his knees. "Karl did all of the maintenance at Moorhaven. His real genius was custom cabinetry. He was an artist that way. Have you seen his carvings in their butler's pantry? The custom bannister, with the lighthouse newel post? The dovetailed shelving in their library? By God!" Gus slapped his thigh. "Nobody does that level of finish work anymore, nobody! Karl only used center cut white oak boards. You can't even find that level of lumber these days. Those old growth forests are gone."

Ben scratched his chin. "Grandpap was the Spenser's paperboy, did you know that? Ten years old, and already working a job. Delivered their papers every morning on his bike, along with their fresh milk and eggs."

"No, I didn't know that." John recalled that morning's discussion of Moorhaven's staff list. No one had mentioned Otto Schlagel running around. John quickly did the math. With a start, he realized that at the time of the kidnapping, Karl Schlagel had been younger than he was now, still less than thirty, with a ten-year-old son in tow. History had played a trick on his mind. Because the event was set in the past, John had assumed that Karl was middle-aged, or older. "No one mentioned that Karl had a son with him."

"Of course the Spensers wouldn't mention Otto." Gus stood and stretched. "Out of sight, out of mind. Dad was just a local yokel kid on a bike. He was invisible." Gus tapped the side of his nose, and winked. "But

Dad had good eyes, and better ears. He knew the shenanigans that went on in that house. Who was sneaking out at dawn, and who was sneaking back in. He caught them at it, when he delivered their milk." Gus snorted. "All of those fine gentlemen in their dinner clothes, tip-toeing across the porch to get to their cars, sneaking out to their fancy Nashes and Hudsons hidden down the lane in the weeds. He knew the scoop."

"Remember the story Grandpap told about the guy in the tux and the suitcase?" Ben guffawed. "Grandpap caught this one guy running down the lane for town, carrying his suitcase under his arm with all of his clothes sticking out of it. The guy tipped him a dime not to say a word, and he said 'I need to get out of here. Those people are crazy.' "

Sarah leaned forward. She tucked her hair behind her ear. "Did Karl ever remarry? After Frieda died?"

"Nope, never." Gus shook his head. "Stayed single the rest of his life."

Ben held up a finger. "Grandpap told me once that Grandpa Karl fell in love with a lady, but that she refused him."

A red four-door Jeep Wrangler Sport came bumping down the rough lane, followed at a cautious distance by a dust-stained pickup truck carrying the rest of Gus's construction crew. The Jeep's driver was waving her arm while merrily beeping the horn.

Ben pointed. "Who's the crazy woman in the Jeep?"

John turned. "That's my sister, Jackie. I wonder what she wants?"

"Let's get going, Ben." Gus stretched again. "Round up the troops. This house ain't gonna build itself."

"Gus," John said quickly. The devil was in the details. You had to listen to people, and ask them to repeat their story again and again, because you never knew when fresh details would surface, or when. "I may have some follow-up questions for you and for Ben, later."

"Ask away." Gus picked at a callous on his hand. "You know where to find us. We've got nothing to hide." He pointed his finger. "Like I told you before, Schlagels had nothing to do with that kidnapping. You cops bungled it back then. Had your blinders on. That baby's killer got clean away."

"Hey, you two!" Jackie shouted. She hit the brakes. The Jeep skidded to a stop, raising a cloud of tan dust. "I have news!" Slipping from behind the wheel, she reached into the open back seat. As usual, Jackie was dressed only in black. She retrieved a crumpled paper sack, and raised it triumphantly over her head. "Sparkling grape juice for everyone! See? I even remembered the twins!"

John offered Sarah his hand. He helped her to her feet. "We're ready for some good news, Jackie. What's up?"

She dug into the sack, grinning like a mad woman, and handed out plastic champagne flutes. "I'm so excited. I just got the email. I passed my licensing exam! I'm a real estate agent now, starting with Atlantic Gold Coast today."

Sarah glanced between the two Jarad siblings. "Did I miss something, Jackie? I didn't know you were working on that." That she hadn't heard about Jackie's effort really came as no surprise. This sister of John's was nice enough, but a little off base, and reserved.

"No one did! I kept it a secret, in case I didn't pass the exam. I've had a great couple of days, I can tell you, sitting on that news. I wanted to wait for the final confirmation." Gleefully, she unwrapped the wire hood, popped the plastic bottle top, and poured sparkling purple juice into their glasses. "It's out in the open now. I'm going to sell those Lost Forest parcels for you, and help you pay this new place off."

"That would be a real help." John took a sip. "I thought they'd have sold by now."

Jackie shrugged. "It's the economy. Fallout from 2008. People want to buy, and the banks want to lend them the money, but no one has the 20% down payment. That's still a bit stiff, especially with our high-end market. It's killing most of the deals. Don't worry, though. Now you have me on the sales team."

"You already sound like an agent." John looked pleased. He raised his glass. "Here's to your success."

"Here's to me." Jackie tapped her plastic flute against his. "And success for us all! I'll make sure you get the family discount, the five percent commission rate, instead of the standard six percent. Drink up, Sarah! Cheers! We're going to be rich!"

CHAPTER TEN

John exhaled slowly and cooled his second cup of coffee. He had reported to the station extra early because his dreams had troubled him again. This time, the Nazis were flitting from tree to tree, chasing him through miles of shadowy woods. He had finally decided to stop running and had crawled out of bed to start his day. He'd been very careful to not disturb Sarah, sleeping by his side. She had difficulty getting comfortable carrying the twins. When John saw that his wife stayed asleep, he had slipped from the bed, grabbed his clothes, and crept out to get dressed in the hall.

In spite of his lack of sleep, John felt surprisingly energetic and clear-headed. Yesterday had been a shit storm of news and surprise events. Today promised to be even more of the same. John loved the thrill of launching each new investigation, that great momentary pause until you found the commonality and things finally started to shape up. In a way, each new investigation felt magical, like blindly stepping off a cliff into a great chasm, trusting that you would, when the necessary time came, suddenly sprout wings, and fly.

CJ trotted upstairs from the basement locker room. The night shift had cycled out. CJ looked geared up and ready for the new day. "Yo, homey. Heard you had a big day."

"You'd better cut that shit out. If Chief Nunn hears you talking smack, she'll can your ass."

"Easy, hoss. I checked her locker. She's not in yet." CJ headed over to the communal coffee station and loaded up. "I read your report on the Spenser kidnapping. Sounds like you won the toss yesterday, answering that Madaket call. I spent the day settling parking space disputes at Harbor Fest."

John took a quick sip of his coffee and scorched his tongue. He winced. "Interviewing the Spensers at Moorhaven is always a treat, like winning a free kick to the nut sack."

"Have to take your word on that." CJ snickered. She plopped into the chair across from his desk. "Fill me in. How did the Chief do with handling the Spensers? She show any nerves?"

"I was impressed. Handled it like a pro." John rested his elbows on the desk. "Nunn said she covered something similar back in NOLA. Asked me to take the lead on this case, on the way over. I'm going to need your backup, CJ, with CSI support, big time."

"You got it."

With a start, John realized that he felt more comfortable letting Chief Nunn bear the public brunt of the Spenser investigation. Once he pushed passed the rancor of his demotion, he felt happier taking a less visible leadership role, and working in the background with CJ on the case. Not being the Chief, or being the face of the investigation and living in the limelight, felt liberating. Now he didn't need to dance to every question anymore, or be politically correct with every single thing he said, terrified of misquote. It was a relief to hand all of that responsibility off to Chief Nunn. He could focus now on his goals, and simply get on with solving the case and getting the answers. "She also said the Bureau might want to weigh in on this one."

"Really? The FBI? Wasn't the Spenser case before their time?"

"Nunn said they still track unsolved high profile cases."

"That will make things interesting around here." CJ dropped her voice. "You know how certain members of the force feel about off-island assistance. Hell, Ted Parsons doesn't even like asking the mainland Staties for help."

"We'll have to help Ted overcome that." John drummed the desk with his fingertips. He felt juiced up. Evidently, his second cup of coffee had kicked in. "If you've read my report, you know where we stand with the Spenser part of this. I'll need you to work with Paul on anything CSI we can get from that trunk. Be sure to cc: the chief on everything you send."

"Of course. I'll give Paul a call. Set something up."

"Paul also said we might see the preliminary Alice Spenser autopsy report later today. If I know him, he worked on it all night."

"Equally good. I can't wait to hear what he has to say."

"That's where we stand so far." John relaxed. "What you don't know is what I learned yesterday from the Schlagels."

"The Schlagels? Like Gus Schlagel, the builder? What does Gus have to do with any of this?"

"His grandfather, Karl, worked as Moorhaven's caretaker at the time of the kidnapping. Karl Schlagel was on the hook as the prime suspect. From what Gus said, it sounds like things got ugly. Anti-German sentiment, you know the drill. Gus is still pretty riled up about the way his family was treated. We'll need to remember that, going forward, and tread gently."

"Thanks for the heads-up." CJ flung her arm on the back of the chair. "Gus Schlagel. I'll be damned. That is so typically Nantucket. We have zero degrees of separation."

"Morning, detectives." Officer Sam Ketchem ambled into the room to start his shift. Sam immediately headed for the coffee station and robotically started brewing a fresh pot.

"Morning, Sam." John massaged his eyes. "You got that right, CJ. I don't need to see a DNA test. I know we're all related -"

John felt the earth shift beneath his feet as soon as he said the words. *Oh, hell. Really? Could it be happening again?* Nell Spenser's notorious Moorhaven cook had been a local woman, Mrs. Ketchem. *What were the odds that Sam Ketchem was related to her?* John leaned back in his chair. "Hey, Sam?" he asked, feeling a solid internal certainty that he already knew the answer. "Mrs. Ketchem, the cook who worked at Moorhaven? She any relation to you?"

"Yes, sir, she was." Sam poured a half a cup of sugar into his mug. "Florence Ketchem, my great-aunt a couple of times removed." Sam gave the piping hot coffee a stir with his finger then licked the sugar crystals off of his fingertips. "We all worked for the Spensers back in the day, when Moorhaven kept a full staff." He slowly walked over, pulled out a chair, and sat next to CJ. "They dropped all of that in the Sixties. Said the staff was too expensive to maintain. You can see it when you go out there now. Moorhaven's not nearly as swell as it used to be."

"I was out there yesterday. Still looked pretty swell to me."

"No, not really, sir." Sam frowned. "Not if you look closely. Moorhaven used to be immaculate. They've let half the lawn return to meadow. All of the trees need to be pruned. They're growing geraniums in the window boxes. Nell Spenser must be rolling in her grave. She hated geraniums. Said they were common. She told Joe Bolton that she'd fire him if she ever caught him planting a single one."

Sam rested his right ankle on his left knee. He cupped his coffee mug in both hands. "My great-grandma, Grace, was their laundress. You wouldn't believe the stories she had to tell. Her older sister, Emma, was their housemaid. You needed a lot of help to keep up with a house that size. All of the laundry was done by hand, loaded through a wringer and pegged out on a line to dry. Good luck if it was raining! And Nell insisted that all of the linen get ironed, too, even the sheets. She thought the family would get rheumatism if the linen wasn't toasted dry." Sam shook his head. "Hard to believe they used to do that much manual labor, but good steady jobs were hard to find." He shrugged. "The Spensers always paid fair wages. I'll give them that. You didn't mess around with that kind of luck. Back then, you kept good jobs in the family as much as you could."

"Crissakes!" CJ laughed. "That house had more Ketchems in it than Spensers!"

"Grandma Florence's daughter Frances worked there, too, as their housekeeper."

"Hold up." John reached for his legal pad. "I have a note on the housekeeper. Ketchem's not the name they gave me. No, it was Dormont, Frances Dormont."

"That's right," Sam agreed. "Frances was a daughter from great-grandma's first marriage to Harvey Dormont. Frances kept her daddy's name."

"Jesus!" CJ looked dazed. "I thought I was only kidding about you people, but I'm not."

Sam sipped his coffee. "There were two Ketchem boys working at Moorhaven, too. Uncle Fred and Uncle Arthur, Florence's nephews from the other side. They worked with Joe Bolton on the yard, and in the garden. Weeding, and such. Had to cut that big lawn using push mowers. They weren't allowed to make any noise, or they got fined a part of their wages. Cut the grass at dawn, as soon as the dew burned off. They used to sing all the way home, at the top of their lungs, to let all of that noise back out."

John had patrolled the road between 'Sconset and Madaket too many times to count. It was a long, dark twenty-eight miles. None of the Ketchems had stayed in Moorhaven overnight. It was decades before the BART shuttle service was even thought of. "How did they get home?"

"Grandpa Roy picked them up in his 1910 Ford Model T open truck." Sam smiled at the memory. "I wish we still had that rattletrap, sir. It was a classic, but it disintegrated. Literally. I've heard this story all my life. Grandpa Roy and Grandma sat up front with one of the girls squeezed in tight between them. Everyone else had to climb in the back. They sat on straw bales. If it was raining, they had to huddle under a canvas tarp to stay dry."

"Jesus." CJ frowned. "Sounds rough."

Sam looked insulted. "They didn't see it that way. They never complained. Beat the hell out of walking."

John flipped through his notes. "The Spensers didn't mention any of these folks to me yesterday."

"No reason why they should, sir. Good servants don't get seen. I remember hearing that much." Sam finished his coffee and stood. "Anything more, sir?"

John tapped his pen against the blotter. He wasn't ready to sign off on the Ketchems just yet. "Is there anyone else in your family still around, who might remember more?"

"Not really, sir." Sam straightened his uniform. "That generation has pretty much passed. My grandmother, Lillian, is still alive, but she's ninety years old and not all there." Sam tapped his temple. "She has an apartment at that mid-island old folks home in Surfside. Never leaves it, not even for a reunion."

"Island Sanctuary?" CJ offered.

"Yep. That's the one. Grandma's been living there for fifteen or sixteen years. Sweet set up, if you ask me."

John was surprised to hear that Lillian Ketchem, or any Ketchem for that matter, was living at Island Sanctuary. John's mother, Jenny, and her Island Girls Garden Club lady friends voluntarily maintained the flowerbeds at the premier assisted living facility. Jenny had mentioned that she never expected to move into the Sanctuary, since the monthly resident care fee there ran from eight to ten thousand dollars a month. John knew the entire Ketchem clan had never owned a hill of beans, and yet Lillian had been living at Island Sanctuary for at least fifteen years. *How on earth were the Ketchems covering that tremendous expense? Where was the money coming from?* "Island Sanctuary? That's kind of pricey, isn't it?"

Sam placed his coffee mug in the sink. "Grandma Lillian's always been an odd fish, sir. Got an inheritance the rest of us missed. Part of some fancy insurance annuity she has with Pacific National Bank. Grandma's never had to worry about a thing her entire life."

"Must be nice," CJ grumbled.

She straightened as Paul Jenkins, the Medical Examiner for Nantucket County, pushed through the Plexiglas door. Paul looked exhausted and jubilant at the same time. He was still enough of an old school gentleman to hold the door open for Chief Nunn, who entered first and smiled brilliantly. Paul hoisted the brown accordion folder he carried in his right hand.

"Hello, people! I brought the Alice Spenser autopsy results."

CHAPTER ELEVEN

"Officer Ketchem, please continue your duties," Chief Nunn directed. "Detectives? Dr. Jenkins? Let's take this into Conference Room A." She led the way. "We'll be more comfortable in there."

As they filed into the room, John noticed that both he and CJ took their customary seats around the rectangular table, following a pattern established at Chief Nunn's very first staff meeting. As the incomer, Paul sat at the head of the table, with Chief Nunn at the other end. John smiled. People were such creatures of habit. It didn't matter who they were. The slightest change, or something slightly off kilter, and you could see them begin to squirm. That inherent human behavior underlined one of John's core investigative beliefs: If you wanted to find out what was really going on, study the people involved in the event. If one of them was acting oddly, or if they started to vary their behavior, that's where the case focus belonged.

Chief Nunn folded her hands. She leaned on her elbows. "Dr. Jenkins? What have you got for us?"

Paul pushed his trendy new rimless glasses up his nose. He opened the accordion folder and set out neat stacks of paper-clipped reports and black and white autopsy stills. CJ had asked Paul once why he still used black and white photos when digital had made color processing so affordable. Paul had explained that he had tried using color, but then realized that he needed black and white to help him maintain his distance. Removing the color was a trick Paul used to help him stay clinical and objective.

He flipped his report open and tapped the cover sheet with his index finger. "I need to warn you, this isn't pretty." He looked up to check his audience and glanced clockwise around the table. "It never is, whenever a child is involved. It still upsets me, after twenty-eight years in this business. You never get used to it."

"I hope you never do," Chief Nunn added softly.

John grew alert. He was anticipating Paul's details, because once you knew how, you sometimes knew who, and once you knew who, you knew why.

Paul took a deep breath. "Alright. Let's make it official. The subject of this autopsy report was an unidentified Jane Doe, a well-nourished, female, Caucasian child approximately 20 to 24 months of age at her time of death, going by her teeth. She had hazel eyes, and auburn hair, and no significant moles, birthmarks, or scars. The newspapers the victim was wrapped in were dated April of 1921. From the condition of the un-embalmed corpse, I wouldn't disagree with that date range."

CJ toyed with her coffee mug. "What was the condition of the corpse?"

"Better than I anticipated," Paul admitted. "Because of the damp conditions, the lid had swollen tight, creating a nearly anaerobic environment. Decomposition was restricted. The corpse naturally mummified." Fanning the autopsy photographs across the table, Paul pulled one free, like a magician with a deck of cards. "I've compared the photographs of Alice Spenser taken before the kidnapping with the subject we found in the trunk. Based on that rather simple comparison, I would be willing to testify that the subject in the trunk was the kidnapping victim, Alice Spenser, in court. That said, I strongly recommend running a DNA sequencing test against any remaining Spenser family members, to confirm the identification."

"Hold up." CJ raised her hand. She looked to Chief Nunn. "DNA tests are expensive. We'll need to run the request past Council for pre-approval before we move on it. It wasn't part of their annual budgeting plan. They'll need to sign off on it first."

Chief Nunn made a quick note. "Thank you, Detective, for the heads-up. I will do that."

Paul shrugged. "I can only offer my recommendation." He flipped to another photograph, turning it sideways with his fingertips. "The subject had obviously been well cared for. I found no signs of sexual trauma, no contusions, or broken bones. There were no signs of any immediate or long-term illness or disease."

Chief Nunn impatiently drummed her fingers. "Dr. Jenkins? What did you find?"

Paul cleared his throat. "I found pre-mortem blistering around the victim's mouth, nose, and under her chin. That evidence points to my conclusion." He crossed his arms. "I believe the subject was anesthetized, probably through the use of chloroform."

"Chloroform?" CJ looked startled. "Who had access to that?"

"Almost everyone. It was the most commonly used anesthetic during the Twenties, until ether replaced it. It also had industrial application on garden pests. In any case, the liver sample I tested showed that chloroform was being metabolized shortly before death." Paul straightened his report. "Chloroform is known to cause fatal cardiac fibrillation and arrhythmia, what is now called 'huffing,' or 'sniffer's death.' The FDA still classifies chloroform as an extremely hazardous material. I don't believe huffing was what happened here." He resettled his glasses. "Because of the presence of the blisters, and because of the victim's age, I believe the usage was involuntary. The trick with chloroform is that, after the victim loses consciousness, the chin must be supported or the tongue can obstruct the airway."

"Please, Dr. Jenkins, just spit it out," Chief Nunn demanded. "What are you saying?"

"Alice Spenser swallowed her tongue." He looked up sadly. "She asphyxiated."

Chief Nunn slapped the tabletop with the flat of her hand. John flinched as the sound reverberated off the conference room walls. Chief Nunn stood. She turned her back and stepped into a corner, crossing her arms. Her shoulders shook for a moment before she straightened, and returned.

What was that about? John wondered. He could see the effort it took her to continue.

"That poor child," Chief Nunn said, blinking rapidly. She whispered: "No one should ever lose a child. It's too hard." Pulling out her chair, she sat back down, placed both hands on the conference table, and cleared her throat. "Dr. Jenkins? What else can you tell us? Any details about the trunk?"

"From the name stenciled on it, we can assume that at some point it came from the Spenser household, but I'd hesitate to say it came directly from any one of them. It is possible that the trunk was discarded, or given away to someone else who used it secondhand."

"Detective Jarad?" Chief Nunn pointed a finger. "There's one follow up for your investigation. Identify ownership of that trunk."

John felt a ripple of irritation. The Chief was being thorough, but she didn't need to tell him how to do his job. "Yes, sir. Got it."

"I've also sampled everything in the trunk for DNA. Once you get the expense approved, I'll send the samples to Nelson Labs." Paul polished his glasses. "I want to note that the test results will take weeks, not days, like you see on TV. That instant timing thing is pure fiction."

"Noted," Chief Nunn said. "Anything more, Dr. Jenkins? Any sign of the ransom money?"

"The fifty thousand dollars? If I had found it, I wouldn't be standing here now," Paul joked. "I do have some interesting information on that, though." He pulled a second manila folder forward and flipped it open. "I was curious about the ransom money. From what I've read about the case online, the Spensers originally didn't tell the police they were going to pay it. They kept the kidnapper's letter a secret, at first. Oddly, the envelope the letter came in was lost. That's a pity; the postmark may have been helpful. In any case, the Spensers sent George Stephens, one of their employees, out with fifty thousand dollars in cash wrapped up in a ransom packet. Stephens said he left the packet, as instructed, at the base of an oak tree on the Moorhaven property. He immediately drove into town and then turned around and returned home, following the kidnapper's instructions to the letter."

Paul tapped his notes. "Alice was supposed to be returned the following morning. When she wasn't returned, that's when the Spensers told the police about receiving the letter and paying the ransom. The authorities were understandably furious. They searched every bit of the Moorhaven property including the garage apartment where George Stephens slept. Ripped the place apart. They never found the money."

"Or," John said, "the Staties found the money and they kept it for themselves."

"Maybe the kidnappers got the fifty grand, but they couldn't return Alice because she was already dead," CJ offered.

"Or," Chief Nunn tapped her pen. "It's possible that the ransom wasn't even connected to Alice Spenser's kidnapping. You said the ransom letter arrived on day two, by US mail. It's possible that the letter was sent by an independent third party, someone who knew what had happened to Alice Spenser, and who wanted to take advantage of the situation to hit the Spensers up for the cash. People are cruel. I've seen them take advantage of this kind of situation before. Robbing houses when people are attending funerals, that kind of thing."

"Logic Tree." CJ cracked her knuckles. "My favorite exercise."

John settled in. Logic Tree was a brainstorming exercise taught at the Academy. It was designed to map out fresh investigative variables and possibilities.

"Who else knew about the ransom letter, other than the family?" Paul began. "Not even the police knew about it, until the Spensers told them on day three."

"Oh, no," John interrupted. "You can bet the Moorhaven servants knew about it on day two, as soon as that letter arrived. If the Spensers were openly discussing it, and you know they were, Moorhaven was filled with people who could have overheard and shared that conversation. I've got a list of the servants. It fills four pages." He sat back. "I think we can assume that everyone connected to Moorhaven knew about the ransom letter on day two. Here's another thing: Even without the postmarked envelope, we know that the letter was delivered on day two. That means it was posted locally. Anything mailed off island would have taken days to arrive, maybe even as long as a week. Ferry service and mail delivery was unreliable in 1921. Day two delivery means that the ransom letter was mailed by someone local, from a local post office, either from 'Sconset or from town."

"Point taken," Chief Nunn agreed. She made a note on her tablet. "Anything more?"

"I've got more." Paul crossed his arms. "The ransom packet weighed approximately five and a half pounds. It was roughly the size of two modern day shoe boxes."

"How the fuck do you know that?" CJ challenged. "Jesus! You are such a nerd."

"Thank you." Paul accepted her compliment. "It's an easy calculation. Each bill weighs one gram, no matter the denomination. With 454 grams per pound, and a $50,000 ransom consisting of 2,500 twenty dollar bills, the packet weighed five and a half pounds." He coughed modestly into his fist. "I should also mention that the ransom wasn't paid in US *dollars*. No one else has mentioned that fact."

Chief Nunn blinked. "What do you mean the ransom wasn't paid in US dollars?"

"The US was still on the gold standard in 1921. Those ransom bills were twenty dollar gold certificates, nicknamed gold backs. The US didn't go off the gold standard until 1933, when President Roosevelt signed it into law."

"What does that mean?" CJ asked, her voice rising. "Those ransom bills were worth real gold?"

"In 1921, they were." Paul smiled. "For every certificate you owned, you could go into any bank or Federal Reserve and demand twenty dollars worth of gold coin on the strength of it, all backed by the US government."

"How about now?" CJ pursued. "If you found the ransom money now, would you get fifty thousand dollars in gold for it?"

"Nice try." Paul laughed. "But no. The Treasury cancelled gold certificates as official currency. You might be able to sell one to a collector, or it would make a nice decorative specimen to hang on the wall, but you can't use them as money anymore. Sorry, CJ."

"I appreciate this creative brainstorming, team," Chief Nunn said. "We're really starting to flesh things out. Anything more? Any talking points we haven't covered?"

"I have one more point," John said. He couldn't help himself. He had to give the Chief a small dig. "I've already listed it on my investigative detail sheet for follow up."

"And what is that, Detective Jarad?" Chief Nunn cocked her head sarcastically. "Care to share it with the team?"

John slowly underlined the point on his pad. "The night of the kidnapping, the Spensers said that two-year-old Alice had been put to bed."

"I recall that detail." Chief Nunn scrolled through her tablet. "It was in the nanny's report. Here it is: 'Nancy Huff had put Alice down for the night'."

John pointed at the autopsy report in the center of the table. "Paul? What was Alice Spenser wearing in the trunk?"

Paul answered without referring to his notes, and without hesitation. "A lace dress, with kid leather shoes."

"Who dressed Alice again?" John dug the point of his pen deeply into the lined paper. "The kidnapper? He knocked her out using chloroform, and then dressed her again right down to her shoes? Mighty thoughtful of him - or her - don't you think?"

CJ rolled her eyes. "Show off," she muttered.

There was a tap at the door. It cracked open. Dispatcher Tina Bradley poked her head in. Her eyes were wide, and her face was flushed with excitement.

"Chief Nunn? Sorry to interrupt. The FBI is here. He's asking to see you."

CHAPTER TWELVE

"Shit." Sargeant Ted Parsons scratched his gray crew cut hair. He glowered from his corner desk. "Now we got to deal with the fibbies? We don't need their help."

"Nunn said the Bureau likes keeping tabs on high profile cold cases." John scrolled through his iPhone, checking for messages. The screen was empty of any green text bubbles, so he relaxed. Even though his wife hated using her cell phone, Sarah had promised to text him immediately if anything came up, since they were keeping an eagle eye on their twin's thirty-five-week minimum gestation window. John was still trying to limit his calls to once a day at noon, and to shake his obnoxious new habit of calling Sarah to check on her two or three times a day, since she said that was making her more nervous, not less. Instead, John had downloaded a weather service app in case they needed an emergency life flight to Boston General. Checking that app obsessively on the sly seemed to satisfy his compulsion. No news was good news when it came to Sarah and the twins.

"If you say so, sir." Ted looked doubtful. He cocked a thumb at the Chief's office. "Look at him. Federal diversity guidelines in the flesh." Ted thoughtfully chewed his thumbnail. "Where do you think he's staying?"

"Tina said he booked a suite at The Sandpiper Inn."

"Typical." Ted scowled. "Another waste of our taxpayer dollars. Probably eating out three meals a day on our chit, too."

John put his iPhone down. He studied Special Agent in Charge Cesar Mayas through the glass partition. John struggled to stay objective until he knew the guy better. So far, all he really knew was that Agent Mayas was an adjunct from the Northeast Bureau out of Boston, that he had dark brown hair and darker eyes, and that he didn't seem to be having any trouble carrying a cardboard box tucked under one arm with what looked like a folding hybrid laptop in his free hand.

Agent Mayas was less than six feet tall. He also looked to be about six feet wide, and judging from the cut of his lightweight summer linen suit, all of that was solid muscle. He had the broad shoulders of a power lifter. The Bureau must have recently relaxed their regulations because he wore a snappy straw fedora with a red and green ribbon hatband, and a well-trimmed goatee. Mayas was certainly styling, although he looked more like South Miami Beach than the island's preppy standard Ralph Lauren.

Chief Nunn had introduced Agent Mayas to the team, and then she pulled the agent and Paul Jenkins into her office and shut the door. John tried to ignore the fact that he and CJ had been so quickly dismissed, like junior force members instead of the detectives on the case, plus the fact that Nunn's office used to be his. These two facts irritated him like having a sharp pebble in his shoe. John shook the disappointment off and reached for his case notes. Buying into that kind of personal drama would do no good, plus he had real work to do.

The Chief's door swung open again, and all three walked out. The Chief was laughing at something Mayas had said.

"No, Cesar, the only thing I truly miss is the boudin, and the grits, of course. Nantucket cuisine is equally delicious. You must try their bay scallops sautéed in garlic and white wine. It's good enough to curl your toes. Team? Let's touch base."

She led them into Conference Room A and picked up a marker under the whiteboard, waiting patiently until every sat. She turned, and the purple marker squeaked in protest as she wrote: "Alice Spenser Kidnapping (Cold Case)" across the top of the board. John tried to ignore the fact that the heading was slightly off center. Chief Nunn capped the marker. She tapped it against her fingertips.

"I've given Agent Mayas a summary of where we stand with the investigation so far. Dr. Jenkins has also shared the Alice Spenser autopsy results. Going forward, team, Detective Jarad will lead the local investigation. I'll liaise with the Bureau." Her sudden wide smile took in the whole room. "I should mention that Agent Mayas can vouch for me. We've worked together before, during Katrina. He was only a trainee then, but you could already see that he had outstanding potential. Welcome, Special Agent Mayas, to the Faraway Isle."

"Thank you, Chief Nunn." The aluminum chair squealed as Agent Mayas stood. His good leather shoes slapped the floor as he walked to the front of the room. "She's right. We did work closely with the NOLA force in August of 2005. We had to, since Hurricane Katrina ripped the roof off our Bureau office on Simon Boulevard. The local force was kind enough to share their space, and their emergency services with us, in an outstanding display of cross-agency cooperation." He reached for the marker. "I'm hoping we can work along similar lines on Nantucket, as well."

John couldn't be sure, but he thought Chief Nunn was blushing.

Mayas started to pace. "It's hard to believe, but in 1921, kidnapping was not a national offense. It wasn't a law on the books until the Lindbergh kidnapping in 1932, when President Hoover first directed federal agencies, including the Bureau, to act. This direction also included the Division of

Investigation at the Department of Justice, and the Secret Service of the US Treasury, whenever a ransom threat was involved."

Mayas set the marker down. He flipped his laptop open. "Prior to that, authority was held at the state level, which is why, sad to say, these Spenser case notes are so sketchy. That said, I'm happy to share what we do have." Glancing up, he checked his audience. "I'd also like to reiterate, as I told Chief Nunn earlier, that I'm here to offer every assistance, to provide advice, and to make available any technical, resource, or forensic help you may need."

"That said," Ted crossed his arms, "we don't need your help."

Agent Mayas ignored Ted's remark. "You may be curious about my qualifications," he continued smoothly. "My official title is a Non-Family Child Abduction Specialist. I'm a member of the Bureau's Child Abduction Rapid Deployment, or CARD team. CARD teams include an agent with a proven track record in violent crimes against children investigations, and the completion of an extensive and focused two-year training program." He began to tick items off his fingers. "As a CARD team leader, I bring local access to the Bureau's in-house behavioral analysts, to the National Center for the Analysis of Violent Crime coordinators, and to any Child Exploitation Task Force members that may be involved. DNA analysis is my special focus."

"Acronym soup," Ted muttered.

Chief Nunn twisted her pen between her fingers. "I'm sure we all appreciate your expertise."

"Thank you, Chief Nunn. CARD teams were developed in response to the National Child Search Assistance Act of 1990, which stated that law enforcement agencies may not observe a waiting period before accepting a missing child report. Every missing child must be immediately entered into the state law enforcement system, and the National Crime

Information Center, the NCIC, which as you know, is quite a change from what we saw with the Spenser situation." He tightened his lips. "Law enforcement entered almost 800,000 missing children into the NCIC database last year. Eight hundred thousand missing children. It's hard to believe. I'm doing whatever I can do to bring those children home."

He swiped his touchscreen. "Of course, the Spenser case presents its own set of unique issues, the first being that the evidence is ninety years old. Usually, abduction investigations need to move quickly. It's commonly understood that the first 48 hours are critical to the recovery of the child. These days, of course, we have the benefit of modern technologies. We're finding video surveillance to be a particularly effective tool."

Ted snorted. "Too bad we didn't have video in 1921. Mystery solved."

"Knock it off, Ted." CJ elbowed him sharply. "You're being a dick."

Mayas picked the marker up. He tapped it against his palm. "The original Spenser investigation considered two theories: one, that the kidnappers were members of a professional East Coast gang, and two, that the kidnapper was someone from inside the Spenser household. The investigation quickly focused on the second option, and it focused on three men: the tutor, George Stephens; Floyd Mulloy, the Spensers' chauffeur; and Moorhaven's handyman, Karl Schlagel. Schlagel was seen to be acting suspiciously at the time, although, from what I can gather from the report, than meant he was showing up drunk to work. Stephens was suspected because he was gay, and Mulloy was suspected because he was Irish."

He frowned. "A state fingerprint expert was brought in. He dusted Alice Spenser's nursery and the house, but nothing definitive was found. Unfortunately, they were still using the silver nitrate system at that time."

Paul Jenkins shook his head. "That test was completely unreliable."

"True, but it was the best resource they had. The expert only recovered smudges. He did make the suggestion that the kidnapper may have worn gloves." Mayas swiped the screen again. "It was also noted that there were no signs of forced entry into Moorhaven, and that the family dog was not alarmed by the intruder."

"Check," John said.

Mayas raised one eyebrow, and continued. "As soon as the alarm was raised, the grounds were searched. Unfortunately, the loose gravel driveway precluded any tracks, and the sandy road was too well used to offer anything substantive. The investigators did take plaster casts of individual tire tracks, but the state had no success in matching them to any one particular suspect. The day after the kidnapping, a ransom letter arrived by USPS. It also offered only smudges, nothing concrete. The envelope was tested, as well."

"Hold up." John pushed back his chair. "We were told the envelope was lost."

"I don't know what you were told, Detective Jarad, but the Alice Spenser ransom letter and the envelope are in our CTAD system." He rotated his laptop. "Here, let me show you."

CJ stood up. She took up a spot at Mayas' shoulder. "What's CTAD?"

"Communicated Threat Assessment Database. It houses the digital versions of every type of threatening or criminally oriented communication we have on file. Bank robbery, extortion notes, or, as you can see, ransom letters."

CJ laughed. "Bet the intern who got that scanning assignment enjoyed the summer."

"I'm sure she did." Mayas stepped aside and shared the screen.

Dear Sir:

Follow this notise. Bring 50,000$ cash made up in one packet. Order Stephens to town alone in car. Leave mony at base of oak tree left seide 100 feet off road under big stone. Drive to town. Do not look back. Do not set a trapp in any way. After we haf the mony in hand we will tell you were Alice is.

"The Spenser letter does offer some key points. It's short, only 65 words. That implies that whoever wrote it knew what he was doing. He was decisive. These CTAD letters are also studied by forensic linguist profilers at Quantico, a resource that wasn't originally available. The linguists search out key word choices, spellings, and phrases that suggest ethnicity and gender."

"This is fascinating," CJ said.

Mayas smiled. "The forensics on the Spenser letter suggests that it was written by a male of European descent. Additionally," Mayas stroked the screen, "the envelope was postmarked April 7, 1921. Nantucket."

John leaned on his fingertips. "Nantucket had two post offices in 1921. One was in town, the other was in 'Sconset. The Nantucket postmark confirms our assumption that the kidnapper was local and not part of a professional mainland gang, because of the time of delivery. Also, if the kidnapper was working from inside Moorhaven, he could easily have mailed the letter from Nantucket town that day, to throw the investigation off the scent, since he or she might have been known in 'Sconset."

Chief Nunn rapped the table. "Thank you for that additional information and insight, Agent Mayas. Alright, team, let's move forward. I believe our next step is to follow up on the DNA samples Dr. Jenkins recovered from the victim and the trunk. Detective Allamand? We'll need samples from the Spenser family for comparison purposes. My hope is that they'll volunteer these. I'd like you to go out to Moorhaven and ask the Spensers for fresh samples. Politely, of course."

"Yes, sir." CJ stretched. "I've got spit kits in my truck."

"I think we can do better than that, Detective Allamand." Mayas lifted the cardboard box off of the floor. He placed the box in the middle of the conference table, and popped it open. It was filled to the brim with yellow tamper evident envelopes. "I thought we might be needing these." He picked up one kit and he spun it between fingers. "I brought FDDU buccal collection kits. Each kit is fully contained. It has everything you'll need for your swab samples, including a foam applicator, pre-inked finger pads, and a pair of nitrile gloves."

CJ looked like a kid getting a new bike on Christmas morning. She took the proffered kit and turned it over and over in her hands. "I've heard of these kits. They're cutting edge."

Mayas slid the box across the table. "Keep them. I can get more."

"Chief Nunn?" Paul stood. He tapped his notes together neatly. "I need to reiterate that it may be a week or more before we see the test results. I can't promise you anything sooner." He shrugged. "I can try pulling some strings with Nelson Labs, but I know they're swamped. Timing will depend on their workload."

"I can get your DNA test results within 24 hours." Mayas slowly folded his laptop. "From our in-house Boston lab, and for free."

Chief Nunn presented a truly impressive standing bitch face. She stared pointedly at Ted before turning her gaze on Agent Mayas.

"Thank you, Agent Mayas," she said. "We'll take you up on that. Apparently, we do need your help."

CHAPTER THIRTEEN

Sarah gripped the steering wheel with her right hand. She rested her left hand on top of her belly. She knew it was normal to be concerned about her pregnancy, but why did she feel so filled with dread about everything else all of the time? Nibbling worry waited for her like a hungry dog when she opened her eyes every morning. Her life felt like some daily version of PTSD, and it all boiled down to one bitter kernel of truth: *What if Mason found her again?* Was carrying this much dread around normal? Her OBGYN, Dr. Diballa, was concerned about seeing the random spikes in Sarah's blood pressure. Dr. D had outlined the dangers of preeclampsia. *Crissakes! I need to cut this shit out. This can't be healthy for the twins. But how do I deal with this? I can't keep dumping everything on John. He has enough on his plate as it is.*

Her stomach growled in spite of the grilled American cheese and tomato sandwich she had enjoyed for lunch. That was another thing to deal with, this endless, gnawing hunger. Sarah dug into her bag for her emergency protein bar, and glanced at the label. Salted caramel. Perfect. Some days she was crazy hungry for salt, some days for sweet. This should satisfy both cravings. Lately, she felt like a huge walking open mouth, Humpty Dumpty, a ravenous egg on legs. Sarah laughed at the image.

At Milestone Road she paused at the stop sign, and turned left, heading for town. John's mother, Jenny, had asked to borrow the truck to save the $150 delivery charge on a load of pine bark mulch for her pet Island Girls Garden Club project at the old folks' home. Sarah couldn't do any heavy lifting, but she had volunteered to drive, so that she could at least participate. She had learned the trick to finding happiness when living an island life: find something to do when she was through painting for the day, and then do it. Volunteering her spare time kept her busy and connected, and it balanced out her days.

The truck rolled up and over the asphalt speed bump into the garden center's main parking lot. Sarah turned for the loading dock out back. Even in the middle of a workday, the Fragile Paradise Garden Supply was packed with well-heeled customers looking for that perfect specimen to fill the gaping hole in their flowerbed, or that empty patch in their vegetable garden. She was in luck. She found a wide parking space next to the forklift near the dumpster. Sarah parked and struggled to free herself from the steering wheel, and she marched inside searching for Jenny.

As soon as she entered the greenhouse, Sarah felt surrounded by a lush, comforting sense of tranquility. The atmosphere felt warm, and it smelled wholesome like moss and good rich earth. Hanging baskets hung on steel rods over her head, and plastic trays of splendidly colored bedding plants lay displayed on tables along both concave opaque plastic walls. The air inside the greenhouse, although slightly humid, felt easier to breathe, probably because of the extra oxygen. Sarah didn't really need anything more to take care of, but maybe a potted plant for her studio might brighten things up? She lifted a clay pot of imperial purple petunias and choked when she saw the price tag: $75. Her innate Pittsburgh frugality immediately rebelled at the inflated Nantucket price. She carefully returned the pot to the shelf, satisfied with her decision to just say no, and she continued her search for Jenny.

A water fountain in the corner chuckled merrily, freshening the delightful breeze blowing in through the door. The breeze gently stirred a peaceful three-note wind chime. An overhead row of Boston ferns kept trying to snag Sarah's hair. She pushed through them and strolled into the main sales area toward the cash register kiosk. A well-built man wearing a turquoise polo shirt was talking to the middle-aged cashier. The man said something under his breath. The cashier laughed, obviously charmed by his attention. Sarah felt jolted by a bolt of recognition. Her entire world sharpened its focus. Her pulse began to pound in her ears. She had to clutch a tray table for support.

"Mason?" she gasped.

He was standing less than twenty feet away. She recognized the shape of his head, and the set of his shoulders. Sarah released the tray table and forced her legs to move, one leaden step at a time, her knees threatening to buckle with each step. Everything in her was screaming to turn on her heels and run away.

Mason hadn't noticed her standing there, yet. She could still dash back to the truck, speed away, find John, and hide. But a new and stronger voice was making itself known, telling her that she was through running away. Nantucket was her home now. Here, she was surrounded by family and by friends. Mason was the outsider, the stranger, and his odious way of living and his obsessive control over her was finished. She was through being bullied by him, or by anyone else, ever again. Yes, she had made a mistake. She had made plenty of them, but that was over and done with. She had learned from her mistakes, and running away had been one of them. She should have told Mason to fuck off directly, years ago. Now she was living her new life and Mason wasn't going to be a part of it, unless she let him, and she wasn't willing to let that happen. With some surprise, Sarah realized that she was glad that John wasn't here to fall back on. Mason was her problem, and she would know once and for all that she had dealt with him on her own terms.

She took two steps closer. Mason even had the same trendy metro haircut she remembered. In spite of her resolve, Sarah couldn't force herself to stand any closer than arms-length away. "Mason?"

He turned. An amused half-smile danced across his lips.

"Sorry? I don't know who this Mason is, but evidently, he's a lucky man."

Sarah dug her fingernails into the softened wood of the kiosk. She stood there, blinking stupidly, as relief flooded through her. This man wasn't Mason. Her relief was so strong that she felt chilled. Gooseflesh crawled up her arms.

"Miss? Is everything okay?"

She swallowed. "Yes, I'm okay. Sorry. I thought you were someone I knew."

"If you're looking for Jenny," the cashier pointed, "she's talking with Henry about that load of mulch she ordered."

"Yes, thank you. I was looking for Jenny," she stammered. Sarah tottered toward the side door, feeling mortified, like a fool. *What was it going to take to finally get over her panicky fear? Would Mason ever fade into her past, or would he always be standing in shadows, grinning like a demon, triggering delusions and paranoia whenever she thought of him?*

Sarah crossed the threshold and stepped into a second glasshouse. This one featured rows of salmon impatiens and half-grown sunflowers. She followed the sound of Jenny's voice around a stack of pallets, and found her mother-in-law animatedly talking with Henry Pollock, the garden center's co-owner. To Sarah's surprise, her sister-in-law Jackie was also there.

"There you are." Jackie crossed her slim arms. As usual, she was dressed in her standard uniform of a black T-shirt, sneakers, and jeans. "We thought maybe you got lost."

"I'll rustle up the boys and load that mulch, Mrs. J.," Henry said. "Shouldn't take long."

"Thank you, Henry." Jenny cocked her head like an alert sparrow. "How are you feeling, my dear? You look pale."

"I'm fine." Sarah waved her off. The last thing she wanted to do was to tell Jenny and Jackie about the misidentification at the kiosk. They'd think she was nuts. She quickly reached for another topic. "How's the real estate job coming, Jackie? Still loving it?"

Jackie dropped her arms to her hips. She looked pleased. With a start, Sarah realized that when Jackie smiled, her whole demeanor changed. When Jackie looked animated, she was pretty. Sarah blushed with shame. Was she so shallow that she had never really looked at this sister of John's before? She felt like she was seeing Jackie as a real person for the very first time.

"I am loving it." Jackie pushed her sleeves up to her elbows. "It's a challenge. There's something new to learn every single day. I'm working with this awesome client. He's the best! Came in as a cold call yesterday. Wants to look at island property, as an investment." She checked her phone. "I'm supposed to pick him up in thirty minutes. He's flying in on the New York shuttle. Wants to look at those Lost Forest parcels of yours, first thing. And he's interested in buying more than one." She returned her phone to her pocket. "That is so smart of him. He wants to buy the vacant parcels on either side, to keep his home site private. I have to say that it's nice working with someone who is decisive, who knows exactly what he wants."

Jenny patted Jackie's arm. "You go ahead then, dear. Sarah can give me a ride to Sanctuary in the truck."

Jackie hesitated. "Are you sure you're okay, Mom, on the other end? You're not going to try spreading all of that mulch by yourself, right?"

"Absolutely not." Jenny shooed her off. "A platoon of Island Girls volunteers is eagerly standing by. Please, dear, I mean it. I come from a long line of wheeler-dealers and freebooters. I'd hate to ever feel responsible for killing a sale."

CHAPTER FOURTEEN

The pickup truck felt logy, because of the heavy load of mulch. It was one more thing to add to their ever-expanding chore list, but the truck needed to be realigned. As hard as Sarah clung to the steering wheel, the truck kept drifting toward the bike lane on the right. Luckily, Milestone Road ran as straight as a ruler. Sarah could easily see any bicyclists or runners on the parallel track in plenty of time, and steer out of their way.

Jenny reached over. She tapped Sarah's arm.

"Really, my dear. I don't mean to be a hovering mother-in-law, but how are you feeling?"

"I'm fine." Sarah skated the truth. Physically, she did feel fine. She didn't want Jenny worrying about her mental state. That Sarah decided to keep private. She was embarrassed to admit that she felt like such a basket case lately. "I drop a pee sample off every Monday to get it tested. Dr. Diballa said that so far, there's no signs of preeclampsia."

"That is terrific news." Jenny settled her hands in her lap. "She didn't mention gestational diabetes?"

"Nope. I am taking this very seriously, Jenny. I've even switched to using acrylic paint. Dr. D thinks I'm one of the lucky ones. She did say that I might need a C-section. I'm not looking forward to that, but when the time comes, I might run out of options."

"I'm delighted that John married into such a resilient family." Jenny smiled serenely. "And how is the new house coming?"

"Good news there, too. They delivered the windows yesterday, no problem. Gus and Ben have already started on the roof. It's amazing how quickly they can put up a house." Sarah slowed to turn left on Hatcher Lane, and then sped back up. "I think it's because they use nail guns these days. When that crew gets busy, it sounds like the Hatfields and the McCoys are at it again. The only decision we have left is where to put John's gun safe."

Sarah chewed her lip. This was the one thing they couldn't seem to agree on. "John wants a built-in safe, in our bedroom closet. I'm not comfortable with having guns in the house, especially, you know, after what happened with Toby."

"Guns are one aspect of John's career that I've never been happy about." Jenny nervously resettled her purse. "When he lived at home, I insisted that John lock his service weapons in his truck. I read once that a gun in the home is twenty-two times more likely to be used in an accidental shooting than in self-defense. That statistic cinched it for me. I don't care how well you secure them. It's too high of a risk, especially with a house full of active grandchildren running around."

She glanced at Sarah worriedly. "Then there's the issue of getting on with life after an accident occurs. Nantucket is such a small community, and we still need to live together." She looked out the side window. "Mercy Talbot is a long-time garden club member. I couldn't expect Mercy to leave our group just because it made me personally uncomfortable. At the same time, she couldn't expect me to step down as President, either." Jenny sighed. "It's been a year since Toby died, and she still won't meet my eyes. I feel so sorry for her. She's so alone. She's lost her husband and both of her children. I can only imagine her grief."

Sarah felt a green apple ripple of apprehension. When she had volunteered to work with the Island Girls Garden Club, she hadn't considered the idea that she might run into Toby's mother. "Will Mercy be there today?"

"No. She sent her regrets. She had a doctor's appointment, one she couldn't cancel."

"Ah." Sarah hid her relief. She knew she should feel some sort of closure, but the horror of Toby's death was still too fresh, too real. She also knew she needed to come to grips with its after-effect on his mother, Mercy. Whenever Sarah ran into Mercy, she felt like she was being judged, as if there was something more she should have done to prevent Toby's death. If she closed her eyes, Sarah could still see that crimson bubble of blood that had stained Toby's teeth as he lay dying in the bottom of the boat. She could still hear his painful, labored lung shot breathing. That memory firmed her resolve. No, she would not let guns threaten the safety of their new home. John would have to find another location for his gun safe. He would just have to deal with the inconvenience.

Sarah pulled into the Sanctuary parking lot, feeling a lot better having made her decision. She drove toward the terraced central garden and the cluster of garden club volunteers in disposable yellow vests that stood by, leaning on their rakes. Quickly pulling a U-turn and using her mirrors, Sarah reversed the truck and parked.

Jenny eagerly unbuckled her seatbelt. "I don't want you to do any of the lifting, my dear. That's what these volunteers are for. Why don't you go for a walk, and enjoy the garden? We should be done in an hour. Relax, and enjoy yourself."

"Okay by me, Jenny. I've been curious to see what you've been up to out here."

Sarah left the parking lot and followed an artful brick path edged with downy daisy-like feverfew. The landscape began to rise, and it expanded into a sloping ballast stone rock garden with a riot of rose shrubs punctuated by clumps of honeysuckle and amusingly fringed French lavender. Sarah strolled past a hedge of Black-Eyed Susans in full bloom. As she rounded a curve, she stumbled onto a resident slumbering quietly in the shade of the mock Victorian gazebo. The elderly woman in the wheelchair was being watched over by an aide, who was busily scrolling through her phone. The aide looked up quickly. She put a finger to her lips.

"Shhh," she whispered. "It's nap time."

The elderly woman was a tiny, shrunken mummy, swaddled in a wooly sapphire blue cashmere cape. Her skin and lips were so gray as to be almost colorless. Her skin hung in crepey folds over the corners of her eyes. It ran in long channels down her turkey neck. Surprisingly, her wispy hair had recently been dyed a bright golden auburn that shone in the sun.

"What's with the hair?" Sarah asked.

"Got me." The aide shrugged. "Gets it done every six weeks like clockwork. Whether she needs it or not."

"It's not nice to talk about me, girls, like I can't hear you." The care patient opened her eyes, which shone with an alert and beady intelligence. "And it's not nap time for me," she croaked. "I just closed my eyes because you, Karlie, are so damned dull." She pointed an arthritic finger. "Always looking at your damned phone."

"Oh, Miz Ketchem." Karlie dropped her phone into a pocket. "Don't mind her. She always gets cranky right after lunch."

"And please don't refer to me in the third person, Karlie. You know it makes me peevish. I'm not dead yet." She studied Sarah suspiciously. "Who're you?"

Sarah felt like she had suddenly been called onto the carpet by one of the nuns. "Sarah Jarad. With the Island Girls Garden Club?"

"Don't end your sentences as a question, Sarah Jarad. It's a dreadful modern habit. You are either with the garden club, or not. Which is it?"

"I'm … with?" Sarah struggled to end her reply with something other than a preposition, but she couldn't come up with anything better on the fly. She had the sudden sinking feeling that she had been trapped by the grammar police.

"Incorrigible." Miz Ketchem studied Sarah's obvious baby bump. "It looks like you, at least, have been keeping busy. Since we're not going to be introduced," she glared at the aide by her side, "I am Lillian Ketchem."

A light bulb went off as Sarah made the connection. She had worked very hard over the winter to memorize the island's more common family names. "Any relation to Sam Ketchem?"

"Sam is my grandson." Lillian slowly wet her lips. "How do you know Sam?"

"He works with my husband, John. They both work for the Nantucket force."

"Sam has mentioned John Jarad before. Have a seat. Karlie? Take a break. Sarah here can watch over me quite as well as you can. I'll push the call button if I need anything."

Karlie looked like she had unexpectedly won a reprieve from the governor. "Do you mind?"

"Not at all." Sarah settled onto a bench. Why not? She had an hour to kill before Jenny needed her mad driving skills again, and besides, for some odd reason the big toe of her left foot had started to throb. It was always something, with the twins.

Lillian blinked up at the sunlight like a tortoise. "It's nice having a new visitor. Sam stops by, of course he does, but it's a duty visit. Not the same thing."

Lillian leaned forward. Sarah could see how much the effort cost her. She could almost hear Lillian's chalky joints creak. Lillian waved Sarah closer.

"I overheard the aides gossiping. Have you heard the news? The police found Baby Alice Spenser."

"I did hear that. My husband John is leading the investigation."

Lillian fell back. "It's an amazing thing. Here I was, thinking that I would take that story with me to my grave. Sam says I shouldn't talk about that terrible night. He thinks the scandal should stay buried. That it doesn't mean anything anymore." Lillian rested her gnarled fingers on her sunken chest. "I heard Karlie and the other girls talking. These aides are so young; they have no sense of history. A new headline grabs their attention, and off they go." She caught her breath. "For those of us who lived through it, though, the past never dies. The older I get, the more real it becomes." She rubbed her forehead with her knuckles. "It's remembering the present that gives me trouble." She chuckled gently. "My mother, Grace, and my Aunt Emma used to talk about Baby Alice in front of the fire many a night, over and over again. Little pitchers have big ears. They both worked for the Spensers during that difficult time. I was young, but I understood what it was they were saying. Oh my, yes, I certainly did."

"Why?" Sarah felt intrigued. "What did they say?"

Lillian slumped against the wheelchair. She suddenly looked sly. "People on the island knew plenty more than they were ever willing to tell the police. Back then, you knew your place, and you kept to it. You protected your own." She raised a trembling finger. "And for all of their money, the Spensers have always been outsiders. *Always*. They've had plenty of chances to do the right thing many a time, but they always chose to defend their class. Chose to trust the police, and that wicked man, that corrupt attorney general, instead of telling the truth about Alice. Oh my, no! They couldn't let that truth get out! That scandal would have ruined the family! So they trusted their hush money, and their connections, and in the end they gained nothing from it. *Nothing*."

"What was so scandalous about the kidnapping, Lillian? Do you remember?"

"Of course I remember! There's nothing wrong with my memory! Everyone's always so worried about me telling tales. Mustn't let those old scandals get out." Her eyes grew filmy, and her blue-veined hands began to shake. "Mother worked at Moorhaven with all of her cousins, and her aunt, every day. Mother was only sixteen, the only laundress there. It was a terrible job, just terrible. Mother had to wash and iron all of that linen, by hand, each and every day, rain or shine. Bed sheets, pillowcases, towels, tablecloths, the whole nine yards! You try getting red lipstick out of a table napkin. Impossible! Mother said that the day the Spensers bought an electric dryer and replaced her sad irons, and she could stop pegging that wet washing on the lines, that was her Independence Day. She could finally stop working like such a navvy. Stopped looking like such a worn out drab. Luckily, Mother only worked at Moorhaven for three years, before she left."

Sarah knew how the grim old working class days in New England had worked. Her mother has shared that wearying tale with her to keep Sarah focused on staying in school. If you were a woman, you either held down a job and brought your paycheck home to your parents to help support the family, or you left home to start a family of your own. "Your mother left Moorhaven to get married?" Sarah guessed.

"I didn't say that!" Lillian snapped. "Mother left Moorhaven to take care of *me*. She didn't marry until after I was born."

"Your mother married your father … after you were born?" Sarah stammered. She recognized the impertinence of her question the instant it left her mouth. *Had she blown it? Had she pushed Lillian too far?* For a person of Lillian's generation, being born out of wedlock would have been seen as a source of lifelong stigma and mocking public scorn. Back in the bad old days, an illegitimate child was most likely farmed out to foster care and hidden away.

"My mother never married my father. Howard Spenser, Junior was my father." Reaching up, Lillian smoothed her artificially auburn hair. "It was a love match, but the Spensers forbade it. They sent Mother away. They couldn't allow their crown prince to marry a common laundress." Lillian's mouth contracted into a nest of bitter wrinkles. She defiantly raised her chin. "Mother married her cousin, Winslow Ketchem, to conceal her shame." She raised her hand to indicate the plush surroundings. "The Spenser Trust paid for Mother's maintenance, and for my support, all these years. The Trust still pays for my care here, at Sanctuary."

Sarah gaped. She had lived on Nantucket long enough to have bumped into the elegant Spensers at art gallery openings and many public benefits. She had heard their fabled and benevolent island history repeated at cocktail parties over and over again. Now she knew it was all a sham, a myth riddled with upper class WASP privilege and deception. She couldn't wait to get home to tell John all about it.

"Lillian, let me get this straight," Sarah said. "Sam Ketchem, your grandson, is a Spenser? Does Sam know that?"

"My dear girl." Lillian beamed. "It's Sam's family history. He knows everything about it."

CHAPTER FIFTEEN

"Sam!?"

John stormed into the station. He felt loaded for bear. When he got home last night, Sarah had met him at the door with a fractured story about the Alice Spenser kidnapping that she had heard from Sam's grandmother, Lillian, the Island Sanctuary resident. The problem was, when his wife got excited, Sarah's stories took on more than a bit of creative license, with detail piling on excited detail until everything got muddled. John needed to find Sam, to set the story straight. He had repeatedly tried calling Sam on his cellphone until midnight, but Sam had never picked up.

"Sam!" John shouted. "We need to talk!"

"Over here, sir." Sam looked up from a laptop plugged into one of the communal desks. He quickly set his coffee mug down. "What's up?"

"I have some questions for you." John marched over. His desk chair squealed in protest as he slid it across the floor. "My wife had an interesting conversation with your grandmother yesterday. You told me the old lady was gaga."

"No, I said she wasn't all there, sir." Sam tapped his temple. "Evidently, there's still enough left to get me in trouble. What did Grandma Lil say this time?"

John started ticking items off of his fingers. "My wife said that, one: there's some kind of scandal associated with the Alice Spenser kidnapping; two, your family has information they never shared with the police; and three, your grandmother is a Spenser descendant, which makes you a Spenser, too."

"That old cat!" Sam sat back. "I really should put a pillow over her face and be done with it, once and for all."

"I want some answers, Sam. I mean it."

"Sir, Grandma Lil loves stirring this shit up. She uses half-truths and gossip to get everybody riled up and to suck them in. It's the reason the Sanctuary aides ignore her. They're used to Grandma Lil's tricks. Actually, it's pretty sad. She's not being malicious. She only does it because she's lonely. Her stories bring people in. Case in point, if I may say so, sir."

"Is any of this true? You are a Spenser?"

"Please, sir, not so loud." Sam rocked forward. "I'd rather that didn't get out. The other fellows will snicker. It's not like it makes a difference. All of that happened a hundred years ago. The Spensers don't bother us, and we don't bother them." Sam grinned crookedly. "We don't hold family reunions. I didn't inherit any money or special superpowers because of their DNA." Sam ruffled his crew cut. "I count myself lucky that I missed the ginger hair gene."

"Okay." John released his breath. "What's this scandal she mentioned? This extra information that your family didn't tell the police?"

"I have no idea, sir, other than the fact that Grandma Lil was born on the wrong side of the blanket. That's the only scandal I know of. I'm not sure what she's hinting at. You'll have to ask her."

John pointed a finger. "I intend to do just that."

Sam laughed. "And Grandma Lil wins again! See what she's done? This way she gets another visitor. Fine by me, sir. Saves me a duty trip."

The station door sighed, and CJ walked in with Cesar Mayas. Mayas had raised the Dapper Dan high fashion stakes by wearing a striped oxford cloth shirt with a contrasting bow tie that matched the ribbon on his hat. He carried a stack of opaque orange binders in his hand. John noticed that CJ was looking strangely bright.

"If they had offered forensic DNA analysis training at the Academy," CJ spoke over her shoulder, "I would have been all over it. That program developed so quickly, my class missed the boat."

"You should take a sabbatical from the force, and pick it up." Mayas dropped the binders on an empty desk. "It's never too late to make a change, and to study a subject that really interests you." He headed for the coffee station and poured out a cup. "Morning." He nodded at Sam and John. "Chief Nunn in yet?"

"Not yet," John replied. The Chief's door was open, but her office was dark. *What am I now? The station's Admin?* John shrugged the negativity off. That kind of focus got him nowhere. He returned his attention to his investigation, where it belonged. "I will be going out to Sanctuary to see your grandmother, Sam. Get the story straight."

"Good luck with that, sir." Sam stood. He smoothed his uniform. "I'm curious to hear how that goes." Picking up his keys, Sam headed off to start the morning's first patrol loop, whistling.

CJ riffled through a stack of sticky note messages on her desk. She looked up, paused, and grew pensive. "Maybe I should take a few post-grad classes, to freshen things up."

"The Bureau offers a preliminary syllabus online." Mayas shook some dry creamer into his mug. He gave the coffee a stir. "You could study from home, on your laptop, at your own speed. It's worth taking a look."

"I'm going to do it." CJ stated. "I've been looking for a new challenge. DNA studies might be the way to go. I like DNA. It doesn't lie."

"It's the forensic finger of fate." Mayas blew on his coffee. He pulled out a chair and settled in. "It used to be, with cases, that if you figured out how a crime happened, then you knew who did it. Now, with DNA evidence, it's backwards. DNA tells you who did it, and then you have to figure out the how." He pulled the orange binders closer, and he pointed at John. "You're going to enjoy hearing the DNA test results, Detective Jarad. I've brought a few surprises."

John sat up. "You've already reviewed the report? What did it say?"

"I sure did." Mayas winked. "First thing this morning. As soon as the email arrived."

"Just tell me, Mayas." John stood. "Did it confirm the victim was Alice Spenser?"

"Patience, Detective Jarad, patience. Let's wait for Chief Nunn. That way, I won't have to repeat myself."

Dickhead. John swallowed his retort. He understood why Mayas wanted to grandstand a bit with the DNA test results, but John hated feeling powerless, like a pawn in a great game. As force Commander, he could have demanded that Mayas produce the DNA test results stat. Now, as a lowly detective, John was forced to submit to the Bureau's authority. It was galling.

Mayas finished his coffee with relish. He held the mug with both hands. "What do you people know about Chief Nunn? I bet having her report here for duty came as a surprise."

CJ scowled. "That decision was cooked up behind closed doors. We had nothing to do with it. We only found out about it after the fact."

"I wondered." Mayas nodded. "You do know why Anetta left NOLA Metro, right? You heard what happened to her husband, Anton, and her son?"

"No," CJ said slowly. "She hasn't really shared any personal information."

"I can understand why." Mayas stood. He returned to the coffee station and refilled his mug. Turning, he leaned against the stainless steel counter. "Her husband and son drowned during Katrina. Anetta was working with us," he tapped his chest, "as part of the first response team. We worked three days straight, without sleep. That bitch Katrina never let up. Anton and Beaudry were supposed to be on their way to Texas, to stay with family. For some reason we'll never know, Anton turned back. Their SUV got swept away. Anetta didn't know. Cell phone coverage was spotty. She thought they were in Houston, safe. It was a month before we recovered their bodies."

CJ gasped. "That's horrible. How old was her son?"

"Beaudry? Two, two and a half. About the same age as Alice Spenser. Beaudry was found still strapped in his car seat." Mayas scratched his chin. "Anetta's a bright woman. I'm sure the irony of this situation hasn't been lost on her." He pushed off the counter and poured his coffee down the drain. "Anetta left NOLA looking for a fresh start, and her very first case is a repeat of what happened to her own child." Mayas shook his head. "Good thing she's tough. Goes to show that you never really know what someone has gone through, that makes them who they are."

The front door sighed again and Chief Nunn pushed through. She had her leather bag slung over her shoulder. Her buff arms were filled with the cold case reports she had taken home to study on her own time.

"Morning, all." She paused, alert, and narrowed her eyes. "What's going on, troops?"

John felt a pang of disloyalty. He had started to feel genuine respect for the way the Chief tackled her duties in such a competent and professional manner. He had even started thinking of Chief Nunn as a kind of friend. He felt ashamed to have been caught gossiping about her personal family tragedy behind her back.

"There you are, Chief," Agent Mayas stated heartily. He lifted his binders. "I've got the Spenser DNA test results."

"Let's have it." Chief Nunn dropped her bag and the folders on top of a filing cabinet. She circled her forefinger. "Conference Room A."

Chapter Sixteen

Agent Mayas fanned the binders down the center of the conference table, and he waited until they had all settled in. As usual, John sat directly across from CJ, with Mayas and Chief Nunn sitting on either end.

"Let's cut to the chase. I know you're eager to hear the results." Mayas handed out the numbered copies. "We were asked to provide DNA test results on two sets of samples, in a support capacity, as part of an ongoing investigation. Detective Allamand provided samples from the direct male line through two males, Howard and Addison Spenser, father and son. The data we needed on the direct female line came from Camilla Dechert, a cousin. The Coroner, Dr. Jenkins, provided a second set of samples culled from the autopsy of an unnamed victim, a two-year-old female child. Both sample sets were tested generically, anonymously, and independently, although, to be honest, we went in hoping for a match."

Mayas flipped his binder open. He tapped page one. "I've included what I know of the Spenser genealogy on this chart. It should help to keep things straight. Five generations of family history can make DNA sequencing complicated." He cleared his throat. "The historic record tells us that Howard and Nell Spenser had six children. Our subject, Alice Spenser, was the youngest. Alice was born in 1919. She disappeared as the result of a child abduction in 1921. Luckily, we didn't need to petition the

Court for permission to exhume her parents for the purposes of this test." Mayas smoothed his hair and took a breath. "The analysis confirms the match. The child victim in the trunk was Alice Spenser."

"Yes!" Chief Nunn slapped the table. Her eyes were shining with excitement.

"There's more." Mayas flipped to page two. "Alice Spenser inherited mitochondrial DNA directly from her mother, as all females in a direct line do." His finger traced a graph. "Because of the sample obtained from Camilla Dechert, we can confirm that Alice was a descendant of Nell Spenser. That information is solid." Mayas looked up. "However, there was a paternal break in Alice's bloodline. Howard Spenser, Senior was not Alice's father."

"What?" CJ exclaimed. "Nell cheated on Howard? I don't believe it. He was the love of her life."

"It could have been the result of a sexual assault," Chief Nunn said slowly.

"Let me finish." Mayas held up a hand. "The analysis states that Alice's father was 'unknown.' We do know that he wasn't a male member of the Spenser family. There was no overlap there. Alice Spenser's father did carry a genetic marker for haplogroup E-M153. It's a unique event sub-Alpine polymorphism. We're in luck. That genetic marker is rare."

"Hold up." It killed him to do so, but John raised his hand. "What's a haplogroup?"

Mayas smiled knowingly. "It's a genetic classification that indicates a population's sub-group. Genes mutate all the time. We follow the genetic markers to identify generations, and any haplogroup distinctions. It helps us sort our data."

CJ clasped her hands. "You said sub-Alpine polymorphism. Are you saying that Alice Spenser's father was German, or Swiss?"

Alice Spenser's father was German, or Swiss? John began to feel the stirrings of a fresh idea as to why Howard Spenser the First might have pursued Karl Schlagel so vigorously.

"Yes. That's exactly what I'm saying. Alice Spenser carried that specific E-M153 genetic marker." Mayas flipped the binder to another chart. "And the evidence goes further than that." He tapped his lips. "It's amazing the level of detail we can uncover. You really should consider a career move, Detective Allamand. I can see that you have the itch."

"Step back, Mayas." Chief Nunn crossed her arms. "Don't poach my team."

"Just making a suggestion, Chief." He smoothed a crinkled page. "Alice Spenser, although a direct descendant of Nell Spenser, was not Nell's daughter. Her mitochondrial DNA was one generation removed. Alice Spenser was Nell Spenser's granddaughter."

CJ looked enthralled. "Could you repeat that?"

"Happy to. The mitochondrial DNA sequencing indicates that Alice's mother had to be one of Nell's daughters, because of a generational shift. Actually, we can deduce more than that. Alice Spenser's mother had to be Daisy Spenser, since Nell's only other daughter and direct female descendant, Millicent Spenser, was only eight years old in 1919, the year that Alice was born."

"You're telling us," John stated slowly, "that Alice Spenser's mother was Daisy Spenser, and that her father was an unknown German male?"

"Correct." Mayas smiled brilliantly. "And that's confirmed by this report."

John leaned back heavily against the chair. His brain lit up like a Christmas tree. He recalled how badly Karl Schlagel had been railroaded by law enforcement at the time of the Spenser kidnapping. "Maybe that's why the Spensers were so eager to have Karl Schlagel locked up. Maybe they were trying to protect their daughter, Daisy, and to protect Alice, from him."

"Or maybe they were just trying to shut Karl up to protect the family from the scandal of a teenage pregnancy," Chief Nunn said brutally. "Privilege can be ruthless that way. How old was Daisy in 1919? Seventeen? Eighteen? She wasn't married, right?"

"No." Mayas studied his chart. "Daisy never married." He looked at CJ. "Any chance you could get a DNA sample from a direct male descendant of Karl Schlagel? That might resolve the question of Alice Spenser's paternity."

CJ pulled her ear. "What do you think, John? Think Gus would object if I asked him for a spit sample?"

"Gus might be open to it, if you asked him the right way. If he won't, Ben might. Ben's a direct male descendant, too." John leaned forward. Another suggestion was rattling around inside his skull, distracting him, calling for his attention. Lillian Ketchem had mentioned to Sarah that she knew of a second Spenser family scandal beside her own. *Did Lillian know the truth about Alice Spenser's paternity?* There was only one way to find out. DNA data was a terrific forensic tool, but people and their memories held the real key. John pushed away from the table.

"I'll be back. There's another line to this investigation that I want to check."

Chief Nunn looked surprised. "Detective Jarad? Where are you going?"

John checked his iPhone. Cruising up on eleven. Nap time at Island Sanctuary. "Don't take this the wrong way." He headed for the door. "I've got a date."

CHAPTER SEVENTEEN

John had to ask an aide to point the way, twice, but eventually he found Lillian Ketchem dozing in her wheelchair on a secluded teak deck overlooking the sea. Lillian was alone, out of the sight of the facility and the staff. John could see why Lillian chose this spot. It was serene, and very peaceful. The tidal breakers shushed against the shore, broken only by a seagull's plaintive *cre-cre-cre* cry. Lillian's knobby fingers were wrapped around a bouquet of daisies resting on her lap. She awoke with a snort and blinked from under her fringe of strangely orange hair.

"Yes? Who is it?"

"Detective Jarad, from the Nantucket force." John squeezed the envelope in his hand. "Mind if I sit down?"

"Not at all." Lillian primly plucked at her wrap. "I love visitors. Please, take a seat."

John sat on a built in teak bench. He rested his elbows on his knees. "I'm investigating the Alice Spenser kidnapping. You spoke with my wife."

"I did." Lillian's eyes sparkled with a mischievous intelligence. "I wondered when I was going to see you, Detective Jarad. I do remember meeting your wife. What a lovely young woman. Expecting, too. You're a lucky man. I am Lillian Ketchem."

"Nice to meet you, Lillian. I also work with your grandson, Sam." John settled in. He wasn't sure how much time he really had, or how lucid Lillian was. "They both mentioned that you might have additional information about the Spenser kidnapping that your family never shared with the police. I know that a great many Ketchems worked at Moorhaven during that time. Is that true?"

Lillian grew still. She was obviously mulling things over. John suddenly felt like a fly struggling helplessly against an invisible web.

"Sam told you that Howard Spenser, Junior was my father?"

"No, I heard that from my wife." John displayed the envelope. "I brought a DNA collection kit. I'm hoping you'll provide a sample, so we can check that claim. We're having a sale on DNA testing this week. Won't cost you a dime."

"Oooh, how do we do this?" Lillian leaned forward ghoulishly. "Will you need to take my blood?"

"No, not blood." John rolled the nitrile gloves on. "You will need to gently run this applicator along your gum line and hold it under your tongue for about fifteen seconds. Then we seal it up, and I send the kit to the lab for testing."

Lillian blinked owlishly. "It's only going to prove to you what I've already said."

"I'm sure it will. I'll also need to take your fingerprints."

"How thrilling! I've always wanted to do this. I've seen it on TV."

Lillian reached eagerly for the foam applicator and popped it under her tongue. Carefully counting to fifteen through her teeth, she removed the applicator with more care than it needed, and handed it back. John completed the test, confirmed that the contact area on the FTA card had turned from pink to white, and returned everything to the EasiCollect envelope.

"What's next?" Lillian held out her knobby hands. "Fingerprints?"

"Yes." John tore the inked pad open. "I'll need your left and right index fingers, which I will ink like this, for the form."

"This would have been easier before I fossilized." Lillian chuckled. She waved her blackened fingers wickedly. "I've never done anything wrong in my life. Why, it's delicious! I feel like a criminal!"

John handed her an alcohol prep pad. "And this will remove the ink."

"You know, I believe I'll leave it on. It will confound my doctor."

"Lillian, you are a troublemaker."

"I am. It's all I have left."

John sealed the protective envelope. He removed the nitrile gloves, placing everything next to him neatly on the bench. "We should have the results with a day or two. I'll come back out, and give you an update."

"I'm simply breathless with anticipation," Lillian said slyly. "Next time, bring me some candy. A Whitman's Sampler, the bigger box. It will cause talk. Imagine! An old lady like me, getting candy from a new beau. How delightful."

"I'll do that, Lillian, if you'll tell me what it was that your family never shared with the police."

Lillian pushed her lips into a pout. She ruminated carefully. "First, tell me what you already know."

"Alright. We know that Alice Spenser was Daisy Spenser's daughter, and not Nell's. We're working now to determine who Alice Spenser's father was."

Lillian squinted. "Any ideas along that line, Detective Jarad?"

John hesitated. He baulked over sharing unconfirmed information. "We're still working on it."

She pointed a trembling finger. "Using more of those kits?"

"Yes."

"Hummm. Modern times. Modern ways." Lillian idly inspected her bouquet. "You're looking for information on Daisy Spenser now? From the time of the kidnapping? From 1921?"

"And from before." John smoothed his shirt. "I've adjusted my timeline. I'm beginning to think that Alice Spenser's kidnapping was the end result of an event, and not the beginning."

"I saw Daisy once, you know." Lillian chewed her lip. "Later. Much later. She passed me on the street. Didn't know who I was, of course. Just another common street urchin to her. She looked regal, like a movie star. Wore the most beautiful custom tailored clothes. Still had all of that spangled strawberry blonde hair. Of course, in 1921, Mother and Aunt Emma both worked at Moorhaven. So did my cousins, Fred and Arthur. Those boys worked in the yard, helping Joe Bolton in the garden. It was a grand time. I heard they had the run of the place."

"Karl Schlagel also worked at Moorhaven in 1921. Karl was the handyman there."

"Oh my, yes. He certainly was." Lillian choked. A thin line of spittle dribbled down her chin. Reaching up carefully, she wiped it off. "I grew up hearing about Karl Schlagel. Glory days! Aunt Emma had the biggest crush on him. It was quite a pash. Of course, back then Karl looked like a young god, an Adonis. Gave all of the Moorhaven girls the vapors, and some of the married women, too."

"Did Karl ever give Daisy the vapors?" John asked.

Lillian studied him carefully. "Between you and me, Detective Jarad, I believe that Karl Schlagel gave Daisy Spenser the vapors earlier, in 1918."

"When she was seventeen."

"Karl was only twenty-six. It's not so far-fetched."

"Lillian." John sat back. "I can see you've given this some thought."

"Time is all that I have left." She slowly turned her head. "I sit in this garden, and I listen to the waves, and to the wind." She waved her translucent blue-veined hand. "All of that makes more sense to me than what I hear those inane aides saying, or what I see on the TV. So I sit, and I listen, and I remember what my mother and my Aunt Emma used to talk over, late at night." Lillian struggled to straighten up. "If you ever want to know what people are really thinking, Detective Jarad, watch their actions. Actions are the real clue. People may tell you one thing, but their actions will tell you what they're really up to."

"Okay, Lillian, I'll bite. What did Daisy do?"

"Do you know the Spenser motto?" Lillian looked at him narrowly, from the corner of her eyes. "*Nos Protegat Nostrum?*"

John stirred. He had taken a picture of that motto at Moorhaven, and he had meant to look it up, but he hadn't had the time. "I'm afraid I don't."

"*We protect our own,*" Lillian said, with relish. "That's what Daisy Spenser did, Detective Jarad. Normally, a young lady of Daisy's social station would have enjoyed a Grand Tour of Europe with her mother, as a final finishing polish before making her debut. But Daisy couldn't go to Europe, because of the war. I heard Daisy felt gyped. She pitched a royal fit. She hated wasting the summer stuck at Moorhaven with nothing to do. Sulked the entire time. Touring California came up as the next best thing. Daisy told everyone that she wanted to visit Hollywood, because she was interested in becoming an actress, like Nell. In September of 1918, Daisy and her governess, Pauline Dalwhinney, traveled to Hollywood, California, by train."

115

"Why didn't Nell go with her? That California trip sounds right up her alley."

"Nell had to skip the trip, because of a late pregnancy."

"With Alice?" John felt baffled. "But we know now that Daisy was Alice's mother."

"Nell stayed home to fake a pregnancy. Daisy went to California to hide one." Lillian shifted uncomfortably. "The Spensers protect their own, detective. They always have. They still do." She tapped her chest with her knuckled fist. "Daisy stayed in California until Alice was born. Then she snuck the newborn baby home. Nell pretended to give birth to Alice in New York in May. When the family showed up at Moorhaven on Memorial Day in 1919, they had month-old Alice in tow." Lillian coughed, and she waved it off. "Back then, a woman didn't have to go to a hospital to have a baby. Children were born privately, at home, all of the time. A discrete family doctor signed a birth certificate, and *voila*! As far as the world knew, Nell Spenser had a new baby girl, and Daisy's reputation was saved." Lillian coughed again. "Remember: Mother and Aunt Emma were working at Moorhaven. They overheard the New York staff gossiping in the servants' hall. They knew what Nell and Daisy were up to."

"How about Karl Schlagel? Did they ever tell him that Alice was really his daughter?"

"No, they never did, but there's no question that Karl found out." Lillian laughed mirthlessly. "My guess is that Karl learned about it sometime in 1921. Why else would he have snatched Alice?"

John fingertips tingled. He felt thunderstruck. "Lillian, if what you say is true, and you knew about it, why haven't you told anyone this story before?"

"*Nos Protegat Nostrum*." Lillian raised her chin. "Because I am a Spenser, too."

Chapter Eighteen

John paused in the Sanctuary parking lot. His mind was swimming with all the new information. *If Lillian was right, Karl Schlagel kidnapped Alice Spenser once he learned that Alice was his daughter. Was that the answer? Could that be right?* John checked his iPhone. Almost one o'clock. He needed to talk to Gus and Ben right away. He wasn't sure if the building crew was still out at the Quammock site. Catching those guys around lunchtime was always iffy. They got ravenously hungry, and they never missed a meal. He speed dialed Gus's number. *Pick up, pick up, pick up.*

"Yes?"

"Gus, it's John. Where are you?"

"At Sayle's Seafood, picking up fish sandwiches. What's wrong now?"

"I need to talk to you, and Ben. About the Spenser kidnapping."

"Say, what is this? CJ Allamand stopped by this morning to take our spit. What's going on?"

"We should talk about this, face to face."

"Ben's back at the house, playing video games. Meet me there."

Gus and Ben lived mid-island. John turned for Old South Road. He tossed his phone into the console, and immediately reached to pick it back up. He needed to call Sarah, to recognize her help in uncovering the solid Ketchem lead. His ability to focus intensely was both a gift, and a curse. His talent made him short sighted, and back in January it had almost cost him his wife when Sarah had perceived his focus on his case as a lack of interest in her. It wasn't that, but John still felt sick when he thought of how closely he had come to losing her. He had sworn that the misperception would never happen again. He had worked very hard lately to keep an awareness of what he was doing, and how it might impact his family and his wife, at the forefront of his mind, because Sarah deserved better, and because that was the version of the man he wanted to be. He thumbed her number next.

"There you are, busy bee! I wondered where you were. How is your day going?"

Sarah sounded cheerful and bright. John swallowed his immediate intensity, and went for calm. "It's been interesting. I went out to Island Sanctuary. Talked to Lillian Ketchem. Thanks for the tip. It turned into an important lead."

"Really, John? I'm so glad. Isn't Lillian a hoot?"

"You're not kidding."

"Was anything she said really true?"

"She volunteered a DNA sample to find out." John checked the envelope on the passenger seat, and reset his focus. "What are you up to today?"

"Helping your mother set up for the baby shower. Don't forget! It's tomorrow at noon."

In spite of his best intent, John beat back the flutter of irritation that he still felt whenever domestic life interfered with an active investigation. "I won't forget," he promised, and he meant it.

"It's kind of a big deal." She whispered, "Jackie's bringing the cake."

Sarah's comment distracted him. He almost missed the turn for Hooper Farm Road. "Sweetheart, you meant Mary Rose." John couldn't blame Sarah for confusing his two sisters. His wife had married into a lot of family.

"No, I meant Jackie. Jenny was really surprised, too. She said Jackie's never volunteered to participate in anything like this before."

"That's true." That was notably odd. Jackie always excused herself from attending any type of family event. "Either Jackie really likes you, or her new job must have turned things around."

"That's what Jenny said, too."

"Honey?" He started down the Schlagels' driveway. The suspension system started to take a beating as the cruiser bounced through dozens of crumbling potholes. "Got to go. Call you later."

"Oh! Okay. Be careful out there. Love you."

He followed the rutted driveway for a thousand yards. When the Schlagels had built their home at the turn of the last century, their mid-island location had been rural and remote. Now, the area had built up. John could see why the new neighbors were complaining. The Schlagels' yard was filled with four generations of discarded building material including a stack of splintered pallets, a pyramid of used brick, and a tumbled mountain of cracked ballast stone. A scrub tree grew up through a heap of cast off wooden ladders. The tree shaded a pile of splintered PVC pipe. Their weathered house wasn't much to look at, either. It was a worn single story with tacked on ells that ran off in three different directions. *The cobbler's kids never have shoes.* Evidently, Gus and Ben spent so much time working on other people's homes that they never spent any time renovating their own.

John stepped from the cruiser, but he left it unlocked. He wasn't sure if Gus or Ben owned a guard dog, or two. He left the door open in case he needed to beat a hasty retreat.

"Hello?" He shouted. "Gus? Ben?"

The cruiser was the only vehicle in the driveway. Evidently, Gus hadn't returned from his sandwich run yet. John spotted a flattened dusty path that ran around one corner of the house. He followed it into a lumpy side yard. Two capped metal pipes stood about a foot above the soil line, spaced approximately twelve feet apart. John recalled that Ben preferred to hang out in a bomb shelter during his free time. A steel hatch-like cover stood propped open nearby. John walked over and peered in. It was like looking down a hollow tube, and it gave him the creeps. He recognized the cascading notes of the Ninja Creed soundtrack. "Ben?"

The soundtrack abruptly stopped. "Who's that?"

"John Jarad. I wanted to talk to you, and your dad."

"Dad's getting lunch." Ben's voice echoed eerily off the concrete. "Come on down, John. You should see this."

John did feel a curious urge to see what Ben had going on down there. One part of him wanted to climb over the lip of the concrete tunnel and following the iron rungs down. The other part of his brain was shouting "*Oh, hell no!*" He stepped in and tested the first steel rung. If it held Ben's weight, it should hold him. John studied the steel hatch to make sure that it didn't come down on his head. He was surprised to see that the locking mechanism was the same simple latch bolt they had on their storm door back home. He had expected to see something more elaborate, like the screw lock on a submarine.

"Ben? Do I need to lock this, or do anything?"

"No. Leave it open. I'll padlock it when I leave."

John tucked his elbows against his ribs, and started down the ladder. Rust flakes bit into his palms. He descended twenty rungs, which he estimated to be twenty feet. Although the air was cooler inside the shelter, it tasted musty, like a bad apple. John stepped off the ladder and paused to wipe the sweat from his hands. He was surprised to see that he was shaking, and not from the physical effort.

He found himself standing inside a perfectly square eight-foot concrete chamber with a smooth concrete floor. A triangular black and yellow Fallout Shelter sign was bolted into the wall on his right.

"See the sign? Take a right around the blast wall, and come on through. Follow my voice."

John stepped around the foot and a half thick, right-angled concrete partition that divided the shaft from the main cell. He found Ben kicked back and lounging on a fake leather recliner. Ben held a tandem gaming console loosely in his hands. For the life of him, John couldn't imagine how Ben had gotten that big chair down that narrow shaft. Ben set the console down. He spread his arms wide.

"Welcome to my abode. Man cave, 101."

"No lie." John continued to duck his head, although he didn't need to. The shelter's ceiling was at least nine feet tall. The main cell was fully twenty foot by fifteen, and not the concave concrete pipe he had anticipated. Ben had obviously customized the place, and made himself comfortable. He had carpeted the floor with a wall-to-wall green tartan plaid. A flat panel monitor was bolted into the far wall.

"I'm impressed. This isn't what I expected to see."

"I know. Grandpap Otto worked on this for over thirty years. It was his pet project. It's pretty amazing."

Ben stood up, suddenly giving the room scale. John felt the walls close in on him. He gulped.

"I'll give you the nickel tour." Ben headed toward the back of the chamber. "Grandpap was always working on another room or another tunnel. He worked down here until the day he died. Told me the tricky part was containing the sand until the concrete risers dried. Can you believe he hauled every bit of this sand out in a five gallon bucket?"

"It sounds like you were really close to him."

"Grandpap was my best bud." Ben shoved a rolling shelving unit aside to reveal another passage, and he started down.

John followed him through. "Would this shelter really protect us from radiation?"

"So they say. It's actually pretty simple. Radiation has to move in a straight line. That first blast wall you came around would pretty much block it." Ben laughed. "The trick was not killing each other while you're down here, stuck with nothing to do."

John suddenly felt cotton mouthed. He hadn't considered that part of it. "How long before you could get outside again?"

"The specs say two weeks to a month." Ben paused in the middle of a second large chamber. He cricked his neck. "I vote with my mother. She always said that when she heard the sirens go off she'd go stand in the middle of the yard, because who'd want to survive?"

"You could be stuck down here for a month?" John couldn't seem to step off the worry train. "Wouldn't you run out of air?"

"That's where this shelter rocks. Let me show you." Ben moved toward a shadowy side chamber. The alcove was completely filled with a compact red and chrome machine. Ben confidently placed his hand on top of it. "This air pump is totally top of the line. Flip this switch, and it pulls fresh air down through six different radiation filters. It can change all of the air inside this shelter in less than seven minutes."

"What if you lose electricity?"

"The shelter is spliced into the island's main electrical supply, but if the grid does go down you crank this handle, and the air pump becomes the backup electrical generator. Grandpap thought of everything. He was really smart like that." Ben rested his beefy hands on his hips. "Anything else?"

"I have to ask. How the hell did you get that recliner down that shaft?"

Ben laughed easily. "Good question." He turned, and headed down another winding tunnel. "It's not magic. There's a second exit. This one stays locked, because it's out of sight of the house. Grandpap didn't want the neighborhood kids playing down here, because you know they would have. I know I sure did, every chance I got. Made me one of the cool kids." Ben smiled wryly. "I still do."

They passed a storeroom door on the right, and John studied a second hatch that looked identical to the steel storm door in his mother's cellar. "I know how this works. We have one just like it, back at the house."

"It's a standard fitting. I brought the recliner, and the gaming monitor, in from this side. I use the ladder shaft because it's closer to the house. Saves me some steps. Still, renovating this place took some work."

"Hey!" Gus's voice echoed through the shelter. "What are you two nitwits doing down there?"

"Food's here!" Ben clapped his hands. "About damn time. Took him long enough." He pointed toward the main chamber. "You go first. I'll hit the lights on my way out."

Hit the lights? Cold sweat popped a line down John's spine at the thought of being left in that shelter in the dark. *One thing for sure, now I know that I need to stay out of any caves.* John was surprised to see how efficiently he retraced his steps to the main chamber, and how quickly his feet followed his hands as he climbed back up the ladder toward the daylight.

Gus stood over the hatch. He held three waxed paper sacks.

"Hope you like haddock, Jarad. I brought you one, too. Fuck. Let's take this inside."

Chapter Nineteen

Gus shoved the unlocked back door open with his work boot. He led the way into the kitchen. John ducked and stepped over the threshold. He wasn't surprised to see that the décor was straight out of the Fifties, gold speckled Formica countertops and all. Gus's wife and Ben's mother, Cathy, had died young, of breast cancer, back in the Eighties. It was obvious that a woman hadn't touched this kitchen in decades. The stovetop was littered with soup cans filled with congealed bacon grease and crumpled handfuls of reused aluminum foil. The place smelled like a rank bachelor pad.

Gus tore some paper towels off a roll near the sink. He carried everything over to the table, and handed John one of the sacks.

"Sit down. Eat." Gus opened the fridge, and he grabbed a beer. "Want one of these?"

"No, thanks. I'm good."

"Figured. You being on the clock, and all."

Gus popped two beers. He set one foaming can down next to Ben's elbow. Ben was focused on drenching his fish sandwich in Frank's RedHot sauce. Ben took one huge bite and grinned around the tasty mouthful.

"Better. Needed some heat."

Gus smoothed his mustache. He squinted, rested his elbows on the table, and leaned forward. "What's this important news? I thought I told you not to stir that Spenser shit up again."

"It's important. I think I know why the attorney general hounded your grandfather. We got the DNA report on Alice Spenser. The report said that Alice's father was German."

Wrinkles creased Gus's forehead. "What is that supposed to mean?"

"I think your grandfather Karl was Alice Spenser's biological father."

The sandwich slipped from Gus's fingers. "Is that why Allamand took our spit this morning? To test out this crazy idea?"

"Yes. And here's the kicker: Alice's mother was Daisy Spenser, not Nell."

"Fuck." Gus fell back against his chair. "Who told you that?"

"Lillian Ketchem. Her mother, and her aunt, worked at Moorhaven. She got the story from them. The DNA test has confirmed the Spenser connection."

Gus pushed back from the table, breathing hard. He stood, and leaned against the counter. "What difference will any of this make, if Karl was her dad? It won't change what happened. Alice Spenser is still dead. You're getting everyone riled up again over nothing. We'll never really know what happened to that little girl."

"I know what really happened to her." Ben belched. "Grandpap Otto told me, when I was seventeen. Biggest damn thing that ever happened to him in his whole life."

"That's crap!" Gus turned bright red. "Why would Pap have told you, and not told me?"

"Because you and Mom never listened to him." Ben inspected the second half of his sandwich. "Grandpap felt like he still needed to hush things up. Kidnapping Alice was a crime. He was afraid he might still get sent to prison, even though he was only ten years old when that shit went down."

"That is a story that he made up," Gus argued. "He had nothing to do with it."

"He was asleep in the back seat of the car that night." Ben mopped his mouth on his sleeve. "He was the one who grabbed the ransom money."

Gus looked about ready to explode. "What the fuck are you talking about?"

Ben rolled his sandwich paper up. He tossed it near the trashcan. "Grandpap said that Grandpa Karl loved Daisy Spenser. It was real, true love. Daisy never told him she was pregnant. The Spensers hushed that up. Grandpa Karl only found out that Alice was his when Daisy came home drunk from a party once and told him, a couple of years later. They used to meet in the garden shed." Ben took a slug of his beer. "When Grandpa Karl found out that Alice was really his daughter, he flipped out. He convinced Daisy to run away with him. Said they'd take both kids, Alice and Grandpa Otto, and make a new life. Somewhere on the mainland, somewhere new. Have a real family. They planned the whole thing, together."

"What went wrong?" John asked.

"Pretty much everything," Ben said simply. He sat back, and patted his belly. "Grandpa Karl picked a real foggy night, so he could drive up close to the house. He got Grandpap drunk on schnapps, and bundled him up. They drove out to Moorhaven to pick Daisy and Alice up. This was the tricky part, because Grandpa Karl needed to sneak into the house to help Daisy with her trunk. She got Alice ready, but Daisy refused to leave without her clothes. Grandpa Karl was worried that Alice might cry, and wake the house, so he took some chloroform out of the garden shed, and he put Alice to sleep. Daisy carried Alice down the back stairs, through the kitchen, and out to the car. Grandpa Karl carried her trunk."

Ben finished his beer. "Grandpap wasn't real sure about this next part. He said the schnapps made him woozy. He fell asleep waiting for the ferry. He woke up because Daisy was screaming, 'I told you she didn't need that stuff! I told you not to do it!' That's when he found out that Alice was dead." Ben crumpled the aluminum can in his fist. "Grandpa Karl panicked. The fog had lifted, and it was getting light out. He was afraid they'd be seen. Daisy was a mess, and they were running out of time. She kept rocking Alice in her arms, and crying, and saying that she wanted to go home, back to Moorhaven. Grandpa Karl didn't know what to do. If the cops found him in the car with the two Spensers, one of them dead, they'd hang him for sure. Plus, he still had Grandpap to take care of. He did the best thing he could think of: he drove Daisy home. She ran up the front stairs and back into that house, and slammed the door. Grandpa Karl drove out to the dump. He buried Alice in Daisy's trunk. Then he drove home, and he finished the schnapps."

John pictured the events of that terrible night. What had started out so innocent and bright, a rosy new future, and how it had descended so quickly into unimaginable tragedy. Everything that Karl and Daisy had done was so completely human, so understandable, so fraught with unconsidered peril. They had tried to escape their trapped and static lives. They had failed, and Alice Spenser had died.

"What did Karl do next?"

"What could he do? He went back to work." Ben shrugged. "Moorhaven was in an uproar. There were cops everywhere. Grandpa Karl couldn't get a message to Daisy. She wouldn't leave her room. He couldn't trust the servants; they'd rat him out, too. The more Grandpa Karl thought about it, the madder he got. Daisy was treating him like shit. The Spensers never told him that Alice was his child. He started to figure that the Spensers owed him big."

John phrased his next line of questioning carefully. It sounded like Ben believed that Karl was the hero of the story, but a crime had been committed. "Karl came up with the idea of asking for Alice's ransom? He wrote the ransom letter?"

"Yeah. He figured that if he had some money, real money, like $50,000 worth, Daisy might change her mind and run away again." Ben reached for another beer. "Grandpa Karl mailed the letter from town, and then he settled in, to wait."

John could see it all playing out before his eyes. Karl Schlagel, the young, decisive, and powerless immigrant, trying only to do what was best for his family, trapped by circumstances beyond his control, risking another action where any exposure could be fatal. *You had to give it to the guy. Right or wrong, Karl had guts.*

Gus scowled. "I can't believe you never told me any of this. What am I? Chopped liver?"

"It was Grandpap's story, Dad. All you had to do was ask him."

John leaned forward. "What about the ransom money? Did Otto ever mention it?"

"Sure he did. Grandpap was in on the pickup." Ben snapped open his second beer. "Grandpa Karl was worried that the drop might be a trap, even though his letter said that the driver should come alone. They hid in the weeds until they saw Stephens in the car. Stephens followed the instructions perfectly. They waited to make sure the coast was clear, and then Grandpap ran out. He grabbed the package, and scrambled back.

Grandpap said he was breathing so hard he almost fainted. The ransom money was all there, every dime of it."

Ben took another long swig. "The next day, Grandpa Karl carried the money back to Moorhaven, hidden in his toolbox." He shook his head. "That took some nerve. If the cops found that money on him, he'd be a dead man. Grandpa Karl snuck up to Daisy's room. He showed her the money. He begged her to forgive him for what happened to Alice, and to meet him again. It wasn't too late. They could still build a life together. Daisy flipped out. She started screaming, called him crazy. Called him a murderer. Said that if she ever saw him again she'd tell the cops what he'd done to Alice."

Ben tossed the empty can in the sink. "Grandpa Karl heard men running up the front stairs. He grabbed the money, and his toolbox, and he ducked into the butler's pantry to hide. He wasn't sure if Daisy was going to expose him then or not. Grandpa Karl hid in that pantry for hours. When things finally calmed down, he snuck outside and ran for home."

"That poor guy," Gus whispered. "I had no idea. No wonder he was so quiet."

"Grandpap said that when Grandpa Karl got home he locked the door and started to cry." Ben glanced around the disordered kitchen. "Weird to think that might have happened right here. Anyway, Grandpap was shocked, because he'd never seen his father cry before. Grandpap said he never wanted to hear a man cry like ever again. He said Grandpa Karl was howling, like he was losing his soul."

John tried to imagine Karl Schlagel's daily life after the kidnapping event. Driving out to Moorhaven every day, repairing the roof leaks and the gutters and watching, from a cautious distance, the glamorous Spensers returning to Nantucket each summer and remembering that soul searing night for the rest of his life. Watching the years roll by as life moved on. He would have seen the newer, acceptable marriages, and more children were born. The generations would have started to shift and to change, and the memory of Alice Spenser would fade. Only Karl Schlagel remembered. *Had Karl ever felt stuck in time as he grew older, and the Spenser family history began to pass him by?*

"Whatever happened to Daisy?" John asked. "Do you know?"

Gus snorted. "I can answer that one. She followed the family ways once the war was over. Embraced the high life. Ran off to New York, then Paris, and London. Spent the rest of her life drinking champagne and swinging from the chandeliers."

Ben raised a finger. "I Googled her yesterday, just to see what I would find. There's a YouTube video of Daisy dancing the Charleston and something called the Black Bottom. Damn, she was hot."

"The Spensers tried to buy Daisy a title, did you know that?" Gus stood. He set his beer can in the sink. "She got engaged to the son of some fancy English duke. They were at a party, and she decided to race home, drunk at the wheel. Drove both of them straight into a tree. They were killed, instantly. She never got that title." Gus stretched. "That's how it was in those days. The rich went on their merry way, and the rest of us, well, we carried on." He twisted his waist. "Some of us have to do the work. Same way as now, if you really think about it."

John considered this new information. He had one question left. "What happened to the ransom money? The $50,000? It never returned to circulation. Do you still have it?"

"Ohmigod!" Gus clapped his hands over his ears. "Don't even start with that! Now we'll have treasure hunters digging up the yard again. No, we don't still have the money, Jarad. We never did have it! And don't think it's hidden in Grandpa Karl's toolbox, because I still use it everyday. I can promise you there's nothing hidden in it. Wherever that ransom money went, it is long gone."

"You don't know that, Dad." Ben stroked his chin. "It might still be out there. Sure would come in handy. I could use fifty grand right now, to cover my booth expenses at the international gaming conference."

"Dimwit!" Gus pushed off the counter. "I've already told you that's not going to happen. Would you please stop saying that?"

"Oh, yes, it's going to happen. I just haven't figured out how to make it happen yet. I've got plans, bigger plans."

"The bigger plan right now is to finish dry walling Jarad's house." Gus tossed Ben the keys. He pointed at the door. "Break time is over. Quammock's that way. Hop to it."

CHAPTER TWENTY

John stood in front of the whiteboard in Conference Room A. He tapped the marker against his palm. He felt relaxed, and remarkably focused. Normally, nearing the end of the day shift, the team started to wind down, but John could see no signs of irritation or fatigue on the expectant faces surrounding the table. Chief Nunn was looking actively curious. Paul Jenkins was busily scrolling through the emails on his iPhone. CJ sat poised on the edge of her chair, her hands clasped in front of her. John had the feeling CJ knew what he was up to. She gave him a conspiratorial wink.

"We'll get started," he said, "as soon as Agent Mayas arrives."

The door double clicked, and Mayas darted in. He was wearing Nantucket Red trousers that still had the crease in them and a loose light blue Oxford cloth shirt, island style.

"Sorry, sorry! I know I'm late, but you're going to like what I've brought." He displayed a legal sized envelope. "I've got the Schlagel DNA test results."

"Impressive." Chief Nunn checked her tablet. "That took less than six hours."

"It's that Boston team. They're the best we have." He shook the report out of the envelope and distributed the copies. "The short answer is on page two." He flipped the report open. His finger drifted under a highlighted paragraph. "The saliva samples Detective Allamand provided this morning confirmed that Karl Schlagel, or a full sibling male of his generation, was Alice Spenser's biological father."

CJ flattened the report with her fist. "I think we can safely say it was Karl, since he was the only male of his family and generation on Nantucket at the time. Statistically, the odds are 1 in 113 billion, in favor."

Mayas smiled. "I completely agree."

"That's what we needed to know." John started to pace. "Thank you, Agent Mayas, for providing the confirmation." John turned. He drew two large squares over Alice Spenser's name, filling them in and then connecting the boxes. *Karl Schlagel* + *Daisy Spenser* = *Alice Spenser*. "I believe we have enough evidence now to state that the Alice Spenser kidnapping has been solved."

Mayas eagerly pulled out a chair. "I can't wait to hear this, Jarad. What have you got?"

"What we really have is a shadow game. In 1921, when the Spenser kidnapping occurred, there were a lot of social pressures in play. We need to keep that in mind, and not take what happened out of context. The players were working against things that may not make much sense to us today." John tapped the whiteboard. "I've talked with descendants of three family groups; the Spensers, the Ketchems, and the Schlagels. Each group provided one piece of the puzzle." John paused. "The story really begins with Daisy Spenser, in 1918. Daisy was seventeen, beautiful, and bored out of her mind. A war was raging in Europe, so she couldn't travel. She spent that summer stuck at Moorhaven, idle, and itching for something to do. Karl Schlagel caught her eye. Karl was the Spenser's handyman. Karl was twenty-eight years old, and he fell for her, hard. When Daisy left in August, she was pregnant. Karl didn't know about that."

John strolled to the opposite end of the room. "Daisy spent the winter and part of the following spring in California. When the Spensers showed up at Moorhaven on Memorial Day in 1919, Nell Spenser carried Alice in her arms. Nell led everyone to believe that Alice was her daughter, and that family myth lived on. From what I've learned from Lillian Ketchem, Daisy only told Karl that Alice was his daughter in April of 1921, when Alice was two." John looked up. "And that's when Karl decided to take his daughter back."

John placed the marker in the plastic tray with a click. "Ben Schlagel said that Karl and Daisy planned to elope. In the early morning of June 6th, 1921, Karl snuck into Moorhaven to help Daisy with her trunk. Karl was afraid that Alice would wake the house, so he brought chloroform, stolen from the garden shed. He put Alice out, and as Paul reported, she died from it."

CJ stopped taking notes. "Was it even a kidnapping, then? If Alice was really Karl and Daisy's child to begin with?"

"That's a question for our legal team." Agent Mayas scratched his chin. "It's a little murky, since Howard and Nell had physical custody. At the lowest level, it was custodial interference."

"In any case," John continued, "Alice Spenser died. Karl Schlagel was a recent immigrant. He couldn't see getting much justice fighting a manslaughter charge against an American child from a rich and powerful family." John leaned back against the whiteboard. "Once Karl and Daisy realized that Alice was dead, they panicked. Daisy insisted on going straight back to Moorhaven, to home. Karl drove Daisy there. She left Karl and ran back into the house, refusing to have anything more to do with him. Remember, she was only twenty. I'm not making excuses for her, but nothing had prepared Daisy for the reality of an event like this. Karl had more life experience. He knew he was running out of time, and he knew what he needed to do."

John started pacing again. He clasped his hands behind his back. "Karl drove out to the Madaket dump. His ten-year-old son, Otto, was asleep in the back seat of the car. Karl buried Alice in Daisy's trunk. Ben Schlagel confirmed this information to me, this morning. Ben heard it straight from his grandfather, Otto, who was there."

"Technically," Agent Mayas tapped his pen against the table, "that's hearsay."

Chief Nunn cocked her head. "It was a tidy wrap up, Detective Jarad, but that's only the half of it. What about the ransom letter? Did Karl Schlagel write it? Mayas, there's your European male. Or did someone unrelated take advantage of the kidnapping situation, as we suspected?"

"Both." John felt a rush of vindication. He was a huge believer in keeping to the grassroots level with every investigation. DNA reports and high-tech forensics were great tools and pointers, but canvassing the local level had offered up the facts, and you could only learn the facts by interviewing actual witnesses.

"Karl wrote and posted the ransom letter after Alice died. According to Ben, ransom wasn't a part of Karl's original plan. It occurred to him after the fact. Ben said that Karl felt bitter about the way the Spensers had treated him, by keeping Alice a secret. Karl also thought the money might help him get Daisy back. It didn't. Karl and Otto conspired to pick up the ransom packet. There's no evidence that an outside or organized criminal gang was involved."

Mayas sat back in his chair. "So where did the money go? The fifty grand?"

"The last point of reference we have is that Karl hid the ransom packet in his toolbox. Gus and Ben Schlagel both say they've never seen any part of it."

"And you believed them?" Mayas' jaw dropped open. He shot Chief Nunn a sharp look. "We could get a warrant, Chief, and search their property to make sure."

"Hold up." CJ warned. "Judge Coffin's not going to go for that. He's a stickler for showing probable cause. I don't think we have that here."

"Why would Gus and Ben lie?" Paul Jenkins polished his glasses with his tie. "They have nothing to gain from it. Those gold certificates are worthless paper. Plus, the minute they tried to deposit even one them, the bank would notify the Federal Treasury."

Chief Nunn straightened. "These are all key talking points. I'll take them under advisement, team, and get back to you with our next steps. Congratulations are in order, Detective Jarad. Nice work. I'll review your report more thoroughly tonight, and start drafting a press release we can share with the Spensers for their review tomorrow. You're going to be quite a hero, breaking the Spenser kidnapping open."

The phone in the center of the table vibrated, and everyone jumped. Chief Nunn laughed nervously. Reaching forward, she pressed the speaker button.

"Yes, Tina? What is it?"

"Chief?" Tina's voice squeaked. "We've got a 911 10-50/PI requesting immediate assistance at Island Sanctuary. First response is already in route."

John felt a cold lump of dread hit the pit of his stomach. *A 10-50/PI meant a personal injury accident.* He punched up the volume. "Tina? Did you get a name with that call?"

"Yes, sir. A Lillian Ketchem. Wait! It's popped to a 10-79. Victim is DOA. They're asking for Dr. Jenkins now, too."

John stood. "That's my case. My witness. I'm on my way."

"I'll follow you out there." Paul pushed back his chair. "I've got the van."

John raced from the conference room. He swept his keys off of his desk and ran for the door. *Lillian Ketchem was dead? A 10-50/PI meant personal injury, so Lillian didn't die peacefully in her sleep. Caregivers surrounded Lillian 24/7. What could have happened? Was it an accident, or something worse?*

He slid into the cruiser, bouncing over a speed bump while in reverse and still buckling the seatbelt. Cranking the steering wheel hard left, John roared toward Milestone Road as remorse and troubling doubt started to frost the edges of his soul. *If Lillian's death was a homicide, was he responsible for putting her in danger?* He had been so caught up in solving the Spenser kidnapping that he had played it fast and loose when mentioning witnesses' names. He had mentioned her name repeatedly, casually, to multiple contacts throughout the interview process. He hadn't taken one step to protect Lillian, thinking that the Spenser kidnapping was so cold that there was no current threat to her safety. *Had he been too shortsighted? Had his questions activated a modern day killer? And if Lillian was murdered, was her death his fault?*

He glanced in the rearview mirror. Paul was on his bumper, filling the window with his Nantucket County Coroner's van. John swung into the Island Sanctuary parking lot. He pulled up short and felt lashed by surprise. Gus Schlagel's Ford F150 King Cab pickup was parked in the extra wide spot next to the handicapped access ramp. *What were Gus and Ben doing here? They were supposed to be in Quammock, working on his house.*

"Officers?"

A middle-aged woman in a pink sweater set was standing near the main entrance. She had a wad of Kleenex clutched in one hand. She was trying to look calm, and failing. "I'm Patience Moran, the Facilities Manager."

John trotted over. "Detective Jarad, Ms. Moran. This is Dr. Jenkins, the Coroner."

"I've met Dr. Jenkins before. Please, come right this way." She tottered away uncertainly on high heels. "She's out back, near the deck."

John fell into step. "What can you tell us?"

She waved her arms weakly. "It looks like she just fell off the deck. We're used to seeing sudden death, of course we are, but never anything like this." She used her security pass to open a door, took a sharp right, and started down a hall. "It's shorter, if we cut through this annex."

John was happy to scurry down the hall. Island Sanctuary was spotlessly clean and filled with comforts, but he couldn't get past the institutional smell, a combination of overly sweet Febreze air freshener and stale urine. He knew it was uncharitable, but John offered up a quick prayer. *Please, Lord. When my time comes, make it quick. Don't let me end up like this.* He felt so relieved when they finally pushed through another side door and stepped out that he released his breath. He hadn't known he was holding it.

The teak deck was as exactly as he remembered it. Two first response paramedics were leaning against a gurney next to the shingled wall. They straightened as he approached.

"We haven't touched a thing, sir." The taller one said. "Dr. Jenkins? It was obvious when we got here she was DOA."

John stepped closer. Lillian's wheelchair was lying on its side near the edge of the deck. John took another steadying breath. He could easily see how the accident might have occurred. Lillian's blue shawl was tangled in the spokes of her wheelchair. He wasn't sure of Lillian's strength, but if she had struggled to shift the chair, it might have tipped her over the edge, and out.

Paul looked down first. "It's not a big fall. Maybe twelve or fourteen feet. She was ninety years old. Wouldn't have taken much to rattle her cage."

Lillian was lying on her side, nestled in a pocket of crushed heather. Her thin neck and her left leg were unnaturally bent and twisted. Lillian's sightless eyes were open, and they stared at the sky. John felt washed by a deep sadness that he couldn't explain. *Had Lillian only hung on to tell him her story?* He had heard of instances like that, where people grimly hung onto life to finish one last thing, and when it was done, they died.

Paul smoothed on a pair of nitrile gloves. Reaching for handholds, he carefully stepped off the deck and started down the slope.

"I don't see any obvious signs of violent disturbance." He knelt, felt Lillian's neck for a pulse, and shook his head. "She's still warm. This only just happened."

John clambered down, following Paul's trail step by cautious step. "What does it look like to you? Criminal negligence? Mishap? Accidental death?"

Paul studied the scene. "Right now I'm leaning toward mishap. I'll need to get her back to the morgue, and autopsy, to be sure." He flicked two fingers at the paramedics. "Alright, you fellows. You can bring her up."

Patience Moran continued to watch from the deck. She was standing next to a young aide, a girl wearing yellow Crocs, and she was wringing her hands. "My God, what a disaster! How am I going to explain this to the Board?"

"Why was she left alone?" John asked.

"I had to pee." The aide sobbed. "She wasn't ready to come in yet. She told me she was fine. She told me to go."

"You shouldn't have left her unattended, Kaylyn," Patience said severely. "You broke protocol. I'm going to have to mention that to the Board."

The aide stepped back. Her eyes flared with anger. "You try telling her "no." She wouldn't listen to me. Besides, I was only gone for a minute."

"I'd better not find out you were on your phone, Kaylyn, or you're in big trouble."

The aide started to sputter. John heard a heavy clunk, and the deck trembled. Gus had dropped his toolbox. He turned to help Ben with his armload of fresh 2x4 framing lumber.

"I noticed your truck in the lot," John said. "What are you two doing here?"

Gus straightened. He stretched his back, and cocked his thumb. "Got an emergency call. They want us to install new guard railings and security cameras, ASAP."

Security cameras? John turned. "Ms. Moran? Do you have security coverage for the deck, or cameras in the garden that might be covering this angle?"

"No, not yet." She raised her chin defensively. "But we certainly will have, going forward. I can promise you that."

The deck shuddered again as the two paramedics hefted the loaded gurney over the edge. Ben Schlagel watched dispassionately as they trundled the strapped black body bag away.

"Oh, yeah. They're going to get sued over this one, big time."

Chapter Twenty-One

John's dream had lost its amusing hide-and-seek quality. The Nazis were still chasing him through the misty woods. Pine needles dampened his footfalls as the relentless hunters steadily gained ground. He caught glimpses of their vaguely uniformed shadows flitting from tree to tree. His lungs were raw, on fire. His breathing sounded ragged in his ears. Lillian Ketchem's sapphire blue shawl was hanging from the branches of a nearby dead tree. He clutched the Sigma's empty clip in his left hand and he raised his Glock in his right as a shrill alarm began to shriek in his ear. John groggily batted the bedside clock radio before realizing that the ringtone was coming from his iPhone.

"Yes?" He felt dazed, disoriented. John rolled over onto his elbow and clamped the iPhone to his ear. "Yes, I'm here. What is it?"

"Detective Jarad? Chief Nunn. I need you to report to Moorhaven immediately. I've instituted an AMBER alert." She drew a deep breath. "Libby Spenser is missing."

"What?" For a moment, John confused the past with the present, and Libby Spenser with Alice. "When did we log the call?"

The Chief hesitated. "911 logged it seventeen minutes ago. I've been trying to reach Agent Mayas. He won't pick up. I'll meet you there."

"On my way." John planted both feet on the cold hardwood floor.

"John?" Sarah mumbled. "What's wrong?"

He leaned over and gently stroked her hip. "Got to go, honey. Go back to sleep."

"What time is it?"

"Two. Almost two."

Sarah threw the covers off and she struggled to rise. "I'll make you some coffee while you get dressed."

"Honey, you don't need to do that."

"Yes, I do." She wrestled with her bathrobe. "Meet you downstairs."

John quickly pulled on socks, slipped into his pants, and buttoned a shirt. He still felt disoriented from his dream. The dream world had been so vivid it seemed more real than his reality. *On your feet, soldier. Rise and shine.* He struggled to clear his head and to focus. *Libby Spenser was missing?* Moorhaven was a huge house, and she was only two. Maybe Libby had wandered off, looking for her parents? Maybe she had decided to curl up and sleep in another room? He fought against the idea of automatically connecting Libby's disappearance with Alice Spenser's tragic history in that great house. *I don't have any data yet. Do not connect the dots.*

He hurried down the stairs into their galley kitchen. Even though dawn broke early on Nantucket, there was no hint of yellow light splitting the horizon. The windows were still completely dark. A dense fog pressed up against them, turning the glass panes into mirrors and reflecting his image. John quickly finger combed his hair.

Sarah stood behind the counter by the coffeemaker. She yawned and pointed the bread knife. "Your coffee is ready." The toaster popped. She quickly slathered peanut butter and wrapped the crude breakfast in a paper towel. "Eat this on the way. You need to put something in your stomach."

John gratefully took the warm sandwich. His duty mindset was already pushing him to hit the road, to get to Moorhaven, to locate Libby, but as he looked at his wife, he hesitated. Sarah was standing near the door, her hands cradling her rounded belly, her bed head hair going every which way. She was so beautiful that his love for her caught in his throat. In spite of the pressing urgency of the moment, John felt washed by a humble gratitude for what he had.

He reached for his keys. "I'm not comfortable with leaving you here alone. Call my mother, or Mary Rose. Have one of them come over and stay with you while I'm gone."

"Are you nuts?" Sarah opened the kitchen door. "It's two o'clock in the morning! I can't call them. They'd have a stroke. Don't worry about me, John. I'll be fine. Women have been pregnant before."

"I'll go, but I'm not happy about this. Keep your phone on the nightstand. Call 911 if you need anything, Sarah. I mean it."

"I know you do, and I will." She flicked the porch light on although all it illuminated was a gray cone of fog. "Text me as soon as you come up for air. I love you."

"Love you more." John rushed out into the night.

It was a good thing that his feet knew the path because the yard was so filled with fog that John had trouble seeing his truck. He climbed in, fired it up, hit the fog lights, and turned for Milestone Road. There were no streetlights mid-island, and as much as he wanted to hurry John had to keep to a 25 MPH crawl. He felt a new appreciation for the benefits of modern technology. *Those whaling ship mariners who circled the globe didn't have fog lights or satellite GPS. They trusted the stars for navigation.*

He had dropped his iPhone on the bench seat beside him. As he finished the toast, John caught himself hoping that the cell phone would ring, that Chief Nunn would report that Libby Spenser had been found, and that the AMBER alert was cancelled.

He overshot the turn for Spenser Lane in the dark and had to cut the wheel sharply to catch it. The dead oak suddenly loomed ahead, its ghostly branches outlined against the slightly paler fog. *It's strange to think how my perception of this place has changed, now that I know more about the Spenser's history.* Before, everything at Moorhaven had been blandly anonymous; now the landscape had layers of fresh meaning. *That oak tree was the site of Alice Spenser's ransom drop.* John pictured Karl and Otto Schlagel crouched breathlessly in the weeds, waiting for George Stephens to drive by in the family's maroon Hudson, and waiting for George to drop the ransom packet. *What had that night meant for George? He was just a random name now, a nearly forgotten footnote to history.*

In the darkest heart of midnight, the truck's headlights reflected off the fog, creating a shining line that split the sleeping meadow into halves. John shivered as he connected solidly with the living past. *Nothing in this meadow has changed in ninety years.* He was seeing things exactly as Karl and Daisy and Otto had seen it on that tragic and fateful night.

He noted a strangely gleaming dome of white light ahead as he rounded the final curve. Moorhaven was lit up like the sinking *Titanic.* Light shone from every single window of the massive house, even from the dormers on the usually dark and shuttered third floor. John hit the brakes, and the truck slid to a stop. Addison and Julia Spenser were haloed in the double doorway, backlit by light from the hall. Fog crawled up the garden steps and swirled around their ankles. They were still wearing what John recognized as cocktail party clothes, although Addison had loosened his tie. He was hugging Julia around her bare shoulders. She looked ready to faint, and she was gripping a single child's shoe tightly in her hands.

John ran up the walk. He took the front steps two at a time. "I got here as quickly as I could."

"Thank God you're here," Julia cried. "We can't find Libby anywhere."

"When did you see her last?"

Julia started down the hall. She paused next to one of the lighthouse newel posts. "Around six-thirty or seven, when we put her down for the night."

Addison followed his wife. "We checked on Libs when we got home, before going to bed. That's when we found out she was gone."

Julia tried to set the shoe down on a table, but she picked it back up. "We always checked on Libby." She choked. "Where could she be?"

"She's not on the third floor," Howard Spenser said.

He was standing next to Camilla on the second floor landing under the great stained glass window. Howard had a checked bathrobe loosely tied over his pajamas. Camilla was wearing a sweater and yoga pants. She clutched a cell phone in one hand and a large chrome flashlight in the other.

"Howard's right," she said. "We've checked every room on the third floor. Twice."

"Baby?" Julia wailed. "Libby? Where are you?"

"She's not in the kitchen, sir." Jamison trotted out of the shadows. He had his pants on over his pajamas. "The back door is bolted. The SafeAlert system is still armed."

SafeAlert was still armed? John looked at Addison and Julia. "Was SafeAlert armed when you got home?"

Addison pressed his fingers against his forehead. "It was. I had to punch in the key code to let us in."

"Wait!" Julia spun around. "That means Libby's still in the house, right? We just haven't found her yet."

"Detective Jarad?" Camilla started down the staircase. "I've called the Assistant DA's office in Boston, asking for help. Her PA promised to give her the message, first thing."

John felt a ripple of grim unease. Libby Spenser hadn't been missing for an hour and the Spensers were already going over his head and calling in the big guns. John knew that the clock was ticking, and that sooner or later some mainland authority would show up to take over the investigation, but he didn't have to like it. He needed to act fast.

"This is all your fault, Camilla!" Julia swiped the tears from her eyes. "We wouldn't be going through this if you had kept your eye on her."

Camilla steadied herself against the bannister. "If you needed someone to stand over Libby's crib, then perhaps you should have coughed up the cash and hired a real babysitter."

"We didn't think we needed one!"

John started up the carpeted staircase. Libby was missing. They didn't have time for this. "Let's start with Libby's room. Which one is hers?"

"Right next to ours." Addison leapt up the staircase.

The carpeted second floor landing widened and split into two great halls that led off in opposite directions. The hallway to the right was well lit, but obviously unused. Dustsheets covered the light fixtures and the furniture. Addison turned left. He passed one opened bedroom door, and stood before the second one.

"This is her room. We found the door open, just as you see it now."

Julia had followed on their heels. She clutched Addison's sleeve. "I'm frightened, Ad. I just want Libby back. I don't care what it takes. I want her back."

"Sweetheart, please. We'll get her back." Addison reached for his wife. He hugged her close. "We need to stay calm. Let the police do their job."

Julia placed her hands on his chest. She looked up, fear and uncertainty reflected in her face. "Like the last time, with Alice? Why is this happening again?"

John halted. It was a good question. *Had Alice Spenser's cold case triggered a copycat kidnapping? Was that what was going on?* He studied the disordered room from the doorway. It was obvious from the rumpled throw rugs that the family had tracked through Libby's bedroom. The scene was heavily compromised, but he wanted to do what he could to preserve any evidence. "No one goes back in here until we've completed a full CSI sweep."

A single high note tinged. It hung in the air like the sound struck from a child's toy xylophone. Addison reached into his breast pocket. He slipped out his cell phone and he stared at the screen. His forehead wrinkled, and his eyes went blank.

He looked up, bewildered. "They sent me a text. They've got Libby. They want five million dollars."

Chapter Twenty-Two

The fog had burned off at dawn, and the bright mid-morning sunlight streamed through the library's mullioned windows. John was surprised to see that several of the cracked diamond-shaped panes had been mended with Scotch tape so old the vintage tape had yellowed. He resisted the urge to pick it off.

Moorhaven was a beehive of tension and forced inactivity. Jamison had cleared an antique partner's desk to use as their command center. Extension cords snaked across the floor from every overburdened wall socket, powering their laptops, tablets, and phone chargers. A plastic drip coffeemaker sat on top of a mahogany lowboy chest of drawers pressed up against one wall. An hour ago, Jamison had glided in on silent feet to deposit a Nantucket basket filled with warm cranberry-orange muffins. Paper wrappers and buttery crumbs littered the desk. It seemed odd to John now, after learning about Moorhaven's history that Jamison was the only staff member left in a house that used to hold dozens.

John felt wound up tighter than a clock. He shook out his hands to release the tension. The initial adrenaline rush from the kidnapper's text message had evaporated, replaced by the steady hyper-awareness of a developing and active case. Addison had texted back confirmation that he had received the ransom message. Now they were waiting on a return response from Libby Spenser's captors. John knew that suspense and delay were two psychological tactics criminals used in their toolkit, but knowing that didn't help to curb his restlessness. He started to pace.

"Patience, Detective Jarad." Chief Nunn looked up from her laptop. Her dark eyes glittered from under her half-closed lids. "I've been through this before, twice. It's a waiting game. They're working our nerves on purpose."

"I know that, sir." John ran his fingers over a row of crumbling gilded leather spines. *Moby Dick, The Heart of Darkness, Rebecca. Classics.* The library shelves were built as one solid unit, beautifully crafted from hand-planed oak. With a start, John realized that he was seeing another example of Karl Schlagel's custom carpentry. He stepped back. The ghosts of the past were alive, and they filled this cavernous house.

CJ was sitting across from Chief Nunn, typing up her report on the CSI sweep of Libby Spenser's bedroom and the hallway. CJ kept squinting at her notes. "I'm almost done. Give me two more minutes and I'll have this for you."

"Steady as you go, Detective Allamand," Chief Nunn replied smoothly. "We should wait for Agent Mayas anyway. I tracked him down. He's on his way."

"I don't understand how you people do this, day after day." Addison Spenser looked spent. Dark purple circles shadowed his eyes. He was sitting hunched on a silk brocade covered couch, holding his cell phone loosely in his hands. A dog began to howl mournfully from the back of the house. Addison glanced in that direction, and then he stood. "Why doesn't Jamison let Fenton out? Do I have to do everything myself?"

The dog abruptly stopped howling. John heard the low-key crunch of tires on pea gravel. He turned to the window in time to see Mayas driving up in a Ford Fusion with rental car tags. Mayas stepped out of car.

He wasn't alone. A skeletally thin woman with blonde bangs wearing a dark silver suit reached into the backseat of the car to retrieve her purse.

"Zandra O'Malley," Chief Nunn spoke into his ear. "Cape and Islands District Attorney. Never met her before."

"She's a piece of work." John crossed his arms. "Ambitious as hell. She's not going to stop climbing the political ladder until she makes governor."

"Good. That means she's hungry. She'll want to help us crack this case quickly." The Chief studied her nails. "That's why I sent for her."

John felt blindsided, and embarrassingly naïve. "You knew Mayas was bringing her in?"

"I did." Chief Nunn firmed her mouth. "This case is national caliber, Detective Jarad. Everyone will want to list this one on their resume."

John felt appalled. As much as he admired the Chief for her cool professionalism, this attitude struck him as stone cold. *Was that all that Libby Spenser meant to her, an anonymous next step toward an end game career goal?* John flushed with anger. *This investigation means more than that to me. This case is personal.* Libby Spenser had been taken on his turf, and on his watch. His line was drawn in the sand. *Fuck career development. Fuck mainland politics. My goal is simple. I'm going to bring Libby Spenser home.*

Moorhaven's front door boomed and echoed. Two sets of footsteps tapped down the tiled hall. The heavy library door swung open. Agent Mayas entered first, followed by the DA.

Mayas stripped off his navy windbreaker with the yellow FBI lettering. He flung it on the back of a chair. "Have you seen the media circus at the front gate? What a pack of hyenas. Good thing the Spensers hired private security. We barely pushed our way through."

Zandra O'Malley spotted Chief Nunn. She crossed the room and stretched out her hand. "Chief Nunn? Glad to finally meet you in person. Sorry for the delay. Hyannis was socked in. The fog cost me half an hour." Zandra spun on her heel and crossed the room the couch. "Mr. Spenser? Sorry to meet under these circumstances, sir. Zandra O'Malley. I'm here to help."

"I'm hoping you can help us with this." Addison shook his cell phone distractedly. "We're at a complete loss. We just want to bring Libby home."

"Of course, sir, of course, and we will." Zandra interlaced her fingers. "Please rest assured that our resources are arrayed to resolve this critical situation as quickly as possible. I'm here to personally act as your liaison with the mainland team."

"Thank you." Addison looked relieved. "I needed to hear someone say that."

"Agent Mayas gave me an update on the way in." She cocked her head. "Where is the rest of the family?"

"Upstairs, resting." Addison sighed. "My wife, Julia, well, obviously Julia's distraught. My father and Aunt Camilla are in their rooms. This has been very hard on them. They're not young anymore."

Mayas moved toward the partner's desk. "That's the best place for them, sir, for now. We can interview them once we've established our base." He flicked CJ's shoulder. "Detective Allamand? Update?"

"Just finished the report on my CSI sweep of Libby Spenser's bedroom." She pointed. "It's printing now."

"Excellent. Of course, the Bureau will do everything we can to support your efforts."

"My samples are ready for the Boston lab." CJ hooked her arm on the back of her chair. "I've packaged them up."

"Equally good. We'll courier them to Boston on the next shuttle." Mayas paused. "Any surprises?"

"There was one odd thing." CJ turned sideways to face the room. "I found a puddle of dried urine next to Libby Spenser's crib."

Zandra gasped. "That's a break in our favor. We can extract DNA."

"I've already tested it for animal protein," CJ replied quickly. "It came from a dog."

Addison snapped to attention. "Oh! I forgot to mention that. Fenton was trapped in Libby's room when we went in to check on her. Fenton ran into the hall when we opened the door."

"Why didn't the dog attack the intruder?" John asked.

"Maybe he was doped." CJ pulled out her keys. "I'll pull a blood sample to check. I've got test kits in my truck." She jiggled the keys in her hand. "Where is the dog, now?"

Addison pointed toward the back of the house. "It sounded like he was in the kitchen with Jamison."

CJ squared her shoulders. "I'll be back."

"Okay, team. Let's recap," Chief Nunn said. "Libby Spenser was last seen around 1700 hours. She was missing when the family checked on her around 0130. 911 notified me at 0150. I immediately issued an AMBER alert. Detective Jarad was first on site. He arrived at 0216. He found five adults in the house: four Spenser family members, plus Richard Jamison, the butler. Addison Spenser received a ransom text at exactly 0300."

She paused for a breath. "The kidnappers stated that they had Libby Spenser, and they wanted $5 million dollars for her return." The Chief raised a hand and pointed a finger at the ceiling. "Here's my next question: how did they get past the SafeAlert system? Detective Jarad confirmed that SafeAlert was armed when he arrived. To me, that suggests that the kidnappers either had access to the security code, or they knew how to bypass the SafeAlert system."

Mayas sat down on CJ's chair. "Bypassing SafeAlert implies a certain level of technical sophistication. That sounds like a professional effort, especially since they knew how to rearm SafeAlert after they left to gain more time."

"Agreed." Zandra folded her arms. "And professional criminals would easily know how to dope a dog."

"We still don't know that the dog was doped," John argued. "That's what Detective Allamand is checking."

"I'm pretty sure it's a given," Zandra snapped.

"Let's stay on topic." The Chief leaned against a table. "Agent Mayas? We're going to take you up on your offer of Bureau support. I'd like you to run this new Spenser ransom text through your CTAD system and check for comparables. If we are negotiating with a professional gang, maybe they've done this before."

"There's not a lot to work with yet, Chief, but I'll try," Mayas said.

"Thank you. Detective Jarad, I want you to develop a list of anyone who might have had access to the Spenser's SafeAlert code like service people, maintenance employees, that kind of thing. Let's cover all the bases."

John felt that unpleasant wave of irritation again. He had been the first one on the scene, and now, with Chief Nunn's secondary SafeAlert assignment, he felt marginalized, like he was being shunted aside. *They should be reporting to him.* John shrugged the negativity off. He was in a subordinate position now. Holding a grudge wouldn't get Libby Spenser home any quicker, and that's where his focus needed to be.

"Yes, sir. I'm on it."

Hunching his shoulders, Mayas flicked on his phone. "Good. The Quantico profiler has some suggestions. Here's what she said about that new text." He read the email and shook his head. "Those scumbags are real pros. Apparently, the ransom text came from a burnable phone through a faked Gmail account." Mayas lowered his phone to his lap. "If they're really smart, they'll continue to use multiple phones off multiple servers from different locations. We can't identify those types of anonymous callers." He sat back. "She also said that our scumbags are most likely white males, Gen X, with at least a secondary level education."

Addison pressed his hands to his temples. "So what do we do next? Just sit here, and wait until they text me again?"

"Yes, sir. I'm afraid so." Zandra sat down next to Addison primly. "That's exactly what we need to do."

The sunlight had shifted through the mullioned windows. The day was getting on. John felt an itch to do something, to do anything. Successful kidnapping cases needed to be resolved within the first 48 hours. The clock was ticking.

"What more can I do to support?" he asked.

Zandra smiled dismissively. "I think we're good, Detective Jarad. We all appreciate the work you did resolving the Alice Spenser kidnapping, but this one with Libby Spenser, well, it's real."

John felt like he'd been gut punched. The blood rushed to his face. He heard it roaring in his ears. The DA had a reputation for being a cold-hearted bitch, but John had never personally felt her lash before. He quickly bit back the *fuck you* on the end of his tongue. He didn't know what her agenda was, but obviously, Zandra O'Malley had one.

And then, as suddenly as it came, John realized that it didn't matter who solved the case, or even who got the credit for it. That was extraneous. The worth of the work was in the doing of it, and in knowing that Alice

Spenser's story had finally been told, and that justice got served. Everything else, including career advancement or glory, was noise.

He blinked. That meant that the same thing was true with his brother's Danny case. John had only been twelve years old when Danny vanished. Twelve was still such a child. In spite of the crushing guilt he had carried for twenty years, there was nothing more he could have done to protect Danny at that time. But he had solved Danny's case, too, so that Danny's story got told and his brother could rest in peace. Now, Alice Spenser could rest in peace, too.

That was the real value in doing this job. Of course, it was his duty to stop, pursue, and catch criminals, but it was even more important that the voiceless victim's side of things got heard. No one could ever take that achievement away from him. When all was said and done, no one remembered the name of the detectives who cracked a tough case. What they remembered was the name of the victim, which was exactly the way it should be.

Chapter Twenty-Three

"Detective Jarad?" Chief Nunn asked. "You look especially thoughtful. Anything more you'd care to share with the team?"

"Yes." John folded his arms. "I think we should explore the idea that this may have been a copycat kidnapping." He glanced at Addison, still seated on the couch with his hands between his knees. "The news about finding Alice Spenser may have reactivated the idea of squeezing your family for ransom."

"That is a distinct possibility," Agent Mayas agreed. "But it doesn't narrow our suspect list down any. A copycat could be a local individual or a professional team."

Addison looked distraught. He ran his fingers through his hair. "Is it better if it's a professional team? I mean, I don't know what's important anymore."

Agent Mayas stood. He leaned back against the desk. "It is slightly better if it's a professional team, sir, because then we know what we're dealing with. We might as well go over this now, so that you can be prepared." He looked first to the Chief, and then to the DA. "Okay if I continue?"

"Go right ahead," Zandra said.

"Yes, Agent Mayas, please continue."

Mayas slowly nodded. "There are rules to follow in every kidnapping event." He smoothed his tie and folded his arms across his chest. "The first is, don't expect this to be over quickly. Negotiations can take weeks or months, sometime even years."

"Years!" Addison gasped. "It might be years before we see Libby again?"

"Yes, sir, it can take years. We need to remember that the kidnapper has been successful, and that this event is just getting started. Any number of things can happen on their end that we simply can't control. There can even be a significant length of time after the ransom is paid before your daughter is returned."

"My God. What a nightmare."

Mayas pushed off the desk. He dragged a chair over the Oriental rug to the couch. "Don't give in to emotion, sir. You need to stay strong and stay focused, until we get your daughter back."

"I know, I know. Yes, of course, you're right." Addison's pale face looked pinched. "What do I need to do? Just tell me. What do I need to do?"

"First off, the kidnappers have demanded five million dollars." Mayas rested both hands on his knees. "The family needs to decide, going in, what your initial low ball offer will be."

"Low ball offer? I am not bargaining over the life of my child!"

"Its not bargaining, sir. It's establishing initial parameters. Kidnapping isn't just about getting the family member back. It's about exercising control. The only real power you have now is that you are the only buyer interested in this particular market." Mayas leaned back. "The family will need to start with a low ball offer to let the kidnappers know that you are not simply going to cave in to their demands."

"It's a game, Mr. Spenser," Chief Nunn said. "They're playing a dangerous game."

"It is a game, sir," Mayas agreed. "And your initial offer doesn't even really matter. They're going to reject it anyway, just to show the family that they're not afraid to play." Mayas reached out. He touched Addison's sleeve. "We'll need to develop our game plan, sir, and expect some back and forth before Libby is returned."

"I can see that now. My God, this is difficult. How do people do this?"

"Yes, sir. Yes, it is." Mayas sat back. "The next thing you need to do, sir, is to demand proof of life when they text or call."

Addison looked haunted. "What is that?"

"Nowadays, proof of life is usually a phone call or a text video. When the kidnappers contact you next, you'll need to insist on speaking with Libby, and hearing her voice."

"What if they say no?"

"Then you must insist on it more firmly, sir, before her ransom negotiations can continue."

"I don't know if I can do this," Addison whispered. He juggled the cell phone in his hands. "I don't know if I can follow through."

"This is where the strong and focused part comes in, sir. Breathe. And don't worry. We'll be prepared for this when they call."

"But where can Libby be? If those men are professionals, she could be anywhere!"

"Actually." John cleared his throat. "I'm hopeful that she's still on Nantucket."

"Really?" Zandra uncrossed her legs. She leaned forward, pressing both hands deeply into the cushion. "What makes you so certain of that?"

"Because I believe that the same fog that delayed you in Barnstable hampered the kidnapper or kidnapping team last night. Ackerman Field and the ferry service have been shuttered since 1700 hours. Chief Nunn issued the AMBER alert at 0150. If the kidnapper, or the kidnapping team, tried to take Libby Spenser off the island by private boat or plane this morning, service personnel would have seen her. To my mind, that means she's still here."

"By God, he's right." Addison leapt to his feet. "You can't fight a Nantucket fog. How do we follow up on *that*?"

"Detective Jarad!" Zandra stressed each syllable. "That statement was unconscionable! You have no evidence for one single thing you've suggested."

"I know how Nantucket works," John said. "That's a part of my evidence chain."

"I'll handle this, Ms. O'Malley," Chief Nunn rose. "Team, Detective Jarad just made a couple of interesting suggestions. I'd like to stress that regardless of the fog last night, the airport and the ferries were both closed and covered by the AMBER alert. Now, I'd like us to maintain our focus, and continue with the line of investigative thought that this kidnapping was the result of a professional team, and discuss how we're going to develop our successful negotiation game plan."

Addison Spenser jumped as his cell phone pinged in his hand. He dropped the phone to the floor and quickly stooped to retrieve it. The room fell silent as Addison punched in his passcode and read the new text message.

"It's from them."

He placed his cell phone in the center of the desk so that everyone could see it and took one step back. John time checked his phone. It was precisely 10:01 a.m.

Libby Spenser is safe. We want $5 million US dollars for her. Get the money ready now. We will text you the ACH wiring instructions tomorrow. Follow our instructions exactly. Try anything funny and we'll send her back to you in pieces.

"Addison?"

John turned. Julia Spenser stood framed in the doorway. Her shoulder length hair was tousled. She was dressed in leggings and an oversized mint green cashmere sweater. Julia's face was as pale as moonlight, and her fists were clenched tight. She looked expectant, hopeful, and fearful, all at the same time.

"I heard the yelling. Has something happened?"

"Sweetheart? Are you okay?" Addison put his arm around her, and he led Julia to the couch. They sat down side by side. "We just got a reply text message. Libby is safe."

"Oh, thank God." Julia sobbed into her fists.

"And we're negotiating her ransom."

"Negotiating her ransom?" Julia's head snapped up. "Just pay it, Addison! Give them the money! I don't care what it costs. I want Libby back!"

Addison took her hands. He held them between his own. "Sweetheart, it's a little more complicated than that. Apparently, we need to negotiate the price. It's part of a process."

"Fuck the process, Addison!" Julia pushed him away. "I want Libby back right now!"

"Dearest, this may take awhile. It's not simply ask, and have. We need to be prepared for that. The kidnappers are demanding millions of dollars. We may have difficulty getting that large amount of money together right away."

Julia looked puzzled. "What do you mean we won't have the money right away?"

"The estate is tied up in the Spenser Trust. The Trust pays for Moorhaven, and the maintenance, and the property taxes. You know that. Dad and Aunt Cam get a small stipend, and it covers my salary, but that's about it."

"But Addison, we have a jet! A private jet!"

"Which also belongs to the Trust. Sweetheart, what I'm saying is, there's no cash. All of the real money is gone. It has been gone, for years. Please, now, don't worry. I'll call Bud Leach at Pacific National Bank. He may be able to give us a quickie mortgage. Of course, I'll have to email the Trustees for permission first, but Moorhaven must be worth something."

"Are you serious?" Julia shot up. "This isn't about a house, Addison! This is about Libby! Are you telling me that all of this is a lie? That we have to go to the bank to negotiate the return of our child?"

Addison Spenser looked at Julia with haunted eyes.

"Yes," he said sadly. "That's exactly what I'm saying."

Chapter Twenty-Four

Sarah grasped the knife firmly in her hand. She hesitated, uncertain of where to make the first cut, since the custom cake was a thing of great beauty. It was luxuriously slathered with whipped cream frosting and dotted with candied flowers, some of which were real. The cake was also half the size of her mother-in-law Jenny's expansive dining room table.

A message had been written across the cake in florid cursive script: *Welcome! Thing One and Thing Two!* The inscription has shocked a few of the older lady guests, but Sarah felt charmed by it. She knew that it was a thoughtful reference to her favorite illustrator, Dr. Seuss. Evidently, Jackie had gone all out to fulfill her promise to bring a cake to Sarah's baby shower. Jackie was still MIA, but the cake had been delivered promptly at ten-thirty by the Sweet Island Dreams Bakery van. *Jackie must be doing really well with her new real estate career. I don't even want to guess how much this crazy cake cost.*

Mary Rose gave her a nudge. "Cut me a big corner piece. The sugar buzz will help get me through my afternoon."

"Go ahead and cut it, dear." Jenny proffered a china dessert plate. "We can't wait much longer. Our guests are getting peckish." She leaned back on her heel and glanced out the window. "I'm going to have to speak to John. It's a shame he's not here. This shower is important."

Sarah ducked her head. She quickly blinked back tears. Jenny had put her finger on the only blot on their celebration. John was also MIA, and he hadn't called ahead to let Sarah know. *I know he's super busy right now, but still, this hurts.* Sarah had been wearing a brave face at the shower, but she had caught a few of the ladies whispering by the powder room in the hall. She had seen the withering pity in their eyes.

"I wouldn't be surprised if John played hooky on purpose." Mary Rose snorted. "Crissakes! Look at this roomful of biddies. He'd be the only fox in the henhouse."

Sarah pushed the knife into the thick cake. She cut a firm line. "I'm sure he's on his way," she lied. "He's busy covering that AMBER alert. They called him out in the middle of the night." She carefully lifted a cake slice and placed it perfectly in the center of the plate. She felt mechanical and artificial, but no one was going to be able to criticize her behavior because of his absence.

"I heard about that in town this morning." Jenny reached for another empty plate. "Libby Spenser. What a horrible, horrible thing. The Spensers must be frantic with worry."

Sarah lifted a second slice. "Of course it has to take priority. I get that." She waved the knife. "We are talking about a missing child."

"Keep slicing, dear. Mary Rose and I will serve." Jenny handed Mary Rose the filled plates. She picked up two more empty ones. "I'm glad that John's on the case. He should be. Libby Spenser needs to be found, and returned to her family. But when he's done that, I really do think it's time for John to rethink his career." She shook her head. "I worry about the risks he takes, with all of the lunatics running around, ambushing police officers at traffic stops. And those domestic disputes! Seems like you read about someone in law enforcement getting shot every day. I really don't know what's wrong with the world these days. And it's keeping John from doing the really important things, like spending quality time with the family."

Jenny's eyes grew dark. "Life is too short. He has a wife and children to consider now. And it's not like the Council, or that new chief of his appreciate what it is that John does."

"That thought has crossed my mind," Sarah admitted. "I thought I was being selfish."

Jenny raised her chin. "It's not being selfish to take a good look at your life, and to correct your course to follow your own goals. The problem is that people hold tight to grudges, or else they settle in. They get comfortable, and then they're too afraid of change to try something different, or something new that might actually be a better fit." She turned as the babble of conversation in the living room slowly died. "What on earth?"

Cooler air tickled Sarah's ankles.

"Hi, all. Sorry I'm late."

Jenny set both plates back on the table. Stretching out her arms, she headed for the door. "Jackie! My dear! Don't you look marvelous!"

"Holy cow." Mary Rose froze in shock. "Didn't see that coming."

Sarah blinked to make sure that what she was seeing was real. Jackie stood poised confidently at the top of the steps leading up from the sunken living room. Sarah barely recognized her. Jackie's customary pulled back tight ponytail had been stylishly cropped to a swinging shoulder length bob. She was also wearing makeup, including magenta lipstick. Most shocking of all, Jackie was dressed in a nubby pink skirt suit that looked liked vintage Chanel with pantyhose and matching sling-back pumps. Even Jackie's work satchel was pink. Sarah blinked again. The vision didn't change.

I can't believe what I'm seeing. Jackie's not dressed like a Goth. If I had passed her on the street, I wouldn't have known who she was!

"Thanks, Mom." Jackie laughed nervously. She lifted two car seats gift-wrapped in clear cellophane tied off with colorful bows. "Congratulations, Sarah! Where can I drop these?"

"Set them over here, dear." Jenny pointed at a stack of opened gifts piled on a window seat. She playfully shook her finger. "You've been extravagant."

"Can't be too careful carrying precious cargo." Jackie laughed again. "I can remember when you and Dad tossed us all in the back of the station wagon. We didn't even wear seatbelts."

"Ah! The good old, bad old days." Jenny beamed. "You must be doing well with your new career."

"I love it, I really do." Jackie strode over. She reached for a plate. "Thanks, Emmer. How's the cake?" She took a bite and waved her fork. "It's my new client. He's totally high end. The sky's the limit with him, and he loves Nantucket. Fell in love with the place. Started off looking at town condos, but now he's decided that he wants to build something new." She took another bite, and spoke around it. "He's renting the Gantrys' old place to live in for now."

Mary Rose frowned. "The Gantrys' place, in Surfside?"

"Yep. That's the one."

"It's got six bedrooms. Kind of a big barn for just one guy, don't you think?"

"Fine by me." Jackie shrugged. "As long as his checks keep clearing the bank." She scraped the frosting off of her plate and licked the fork clean. "I have to say it's nice working with a client who really knows what he wants. You'd be surprised." She shook the fork. "Most of them don't.

He's looking at a couple of those Lost Forest parcels, too, Sarah, that you and John have for sale, including that big corner lot."

"Selling that would be awesome, Jackie. It would really help us out."

Jackie winked. "I'm going to sell him something. I took him by your new house site, too. He loved, loved, loved the Quammock location. Adored driving along the coastal road. I told him "no way," but he wanted me to ask if there's any chance that you and John might sell him that property, instead?"

Sarah flinched. She felt a cold finger of dread touch the space between her shoulder blades. *Settle down. Don't overreact. Jackie just wants to impress her new client by showing him all of Nantucket's housing options. Quammock is a great site. I just wish she'd asked us about it first. This feels like an invasion of privacy.*

"Jackie! What kind of a question is that?" Mary Rose sputtered. "Of course they don't want to sell Quammock. They're building their dream home there."

"Business is business." Jackie shrugged. "Thought I should put it out there, just in case."

Claire Burdett turned. "Sarah? I've been meaning to ask. How is that new house coming?"

"So far it's been great, Claire. They just finished the roof."

Patsy Wraeburn stepped up to the table. She reached for a second piece of cake. "A new house, expecting twins, and the Arts Guild grand prize! You certainly are having quite a winning streak this year."

"That's right." Claire adjusted her wrap. "My Nate called from Napa on Sunday. He saw *Altar Rock* online. You know Nate's an artist. He said that everyone is talking about the award."

Sarah crushed a small flutter of panic. *Relax. This is just conversation. I am not going to let fear ruin this baby shower for me.*

The doorbell rang, followed by a loud rapping knock. Sarah felt another cool draft stir the air in the stuffy living room.

"Hello, the house? We're coming in."

A stout woman with tortoiseshell glasses limped across the slate floor. She carried a gift-wrapped box bearing a huge silver bow. A lanky teenaged girl with long blonde hair, and a younger boy wearing a red hoodie trailed behind her. They both held back, looking shy and uncertain.

"Amanda!" Jenny stepped forward. "I'm so glad you could make it. Sarah? You remember Amanda Ketchem, from your wedding? And these are her children, Heather and Boyd."

"Of course." Sarah reached for the gift. "How are you? Thank you for coming."

"I'm sorry. We can't stay." Amanda's eyes were red-rimmed and swollen, as if she had a cold or had recently been crying. Pulling a crumpled Kleenex from her pocket, she wiped her nose. "My grandmother Lillian died. I need to go make the funeral arrangements."

"Oh, my dear!" Jenny gasped. "I'm so sorry to hear that. Is there anything we can do?"

"No, not right now, Jenny. Thank you." Amanda dragged her fingers through her hair. "We'll let you know about the service. I'm assuming it will be St. Michael's, but that's still up in the air." She puffed out her cheeks, and sighed. "There's so much to do!"

Tana Starbuck joined their circle. She clutched her pearls. "What happened? Who died?"

"Lillian Ketchem," Susanne Hussey said. "Died from a fall. My husband Tom told me all about it at dinner last night." She *tsked-tsked*. "Happened at Island Sanctuary. Such a shame."

"She broke her neck," Boyd interrupted.

"Dude." Heather glanced up from her phone. "Dial it down. Jesus! She was your great-grandma."

Lillian, that wonderful old lady was dead? Sarah felt a sudden rush of sorrow. She looked around for an empty table or chair. She felt completely awkward standing in front of the grieving family while holding the gaily-wrapped gift in her hands. "How old was she?"

"Ninety." Amanda sniffled. "Paul Jenkins said it was pure accident. No sign of a struggle, or any distress. Thank God for that. At least it was quick. He said she didn't suffer. I know Gram was a total pain in the ass, but I miss her already."

Susanne pointed her finger. "You should sue that place. Tom called it criminal negligence. He's a lawyer. He should know. Tom said she was left unattended. If I were you, Mandy, I'd give Tom a call."

Amanda blanched. "We're not anywhere near ready to look into that, Sue."

"Oh, my!" Claire glanced at her gold wristwatch. "Look at the time! I promised Maggie that I'd pick her up after soccer practice. She's carrying her gear."

"Is it that late?" Patsy reached for her purse. "Thank you for the lovely party, Jenny. And Sarah? Best of luck. We'll be waiting to hear the good news."

There was a general clinking of china and a silken rustle as the ladies began to abandon their cake plates and to gather up their coats. Jenny climbed the three small steps by the door. She hefted a bushel Nantucket basket.

"Ladies? Don't forget your cell phones."

Whew! Made it. Sarah relaxed. *That's over with.* A fancy tea party filled with island ladies wasn't big on her to-do list, but Jenny had thought it important, so Sarah had gone along with the idea. She would have preferred to stay at home, dressed in her sweats and noodling around with sketches for a new painting or two. Right now, though, all Sarah wanted to do was to get off her feet. They were aching so badly she could feel her pulse in her big toes.

"I'll give you a ride home." Mary Rose dug into her purse, hunting for her keys. "John can come back later with the truck. Girlfriend, you made out like a bandit. I don't think there's room enough in my car for all of these shower gifts."

The dam burst. As much as Sarah loved being a part of the close-knit Nantucket community, she had counted on John to be by her side, to be her anchor, her safe harbor, at the baby shower. *Where are you, John? You were supposed to help me with this.* Sarah scurried for the powder room, choking on tears.

"Why is she crying?" Jackie wondered. "She didn't even really know Lillian Ketchem."

"Jesus, Jackie! It has nothing to do with Lillian. She's crying because John didn't show up for the shower."

"Oh, well. He's just like Dad. She'd better get used to that."

Chapter Twenty-Five

There was a tap on the door.

"Sarah? Dear? You can't hide in the powder room forever. I've had three cups of tea, and this is the only lavatory on this floor."

"I'll be out in a minute, Jenny."

Sarah checked her face in the mirror. She looked dreadful. Her eyes were puffy and red. She quickly held one of the guest hand towels under the cold tap and applied it to her eyes. The cooling sensation felt wonderful.

What is wrong with me lately? I feel like I'm losing my mind.

She fumbled with the lock, and stepped into the hall. "I'm sorry, Jenny. I don't know why I'm so weepy. Must be the hormones."

"Go take a seat, dear. I'll be right with you. I really do need to use the loo."

Sarah wandered back into the living room, now blessedly silent. She had grown up in a small, tight family in a quiet house. *I knew when I married John that I'd get thrown into the mix, but I never anticipated this. Every one of these family events is a mob scene.* She pulled a Windsor chair closer to the window and sat, resting her hands on her stomach. *At least the twins will be fine living like this. They'll grow up surrounded by cousins, but for me, this takes work.*

"That's better."

Jenny grasped the wrought iron railing. She successfully navigated the three small steps. Using her foot, she scooted a tufted ottoman across the floor. "So tell me, my dear. What's wrong? I hate seeing you upset like this. It wasn't the party, was it?"

"No, it wasn't the party, Jenny. That was lovely." Sarah twined her fingers together. She needed to talk to someone, and Jenny was the closest thing to a mother she had. "I know this is going to sound nuts." She sniffled as more tears threatened to spill from her eyes. She could taste the salt on the back of her tongue. "I love John, I really do. We're having twins. We're building our dream house. Everything is going our way." Sarah shook her head. "I don't know why, but I don't feel happy."

Jenny's eyes softened with compassion. "What are you unhappy about?"

Sarah laughed through her tears. "That's what I don't know!"

"Are you worried about delivering the twins? Is that what this is about?"

"No, not really. Dr. Diballa said everything's fine. So far, so good."

"Is something else worrying you?"

Sarah took a shuddering breath. She faced her darkest fear.

"Yes," she admitted. "There was a man, a guy I used to know back in Pittsburgh, way before I met John. We were engaged. It was a disaster." Sarah combed her fingers through her hair. She found a snarl and nervously started to pick it out. "He was abusive. I was a fool. I kept thinking that if I hung in there long enough that Mason would change. It took me two years to figure it out. Mason wasn't going to change. Ever. So one day, when he was away on a business trip, I packed up and I left him." She sniffled. "That's how I ended up on Nantucket. I was running away."

"I see," Jenny said. "So, you're worried about this Mason?"

"Yes," Sarah confessed. "Ever since *Altar Rock* won that Arts Guild award I've been living on pins and needles. I'm a nervous wreck." She shook out her hands. "I'm so afraid that he's going to find me that I can't sleep. The other day, at the garden center, I thought I saw him. I panicked. I wanted to run back to the truck and hide. It took everything in me not to do that."

"Hum. Have you talked to John about this?"

"Not really. He's been so crazy busy lately. I keep waiting for the right time, but it never comes. There's always something going on with him." The tears threatened to spill over Sarah's eyelids. She fanned her eyes with her hands, hoping that it would help. "The only time we ever really talk anymore is when he sends me a text."

"I see." Jenny reached for a needlepointed pillow. She tucked it behind her back. "Alright, Sarah, here's my advice, for what it's worth. You need to talk to John, and you need to share with him how you feel. From what I'm hearing from you right now, John doesn't know this is happening. That's not fair to him. John trusts you to be honest. That is how marriage works."

"I know that, Jenny. I do." Sarah linked her fingers. "I think that's my problem. I don't trust people anymore, after what happened with Mason."

"I see what's really going on here." Jenny relaxed. "This is about faith, my dear, not trust. Mason made you doubt yourself. You lost faith in your own judgment because of what happened with him, but I have an answer for that." Jenny reached forward. She patted Sarah's knee. "You need to give it time, plenty of time, but as you keep making good decisions, you'll regain trust in yourself."

"So, you're saying that I need to be patient."

"Yes, and to continue making good decisions." Jenny smiled. "My dear, no wonder you're so upset. Look at your life! You and John are going a lot of transitions right now, and you're right in the middle of most of them."

"Great," Sarah said sarcastically. "So when do I start to feel better?"

"Don't you feel better now?"

With a start, Sarah realized that she did. Talking with Jenny had helped. "I do. Thank you, Jenny. I really do."

"Good. I'm glad. That's what I'm here for. Now, you just need to talk with John. That's your homework assignment."

The front door clicked. There was a rapid slap of shoe leather down the slate hall. John slid to a stop at the top of the steps. He met Sarah's eyes.

"Sorry, I'm late. I got hung up with the AMBER alert on Libby Spenser. Lost track of the time."

Jenny pushed up off the ottoman. "I'll be in the kitchen." She tugged John's sleeve as she passed, and gazed at him over the top of her bifocal glasses. "You need to talk with your wife, son."

John unzipped his jacket. He glanced at the stack of shower gifts. "Honey? I've fucked up big time, didn't I?"

Sarah wanted to shout with frustration. She wrestled it down. Pointed accusation and recrimination would only escalate and get them nowhere. She and John needed to talk. Sarah reached into the depth of her soul to find the strength to be fair and honest. "It's okay," she lied.

"No, honey, no. It's not okay." John dropped his jacket. He sat on the ottoman and reached for her hands. "I can see you're upset, and I'm sorry. I never wanted that to happen."

"Oh, John. Where were you? You were supposed to be here with me. You're breaking my heart."

"Don't say that. I know I let you down. All I can say is I'm sorry. I know that I promised you better than this."

It took some effort, but Sarah held the line on honesty. "Yes, you did."

"Fair enough."

He stood, and settled his fists on his hips. "Sarah, I realized something on my way over here. I've realized that I spend more time with some of the force than I do with my own family." He shook his head. "That's not right. Somehow, I feel like I've gotten off track. I got involved with law enforcement because of Danny. I wanted to solve Danny's case. Well, I did that. It's solved. Now I'm wondering: Why am I still doing this, if it's making everyone around me unhappy?"

"But I thought that you loved your job?"

"I do. I did. But the job has changed. The force has changed." John stared at the floor. "I used to feel like it was a part of my job to be engaged with the community, to work with folks at the local level, and make things better. Cool the feuds. Find shelter for a woman and kids when her drunk boyfriend threw them out into the street. Make sure the kids got home safely from school. We used to be a part of the same team." He frowned. "I don't feel that way anymore. Something has changed. The force has gone techno. Sarah, you should see what we do now. Email searches, satellite facial recognition scans. That is not what I signed up for."

John compressed his lips. "That's not all of it. I've been feeling marginalized since my demotion. The assignments I've been getting lately don't satisfy me like they used to do. I hate thinking it's ego, but I've been feeling mothballed. Pushed aside."

"Maybe it is time to try something new."

"And toss my Masters degree? Writing that thesis took me two years!"

"Your degree is still useful, if it led you to this place." Sarah relaxed. "John, if you could do anything that you wanted to do, anything at all in the whole world, what would it be? What is the one thing that makes you the happiest?"

"Besides you?"

"Yes, besides me, you goofball. Be serious."

He thoughtfully scratched his chin. "The sea. I love being on the water. That's why I could never leave Nantucket. Not permanently. No way. If I got to pick, I'd want to do something ... fundamental. Something that connected me to the natural world, every single day. Maybe, I don't know, a charter boat fisherman?"

"So why not look into it? Once Jackie sells those Lost Forest lots for us, we'll have the money to invest. Why not buy a boat? John, you're thirty-two years old. If you're going to do something different with your life, now is the time to do it."

"I could do it, you know, if I really wanted to." He tugged his ear. "Wow. That's a scary thought. Leaving the force is a very big step."

"The only one stopping you is you. I'm all for it, if it would make you happier." Sarah felt the pressure of a foot. She shifted in the chair. "Just so you know, the twins are voting 'do it,' too."

"It would be a boatload of responsibility. Pun intended." John started pacing. "I would be my own boss again. I like that idea."

"If not you, then who?"

John glanced up. "What if I fail?"

"What if you succeed?" Sarah laughed. "Stop trying to come up with reasons not to try." She settled back in the chair, and pointed at her belly. "I never thought that I'd end up doing this. Sometimes, you just have

175

to trust the path to lead you where you're supposed to go. Sometimes it's up, sometimes it's down." Sarah wiggled her fingers like she was playing a keyboard. "Sometimes it's kind of sideways. I was a mess, two years ago. Then I met you, and things got better."

John sat down again. He rested his hands on her knees. "Sarah, you are the one thing I can count on. Please, don't ever change."

"I can't promise you that. I will promise that I'll try to never let you down."

"Ouch." He winced.

"That's not what I meant." Sarah took a deep breath. *Why is this so hard?* She willed herself to honest, and to be brave. "John, this family we're building means everything to me. You, the twins, all of your crazy relatives. This is my new world, and I'm going to fight for it. I know that our marriage is still young. I know we're still working things out." She took another breath. "What I'm trying to say is, I'm here for you, and I always will be. You can count on that."

He reached for her hands. "Honey? Do you remember our first date?"

"Sure I do, the picnic at Sesachacha Pond. It was the first time you ever kissed me like you really knew what you were doing."

"Funny girl. Here's an idea: Let's have another picnic, just you and me, in Quammock, at the new house site, tomorrow. Bring the twins."

"John, I'd love to do that! Can you take the time off? What about your case?"

"I'll work my schedule around it." He tightened his grip. "I'll have my cell phone with me. They can call if anything urgent comes up." He helped her up. "Why not look at things a little differently? Maybe it is time to move on. Honestly, Sarah? I'm terrified. The last time I felt this excited was the day that I met you."

CHAPTER TWENTY-SIX

John leaned in and studied his Excel spreadsheet. *Almost done. One last double check, and I'll go get Sarah.* Satisfied with what he saw, he hit the control "p" quick key and sent the report to the station's shared printer. It had taken all morning, but he'd been in luck. Jamison had emailed him a list of every contractor or service person that had Moorhaven's SafeAlert access code. *The only ones left to check on are Gus and Ben.* John had tried calling both of their cell phones, but neither one had picked up.

The station was buzzing with focus and energy. Mayas was ensconced with Chief Nunn in her office. Mayas had imported two additional special agents, associates from the Boston Bureau. They had commandeered Ted Parson's desk and John's extra chair. Ted had stormed out of the station in protest to run an unscheduled Wauwinet patrol loop. John had taken the bull by the horns. He had walked over and introduced himself. Frick and Frack had politely looked up, nodded, and silently gone back to "interfacing" with Quantico. John snorted. *Local peon is dismissed. Fuckers. Crissakes! This shit never ends.*

He passed the coffee station on his way to the printer. CJ was thoughtfully pouring out a cup. When she saw John she laughed. She used her elbow to point at the counter.

"Who brought in the Whitman's Sampler?"

"That's mine," John said. "I bought it for a friend. She doesn't need it anymore."

"I haven't seen one of those in years. I didn't even know they still made them."

"Congdon's Pharmacy carries them in the back. I had to ask them where."

"What the hell. I'll risk a tooth." CJ popped a square caramel into her mouth, and talked around it as she chewed. "What are you up to?"

John started. "What do you mean?"

"Why are you so jumpy?" She narrowed her eyes. "I meant, what are you developing?" She cocked her thumb at the two special agents. "Tight quarters with them here. It's fascinating to watch them work, though. Their world is so much more ... global. We focus on our jurisdiction, but their vision is huge." CJ reached for the powdered creamer. She slowly shook some into her mug. "Mayas stopped me in the hall this morning. He suggested that I should visit the Boston Bureau. See it in action, how stuff really works." She glanced up. "He said he could find me a place on the Boston team, if I was interested."

John felt startled. Evidently, he wasn't the only one thinking about a career change. "Are you considering that, CJ? Would you leave Nantucket? Move to Boston, and go work for the fibbies?"

"I'm not sure." She chewed her lip. "It's kind of exciting to get asked, though. I do love forensic DNA analysis. Quantico is developing cutting edge technology. There's some amazing research going on in that field right now, at the micro level. I don't know, John. I'm thinking that I might like to be a part of that."

"It wouldn't hurt to look into it," he said carefully.

CJ laughed. "Oh, I know. You're shocked by the idea of leaving Nantucket. You're such a lifer. You'll never leave the force. They'll haul you out of here with your boots on."

John's conscience prickled. CJ was one of his closest friends. He couldn't remember a time when he hadn't known her. He hadn't mentioned to her that he might be considering a career change of his own, yet. It wasn't that he was trying to keep the idea of buying a charter boat a secret, but John felt the need to keep the idea close to his vest until he made a decision. He preferred to be straight up, because lying was too complicated and hard, but it was best to be prudent. He was surprised to discover that there was a slightly delicious feeling in being duplicitous.

"Detective Jarad?" Chief Nunn called. "How's that report coming?"

"Right here, sir."

John scooped his spreadsheet off the printer and headed in, stepping around the trip wire gauntlet of cables that crisscrossed the floor around Ted's desk. Chief Nunn's door was half open. She sat hunched over her desk, staring at her PC. Mayas was sitting in the armchair to her right. He was staring at his laptop.

"Wojchak says we should see the warrant within the hour." Mayas quickly typed a reply. "VRBO and AirBnB will work with us, once we have it in hand."

"VRBO?" John asked.

Mayas looked up. "Yes. That fog may have helped. If the kidnappers hadn't planned on staying overnight, they'd need quick accommodation. Searching online rentals from the last forty-eight hours might turn Libby Spenser up, if she's still on the island, as you suggested."

"She's not getting off this island." Chief Nunn jotted a note on a legal pad. She tapped her pen against the pad and smiled with grim satisfaction. "Port Authority has triple checked every vehicle or container since harbor traffic reopened. I'm going to hear about searching those private jets for the rest of my career. Too bad, so sad. Sorry to inconvenience you, sir. Honestly, what are those people thinking? We are searching for a missing child." She looked up. "It's day two, Detective Jarad. What have you got?"

John handed them each a corner-stapled copy. "Richard Jamison confirmed that twenty-seven people besides the Spenser family members had access to Moorhaven's SafeAlert code."

"Good." Mayas ran his finger down a column. "No real surprises here that I can see. Looks mostly like local contractors or some service personnel, like the cable guy or the electric company. Detective Jarad? What's this data reflected in column D?"

"Column D reflects the last date that person tried to access Moorhaven's security keypad. Jamison confirmed that he changes the access code every ninety days. Column E indicates whether or not that person used the current code, or if they were refused and had to call it in."

"Nice detail." Mayas tapped the page. "At least the Spensers rotated their security code. Most people don't even do that much."

"Solid work so far." Chief Nunn flipped the page. "I want you to follow up on this, Detective. Reconfirm the access code that each one of these people is currently using. Timing might help us eliminate most of these local names." She tapped her lips. "I still see this as a professional snatch. In any case, I want to cover all of the bases."

Also known as a little cautious C-Y-A. "Yes, sir." John felt a spark of guilty conscience. *I might be having a little too much fun with my career change idea. Jesus! It's liberating to think I might not be doing this anymore, but Libby Spenser is still missing. I need to keep my focus on that.* Canvassing the list of island contacts meant more grass roots legwork, but that was how this job got done. John cleared his throat.

"The only gap in my report is confirmation from the Schlagels. They haven't responded. I'm going out to their house next, to see if I can catch Gus or Ben in person and button it down."

"Good. Sounds like a plan." Chief Nunn returned to her PC. "Keep us apprised."

John checked the wall clock as he left Nunn's office. Eleven twenty-two. *Perfect.* He had time to pick up the pizza, swing by mid-island to check on Gus and Ben and still meet Sarah for lunch. *Why do I feel like a teenager dodging the principal and playing hooky from school? I'm not doing anything wrong. I'm just out of my usual comfort zone.*

Tucking the spreadsheet under his arm, John swung by his desk for his jacket and his keys, doubling back to pick up his iPhone. *Crissakes! Where is my mind? It's all well and good that I'm looking forward to seeing Sarah, but I need to stay present, and alert. Law enforcement is all about focus.*

He pushed the door open, trotted across the lot, started the truck, studied the traffic pattern and headed west on Orange Street. His stomach rumbled, and John laughed. He had online ordered an eight cut Parma sausage, onion, and mushroom pizza because it was Sarah's favorite. *I'm good for three of those slices.* Sarah would protest that she was full, and then polish it off.

He happily handed his debit card over at the drive-through window at Slice of Heaven, and reached for the sturdy cardboard box. The rich aroma of tomato sauce, onions, spicy sausage, and cheese filled the truck. John considered the idea of folding one slice and eating it on the way out to see Gus and Ben. *Shame on you! Can't you wait twenty minutes?*

He turned left on Milestone Road, and placed his hand on the warm pizza box to keep it from sliding around the bench seat as he navigated the Schlagels' sketchy driveway. The brakes squealed as the truck rolled to a stop near their scrap lumber pile. Their construction truck was nowhere in sight. The house, and the yard, looked deserted. Even the bomb shelter hatchway was closed.

Crap! This might take more time than I had planned on.

He jumped as a case of bottled water landed on his hood. Ben Schlagel leaned his cabled forearms on the passenger side door.

"Hey, John." Ben smiled appreciatively. "Something sure smells good. That pizza meant for me?"

Jesus Christ! John's heart was thumping so hard he saw stars. *Where is my brain? I just let Ben Schlagel sneak up on me. Didn't even catch sight of him in my mirrors. I need to cut this daydreaming shit out. It could get me killed.*

CHAPTER TWENTY-SEVEN

"Dad's not here," Ben said. "Pearlie Wilkins called. Pearlie saw someone prowling around your site after the crew went on break. Dad went to check on it. You know how some folks get sticky fingers. He didn't want your new windows walking off."

John tried to relax. His nerves still jangled. "I'm on my way out to Quammock now. Picking up my wife for lunch."

Ben's brow furrowed. "So what are you doing mid-island? A little out of the way, isn't it?"

"I need to confirm the SafeAlert code that you and your dad use for Moorhaven."

"Because of Libby Spenser? That new kidnapping?"

John stole the Chief's line. "We're covering the bases."

"Easy enough." Ben shrugged. He reached into his brown coverall bib. "I store it in my phone, since it changes so much." Ben used his broad thumb to swipe the screen. "MH2016R. Sound about right?"

John checked the spreadsheet. "Yes. That's current. Thanks for checking."

"Not a problem." Ben stepped back. He linked his hands together. "It's kinda weird another kidnapping happened at Moorhaven. A copycat. Know what I mean?"

"I do know what you mean."

"So what do you think? Professionals? Some East Coast gang, like CNN said?"

John felt mulish. "That's what they said. Me? I'm not so sure. It was local ninety years ago. Might be local this time, too."

"Jesus! I can't believe you said that." Ben rested his fists on his hips. "Dad's right. You do have a bee in your bonnet." Ben pointed his chin at the kitchen door. "I can promise you we had nothing to do with it this time. Go ahead and search the house if you don't believe me. I give you permission."

John felt a riffle of embarrassment. Ben's face shone with honesty. "I believe you, Ben. This case has me questioning everything, and everybody." He restarted the truck. "Just out of curiosity, though, if Gus is out at the site, what are you doing home?"

Ben roared with laughter so loud the sparrows flew from the holly bushes. "Damn, John, turn it off! You have got it bad. Dad left me here to finish payroll. We need to get it to Pacific National by three or the fellows won't get their checks. He even padlocked the shelter and took the key, so that I can't get to my games until I'm done. Satisfied?"

"Sorry. You're right. I can't seem to turn it off anymore."

"Professional caliber OCD. That's what they pay you for." Ben picked up the case of water, tossed it onto his shoulder, and walked over to the circular hatch. He lowered the case to the grass. "Have to be my next trip down." He turned, and looked surprised to see that John was still there. "Text me if you need anything else."

"Will do."

John executed a three-point turn and headed for home. *One last confirmation and I'll be done with that SafeAlert report. Detail, details. The work is important, and I'm giving it 110%, but I do miss being involved at the senior level. That scene in Nunn's office this morning was just plain awkward. Maybe it is time to leave law enforcement. Finish this case, drop the mic, and move on. I do like that charter boat idea. Interesting. That idea doesn't sound nearly as far-fetched now as it did yesterday.*

Sarah was standing on the porch. She waved, and John's breath caught in his throat. *This is where my reality is. How did I get so lucky?*

Sarah looked stunning, even dressed in his old barn coat because her jackets were now too snug to fit around her waist. John parked and he got out to open her door.

"Aren't you being gallant?" She teased. "I could get used to this. You never opened my door before I got pregnant."

"I'm paying more attention to my wife." He closed her door and walked around to the driver's side, removing his holster and locking his Glock in the truck's gun safe. Sarah hated it when he carried his pistol. The G17 reminded her of bitter things. He slid back behind the wheel, and watched her wrestle with the seatbelt.

"Need some help with that?"

"No, I've got it. Damn the thing!" She finally clicked the buckle. "There. That pizza smells delicious."

He backed down the driveway. "I almost dipped into it on my way here."

She laughed. "You have more willpower than I do." Her fingers drummed the door. "How's your day been? Anything new on Libby Spenser?"

"Mayas brought in two more of his fibbie friends from Boston to help."

"Is that a good thing?"

"Of course it is," John admitted. "It's just weird having them here. Ted's fit to be tied."

"Given any more thought to buying a boat?"

"I did think about that." John slowed to make a left and continued east toward Quammock. "Funny thing. Before yesterday, I'd never even considered leaving the force. Now that I've started thinking about it, it seems more and more like the right thing to do. I noticed it again this morning, when I was talking to Chief Nunn. I felt detached, like law enforcement was already a part of my past."

"That's the way it happens." Sarah turned. "Once you start going down a path, it feels hard to go back. There's resistance, like you're working upstream against a current."

"That's exactly what it feels like. I feel like my future has split into two different directions, and I've already started down one of them." John slowed even more as the truck left the pavement. "Hang on to something. This road is getting choppy from all of the construction."

"Got it." Sarah pointed. "Someone's coming."

"I see it." John recognized the battered truck. "It's Gus. Ben said that he was out here." John slowed to a stop. He rolled his window down as Gus pulled up.

"Hey, John, Sarah." Gus's hair looked like windblown eiderdown. "How are you two doing? Sarah? How are those babies?"

"They're fine, Gus. We're hanging in there."

"Good." Gus smoothed his mustache. "Stopped by to check on your site. Pearlie said he saw someone poking around. Damn these people! They're like nosy circus monkeys." He shook his head. "Checked things out. Didn't notice anything obvious missing."

"Ben said you were out here. I stopped by to see him."

"You did? Has he finished the payroll?"

"He said he was working on it."

"Good." Gus looked concerned. "Why did you want to see Ben?"

"I needed to see you both, to confirm the access code you've been using at Moorhaven. It's part of the Libby Spenser investigation."

"Oh! Okay. MH2016R." Gus tapped his temple. "Nothing wrong with my memory."

"That's it. Thanks, Gus."

"Let me ask you something." He leaned on his steering wheel. "Are you two planning on getting out of that truck when you get to the site?"

"Yes. We're having a picnic," Sarah said. "We're on a date."

"Then hold up a second."

Gus's door creaked open. He stepped out, pounded his hip, and groaned. "Damn this arthritis! Kids, don't ever get old. It's not for sissies." He hobbled to the back of his truck and lifted two bright yellow hard hats. "I know you're going to ignore everything I'm about to say, but I'm going to say it anyway." He passed the hard hats through Sarah's open window. "Your new house is an active construction site. I run a careful outfit, but not everything is locked down. I'd feel a whole lot better if you'd at least wear these while you're climbing around."

Sarah sat the hard hat on her belly. "I won't be doing much climbing around, Gus."

"Wear one anyway." He shook his finger at her playfully. "And carry your cell phones in your pockets. Don't leave them in the truck. In case you run into trouble. Cell phones were a great invention. And don't fall through the floor. Anyway, that's pretty much what I tell my crew, and they've all survived, the dimwits."

"Yes, sir." Sarah saluted. "Will do."

"Go have some damn fun with it." Gus clambered back behind the wheel. He gave them a thumbs-up. "You two should have about an hour, before the crew gets back from lunch." He pointed at John, and winked. "Don't do anything I wouldn't do, twice."

The hard hat clunked against the roof of the cab as Sarah tried it on. "This thing must weigh ten pounds! How do they wear these?" She laughed again. "Gus is such a charmer. I'm half in love with him."

"Yes, but I come bearing pizza."

"You win." She patted her stomach. "For more than a couple of obvious reasons."

It had rained heavily during the night. The construction site was an enormous muddy swamp. John pulled the truck around back onto the concrete pad already poured for the garage. "Let me get your door."

"You need to cut that shit out, John. I'm going to get spoiled."

"Then at least let me carry the pizza."

He gave Sarah his hand. They climbed up the roughed in staircase to the framed second floor. Their new house was designed to be upside-down, with the bedrooms on the ground floor and the living area above, to take full advantage of the spectacular ocean view. Even with the three hundred yard setback from the cliff, there was nothing manmade for as far as the eye could see, only the endless gray-green ocean rolling out to a slightly darker horizon.

John put the pizza box down on pile of framing lumber, and he turned to study the sea. He felt the tension melt off his shoulders. *This is my future. I'll never get tired of looking at this.*

Sarah sat down on the lumber. She popped the pizza box open, and handed him a slice. She bit into her slice, and spoke around it. "I still can't believe that this is going to be our new house."

"Thank you, Uncle Ethan." John sat down next to her. He folded his slice lengthwise, took a hefty bite, and gestured with his free hand. "Imagine this with the walls in, and the French doors, and the deck, and all the windows." Setting his half-eaten slice down, he framed the view with his fingers and thumbs. "It's going to be amazing."

"It's pretty nice right now." Sarah dropped the crust back into the box. She dusted crumbs from her fingers. "I still can't believe this is ours. Sometimes, it feels like a dream, but a good dream, you know? The kind of dream where you don't want to wake up." She looked at him over her left shoulder. "A big part of that is because I love you, John Jarad, with my whole heart."

"Sarah." John pulled her into an embrace, and their hard hats clunked.

"Ouch!" She laughed.

"I know we've been through a lot lately. I know I'm still working through some things."

"We're still working through some things," she agreed.

"That's right. We're still working through some things," he repeated. "But this is what's real to me. I want to live here, with you, forever. You, me, and the twins. This will be our home." He tightened his arms. "I want to see our kids grow up in this house. I want to see our grandkids get married in our yard. You and me, we're going to dance at their weddings." He hugged her close. "Don't ever forget what you mean to me, Sarah. The rest of it is just noise."

"That's very romantic," her hair muffled her voice, "but I'm starving. Could you pass me another slice?"

John snorted at her remark. He reopened the pizza box. "Don't ever say that I haven't been trying."

"I would never say that." She brushed her hair back and reached for another slice. A familiar ringtone trilled from her pocket. She set her second slice back down. "Obviously, the universe wants me to diet." Sarah unlocked her phone, and all of the color drained from her face.

"Sarah? What is it?"

"I know this number." She started to tremble. "It's Marjory." She glanced up repeatedly, her eyes wide. "Why would she be calling me?"

"I'm sorry." John drew a complete blank. "Marjory who?"

"Marjory, Mason's mother."

He pointed. "Put her on speaker phone."

"Good idea." Sarah fumbled with the button. "Hello, Marjory?"

"Is this Sarah Hawthorne?"

"Yes, it is." Sarah tucked her hair behind both ears. "I mean, it was. Yes, it's me, Marjory. What's wrong?"

"Sarah?" Her voice sounded slightly breathless. "I know we've never been close, but I felt that I needed to call. Something's happened. You should be told."

Sarah looked blank. "Told what?"

"Mason is missing. I went to check on his condo, yesterday. He hasn't been there in weeks. His mail was stacked behind the door. The smell from the trashcan was appalling."

"Marjory? Where did Mason go?"

"That's what I don't know. But I found a notepad on his desk. It had your married name, Sarah Jarad, and this number written on it. I think Mason's hired a detective. And you're living on Nantucket now, right?"

Sarah stood. She stared at her cell phone in horror. "I knew it! I'm not going crazy! Mason is here. He's on Nantucket."

"What was that? Sarah? Please be careful. Mason's been acting odd lately. I'm not sure he's been taking his meds." Marjory paused. "I know my son. It's not his fault. He's just like his father." She paused again. "I'm afraid Mason might go after your husband, to punish you for leaving." Marjory's voice grew even softer, to a whisper. "He'd want you to hurt, and to hurt for a long time."

Sarah grabbed for her cell phone and missed. It bounced off the plywood subfloor and shattered. There was a sudden rattling of a falling plank from the back of the house. John stood as she spun around to face the noise. Her lips were so clear they were colorless.

"Stay here."

John handed her his cellphone and reached for his service piece. His hand came up empty. "Fuck! I locked my Glock in the truck."

"Let's get to the truck." Sarah grabbed his sleeve. "Both of us, right now. This minute."

Left weaponless, John changed his mind. *First things, first. Make sure Sarah and the twins are safe.* He gripped Sarah's arm and helped her down the steps.

The staircase suddenly shuddered and rolled, as if the house had been struck by a tremor. Sarah jumped off the bottom step as a section of the garage's cinderblock foundation tilted and began to fall.

"John! Look out!" she screamed.

This is so strange. John's lungs felt compressed to the point of airlessness. The world had turned golden brown. He couldn't breathe. *Lived all my life surrounded by water. Never been afraid of drowning. My biggest fear was getting buried alive, in sand.*

CHAPTER TWENTY-EIGHT

John reached for a Kleenex. He leaned forward and hacked up more superfine dust. It wasn't pretty, but Doc Folger at the Cottage Hospital ER said that her main concern now was that he would contract particulate pneumonia. The MRI had shown that his ribs were bruised, not broken, which was a good thing, although he hurt like hell with each racking cough. John straightened, and reached for the ibuprofen. Doc had also said he could take up to 1200 milligrams a day without incurring permanent liver damage. He had cruised past that dosage at breakfast. He shook another couple of extra strength tablets out of the bottle, and washed them down.

"What are you doing here?" CJ stood over his desk. "Why aren't you at home? The union steward's going to flip if he hears about this."

"Don't tell him." John coughed up another nasty yellow luggie, and he groaned.

"How is Sarah? She okay?"

"She's fine, thank God. The twins are fine, too." His tongue still tasted like dirt. "My mother is staying with her. Doc Folger kept us overnight for observation. It was just an accident, CJ, a stupid, careless accident."

She sat, and rested her hands on her knees. "Are you sure about that?"

"As sure as I can be." John wiped his mouth. His face felt chapped and raw. "The crew saw the risers collapse. They heard Sarah screaming. Found her trying to dig me out with a board. Good thing they had shovels. Said they didn't see anyone else on the site, or leaving as they came in." He coughed again, and gently supported his ribs. "Doc wants me walking around, vertical, coughing this shit up, for as long as I can stand it."

"You sound like such a bad-ass." CJ leaned on the desk. "Anything I can do, to help?"

He raised his mug pitifully. "Could you get me a refill?"

"Just this once." She snatched up the coffee mug. "I'm not your admin, Detective Jarad."

"I would never think that." John wheezed. He reached for his pen, and glanced at his old shuttered office. Chief Nunn and Agent Mayas were still hard at work in there, with the door closed. Because the Libby Spenser kidnapping had entered day three, Mayas had requested even more FBI resources. Frick and Frack were on their way to the airport, to pick up their arriving colleagues. The Spensers were now relentlessly requesting hourly updates. Scuttlebutt said that Julia Spenser was taking Xanax for anxiety. John frowned. *In spite of all the new techno gadgets and the fibbie resources, this approach still feels wrong to me. It wasn't a professional gang the first time, with Alice. Any yahoo can buy a disposable phone.* His ribs flared in protest as he tugged a legal pad closer.

"Little cream, no sugar." CJ set his mug down dangerously close to his elbow. "What are you doing?"

"Logic tree." John started drawing bullet points down the left side of the sheet of paper. "If Libby Spenser's kidnappers were local, who would our suspects be?"

"Now, you're talking." CJ sat. She scooted the chair closer.

"First up. Let's consider the Spensers."

"Why would they kidnap Libby? They have all the money in the world."

"They don't have all the money in the world." John pointed his pen. "Addison Spenser said he'd have trouble getting the five million dollars together. Evidently, the money is tied up in a trust."

CJ frowned. "When did Addison say that?"

"When you were out testing the dog."

"Fenton?" She tapped the desk and pointed. "That test came back negative, by the way. That dog was not doped."

"Which means, to my mind, that Fenton trusted the kidnapper. Why else would he have let him, or her, take Libby without raising a fuss? Fenton was sleeping next to her crib."

John recalled the dustsheets covering the furniture in Moorhaven's disused hall. "Any one of them could be hiding Libby in the closed up wing of that house. Moorhaven is so big we'd never know she was there. The kidnapper could have hidden Libby during our initial search." John sipped his coffee, and he scalded his tongue. "We don't know what the Spensers are really up against. Kidnapping Libby might be a way to force the Trust to release some cash."

"I'll buy that. Who do we start with? Howard Senior?"

"Let's start with Howard, but he seems like a pretty weak choice to me. He's already getting his living expenses, and an allowance, from the Spenser Trust. Unless he has a secret drain, I can't imagine what more Howard needs."

"How about Addison?"

"Same thing. Except Addison's collecting a salary, not an allowance."

CJ sat back. She crossed her arms. "And I don't see Addison kidnapping his own child for money. He seems devoted to Libby. I can't see Addison putting her through that. What about his wife, Julia?"

John paused. "What do we really know about her? What's Julia's background?" He made a note. "She seemed surprised to find out the family was broke."

"You think maybe Julia's a gold-digger?"

"Possibly, but then again, she seemed genuinely distraught the night of the kidnapping. Paul said she's taking anxiety meds. Would Libby's kidnapper do that, for local color?"

"There's no proof that Julia's actually taking the pill," CJ stated.

"True, true."

"How about Camilla Dechert?"

"Now, she'd be smart enough to pull this off. From what I've seen, Camilla runs the place. Plus, for some reason, I think she's wearing a wig. Maybe Camilla has health issues we don't know about, like paying for private chemo? Let's put a star next to her name. Who else is there? The only staff they have is Richard Jamison."

CJ pointed. "Don't even try to tell me that the butler did this."

John choked out a laugh. It hurt.

"Why not? Jamison had access. The Spensers trust him. Libby would have trusted him, too. Plus, he's invisible. Jamison can go anywhere, anytime, unseen. Maybe he's unhappy with his salary, or the Trust's pension plan. He's got to be getting close to sixty. Maybe Jamison's worried about having enough money saved for retirement." John circled the names on the pad. "I think all of these are worth another look."

The metal shutters clanged as the office door swung open.

"Detective Allamand?" Chief Nunn called. "In my office. Now, please."

CJ stood. "This might be it, John." She straightened her jacket. "Mayas might be offering me that CSI position with the Boston Bureau."

John's mouth went desert dry, and not from the remnant dust. "If that's what you want, CJ, go for it. Good luck."

He dropped his pen. Life was all about change, and he wasn't the only one going through the process. This was a terrific new opportunity for CJ. John hoped that she got it. He tried not to think of the hole she would be leaving in her wake. *My life will be diminished without her in it.*

But CJ wasn't the only one seeking a new direction. He was, too. And with a start that made him sit up, John remembered that Ben Schlagel was also working to build a different future. *Ben said he needed fifty thousand dollars to enter that gaming competition, and that he was having trouble raising the money.*

Slowly, John stood. Ben had dropped a case of water yesterday next to the circular hatch. *What if Ben was hiding Libby Spenser down in the bomb shelter? No one would hear her crying, underground. Ben also had access to Moorhaven's SafeAlert code. He's savvy enough to use burnable cellphones to avoid detection. Yesterday, Ben said that the hatch was locked. Was that his way of keeping me out of the shelter, because Libby was in it?*

There was only one way to find out. Snatching up his keys, John limped for the door.

CHAPTER TWENTY-NINE

John spun the wheel, and headed for mid-island. The truck coughed when he floored the accelerator. *This all started after we found Alice Spenser. Until then, all of this was history, faded memories, and a forgotten dream, nothing more than old newspaper stories and a trunk full of dust.* He made a quick left on Milestone Road. *Was Libby Spenser a copycat kidnapping? Did finding Alice Spenser reactivate the ransom idea? Ben was looking for quick money. Was Ben foolish enough to jump at this chance and take Libby?*

He gripped the wheel with his left hand, using his right arm to support his sore ribs as he dodged the swampy potholes and gravel patches in the Schlagels' driveway. *There's no way Judge Coffin would grant me a search warrant. I don't have probable cause. This is all supposition. But if Libby Spenser is down in that bomb shelter, we're running out of time. If this does go down, I can lie about why I was on the Schlagels' property. I can say that I stopped by for an update on the damage to my new house. It's lame as hell, but it might fly.* John swallowed drily. *It's all I've got.*

He swung into the side yard, and parked. The Ford 150 was gone. The house looked deserted. *All I want to do is to check that hatch.* As John closed his door, he heard CJ's long-standing warning in his head: *You're always such a cowboy. That's what keeps getting you into trouble. What's so hard about calling for backup?*

As usual, CJ was right. John reached for his iPhone. *I can't call Chief Nunn. She'll insist that I back off, and that we follow protocol. We don't have time for that.*

He speed dialed CJ's number. It rang four times, before rolling to voicemail. "CJ? I'm at the Schlagels' place. I think Ben Schlagel took Libby Spenser. Ben had access. He's been looking for easy money. I'm going to search their bomb shelter. Back me up on this."

John ended the call. He zipped the iPhone in his pocket. The circular hatch was twenty feet away. He limped over, feeling his heartbeat thudding in his throat with each step. The hatch was shut, but the padlock was missing from the hasp. John knelt carefully. He reached for the handle, and gave it a solid tug. The hatch refused to budge. He tugged harder. His ribs lit up with searing white pain, and John saw a shower of stars. *Someone must be down there. This hatch is locked from the inside.*

He stood up. Two parallel ruts of crushed grass led deeper into the yard. The hair prickled on the back of John's neck. *Carrying thirty-pound Libby and his supplies down that ladder shaft would have been tough. Was Ben using the larger rear hatch for access?* He quickly crossed the yard, and stood over the square storm door. *Ben said this hatch was always kept bolted, so that the neighborhood kids couldn't get in.* John grasped the handle, and he pulled. The steel door swung open easily, until the interior hinge snapped into place.

John retreated to his truck. Unlocking the gun safe, he grabbed his tactical duty light and snapped the clip to his belt, opposite his Glock. The thought of getting trapped inside the bomb shelter in the dark made his head swim. He took a steadying breath, and returned to the opened steel door. *If I'm going to do this, let's get it done.*

He stepped over the threshold into a low sloping tunnel lit by a row of 60-watt bulbs in yellow plastic construction cages strung down the center of the ceiling. His senses went on high alert, and he released his

Glock. The muscle memory in his hand protested as he tightened his grip. The 9mm wasn't his old familiar Sigma. Even after the dozens of hours of range practice, the Glock still felt odd in his hand.

He stepped down the tunnel. A mildew stench permeated the concrete walls. The only sound John heard was the slap of his footsteps against the smooth floor. The deeper John went, the quieter the shelter got. There were no sounds of any fans, or the TV, or of any other life. He began to imagine the weight of the tons of cold sand pressing against the rough homemade walls, and he popped with sweat. John pushed the terrifying and imaginary image away. *Stay focused. If Ben were down here, where would he be?*

A line of muddy prints had dried on the concrete floor, the imprint of a man's steel-toed boot. Raising the Glock, John followed the faint trail. From what he remembered from Ben's brief tour, this tunnel led into the larger central chamber where Ben stored his games. John glanced down again, and he pulled up short. The dried prints turned left, sharply. They stopped in front of a steel storeroom door, bolted at eye level. Reaching up with his left hand, John drew the bolt.

The steel door creaked open like something out of a horror movie. John flinched as the stink of fresh urine stung his nose. He pushed the door open and leaned against it, rolling up on his toes, anticipating a response. The echo from the door faded. The shelter fell silent again.

The storeroom light was on. John rolled up against the hinge, raised the Glock to eye level, and looked in. An air mattress lay on the floor, covered by a rumpled bundle of pink blankets. The case of water was pushed against one wall. John's heart sank. *Oh, no, Ben. I didn't want this to be true.* John heard a whimper, like the sound a sleeping puppy would make. Libby Spenser suddenly sat up. She rubbed her face, and peeked through her chubby fingers.

"Daddy?"

"Hey, baby girl." He double-checked the tunnel. *All clear.* John holstered the Glock and stepped into the storeroom, forcing himself to slow down as he approached Libby. *Slow it way down. Don't startle her.* Reaching for the floor for support, he knelt.

"Hi, Libby. How are you? I'm here to take you home."

She remained motionless, staring at him with big eyes over the thumb in her mouth.

John felt charged by electrical energy, magical, like something from a powerful dream. *I can't believe I found her!* He pulled out his iPhone to call it in. The white screen lit up, and the omnipotent feeling faded. The concrete shelter was blocking his cellular connection. *No bars. I'm going to have to do this the hard way.*

Libby was wearing a blue two-piece sleep set with a rabbit on it. John began to gather the blanket up. "Libby? We need to go now. I'm going to take you home to your mommy and daddy, okay?" John's heart broke as she began to tremble. Libby whimpered again.

"Scared." She protested, shaking her head. "Scared."

"Close your eyes, baby. I've got you." John picked Libby up, stifling a groan at the effort of rising off balance out of a deep squat with Libby in his arms. She continued to tremble as he turned for the door, reaching up to clutch his jacket tightly with both of her hands.

"Goddammit, Jarad." A voice echoed down the tunnel. "Dipshit! I know you're in here. Your goddamned truck is parked in the middle of my yard."

Libby spasmed. She kicked John in the ribs. The blanket grew warm and wet as her diaper failed. John fell back against the wall as he recognized the voice. His world spun a one-eighty. *Ben Schlagel didn't kidnap Libby. It was Gus.*

"Should have left things alone, Jarad. I was going to give her back. No one had to get hurt. She's only two. She'd never remember any of this."

A metallic clang and a rattling clatter reverberated down the tunnel. *He's resealed the rear hatch. Now we're in for a fight.* Shifting Libby to his left side, John released the Glock. He held it at the ready.

"You had to go and make things complicated." Gus was getting louder. "You messed things up. Just like that Ketchem bitch. Couldn't keep her big yap shut."

The icy truth rattled John's bones. *Lillian Ketchem's death wasn't an accident. Gus murdered her.* John tightened his grip on Libby and on the Glock. *Greed is one thing. I get that, I do. But murdering a helpless woman is something else. You crossed the line there, Gus.*

"I've got Libby Spenser," John shouted. "She's coming with me."

"So you say, dipshit. Good luck with that."

His work boots scraped the floor as Gus limped closer.

"You're just another goddamned mess I have to clean up."

Decision time. Libby was nestled tight against John's collarbone. *What are my options? I'm not afraid of facing Gus one on one, but I won't risk Libby.* John studied the tunnel. *I can move quicker than Gus can. Can we get to the ladder hatch first, and get out that way?*

He hefted Libby to his shoulder and turned left. *Don't overthink this. Just remember what you saw that day down here with Ben, and go.* John double-timed it down the tunnel as Libby began to shriek in his ear.

"Hush, baby girl. We're getting out of here."

He raced down two hundred feet of tunnel until it spilled into the central chamber. Raising the Glock, John scanned the area. *All clear. Should I take cover, make a stand?* Libby's continuous shrill shrieking would give their position away. She was actively struggling now, kicking both feet and flailing. John was having trouble holding her and the Glock. *Should I put her down, and set up an ambush?* His will stubbornly rejected that idea. Now that he had Libby in his possession, there was no chance he was going to get separated and leave her behind. *Decision made. Ladder hatch it is.*

He quickstepped around the recliner and crossed the room, abruptly stopping as he neared the far wall. Fear jolted his nuts as John noticed two tunnel entrances leading away. *Was that right?* John blinked. *I don't remember seeing a second entrance down here that day with Ben. Which tunnel leads to the ladder hatch?* He resettled Libby against his shoulder. *I don't know for sure. Okay, which one do I pick?*

The entrance on the right was slightly larger and more rounded. John followed it as he mentally began to prepare for Plan B. *If we have to double back, Gus might catch us. I hope that doesn't happen, Gus, because I am taking this little girl home to her family. If I have to, I will blow through you like the breeze.* John heard a whining electrical sputter like a slowing net winch, and the tunnel went black.

CHAPTER THIRTY

Libby shrieked.

Fucker! He's not dumb. Gus knows this shelter like the back of his hand. Now he has the advantage. I'd have done the same thing in his shoes.

John holstered the Glock, and quickly unclipped his duty light.

"Hang on, baby. Light is coming." He shifted Libby to the crook of his arm, balancing her off of his hip, and double-clicked the base of the duty light to select maximum wattage. The pitch-black tunnel lit up like sudden glory.

John resettled Libby and hustled down the tunnel, making up for the slight delay. *This tunnel seems longer than I remembered.* He froze as the cone of light bounced off a solid cinderblock wall. *Shit! Did I choose the wrong tunnel?* An oblong gray square of shadow danced along the wall's right edge. *Hold up. This is the blast wall behind the ladder shaft.*

John circled the wall. He stood looking up at the twenty-foot ladder. The shaft looked narrower than he remembered. Libby was still shrieking. Her terrified cries pierced his ears. *How am I going to do this? I can't hold Libby, the duty light, and climb the ladder at the same time.* He stooped, and his ribs sparkled with pain points. He set the duty light on the floor. The powerful halogen beam lit the entire length of the ladder all the way up to the hatch. Gripping Libby with his left arm, John grasped the first iron rung. He started to climb.

The first four rungs were easy. Step, step, grab. Step, step, grab. *Sixteen more to go.* Libby kept screaming as John snatched at each rung, pulling them higher one rung at a time. He was drenched with sweat. His right shoulder began to shake. It threatened to seize up. John ignored the pain. *Six more. Keep going.* Libby worked one of her legs free, and she kicked him in the ribs. Black spots swam before John's eyes. For one brief second, he considered surrendering to the darkness. He shook his head to clear it. *Not going to happen, on my watch.*

He tightened his grip on the ladder, and pinned his focus on the circular hatch. *Where was Gus? We're running out of time.* He reached the top rung and pressed his left shoulder against the concrete shaft, looping his arm around Libby and the top rung for support. Reaching up with his right hand, John frantically felt for the hatch cover above his head. *Don't over think this. It's the same latch we use back home. You've done this a million times.* John quieted his mind. He willed his fingers to automatically remember the locking sequence. *Turn the bolt to the left until it clicks and then slowly slide it up. Just like that.* The hatch popped open.

John pushed on the hatch using his right hand and the top of his head. Rust particles stung his eyes. He blinked them clear. He pulled Libby tight. She stopped struggling as they rolled over the lip of the hatch cover into the daylight. Cradling Libby against his chest, John stood. He drew the Glock. His legs were shaking so badly he could barely stand. Using his boot, John kicked the hatch cover shut. He glanced around. *How do I lock this? The padlock is missing. Climbing that ladder won't slow Gus down for long. Time to get out of here.*

Keeping his eye on any movement from the hatch, John shouldered Libby and stumbled toward his truck. *As soon as we get down that driveway, I'm calling this in. Trust me, CJ. I have learned my lesson.* John heard an oncoming diesel rattle, and he looked up. The Schlagel's Ford F150 was bearing down on them, with Ben hunched behind the wheel.

John went ice cold. Raising the Glock, he dropped Libby to his hip and cradled her in the crook of his elbow. John focused on the truck, unblinking.

"Don't push me, Ben. I'm done," John shouted. "I have had enough." He kept the F150 covered as it swerved to his left. *What was Ben doing?* John blinked in disbelief as Ben drove the truck over the circular hatch. Ben slammed the truck into park. He slid from the King cab and raised his hands.

"Don't shoot me, John. I'm on your side."

"Keep your hands where I can see them. I don't know that."

BAM. The hatch slammed against truck's undercarriage. BAM. BAM. BAM.

"Stop it, Dad," Ben yelled. "Cut it out. Keep that up and you'll crack the oil pan." He studied John quizzically. "What happens next? Do you trust me, or not?"

John kept him covered. "I haven't decided. Don't do anything fast."

"You've got the gun." Ben slowly moved toward the truck bed. Reaching in, he lifted a rattling length of steel chain, and held it loosely in his hands.

"What are you doing with that?"

Ben looked surprised. "I'm locking him in." He carried the chain over to the square hatch. Kneeling, Ben wrapped the chain through both handles and tightened the chain until it was secure. He stood, and slowly dusted his hands.

"Don't blame him too much for this, John. It's not his fault. Dad's been acting squirrelly, lately. Worried he didn't save enough money for retirement. He's not mean, just dumb." Ben frowned. "I knew he was up to something. Never thought it was this. Never thought to check that storeroom. We never use it." He pointed at Libby. "She okay?"

"I'm taking her to the Cottage Hospital. Get her checked out."

"You okay to drive? You look pretty done in."

"I'm fine." It took some effort, but John straightened. True, he could call 911 and wait for the paramedics, but it would be quicker if he drove Libby there.

"Tell them I'll be here, waiting." Ben's broad shoulders slumped. "I'll let Dad out when they're ready."

"Let's go, Lib." John holstered the Glock. He limped for the truck. "Let's get you home to your mom and dad."

Libby had settled down in the daylight. She was a royal mess, but she contentedly sucked her thumb as John buckled her in. His mind chose that exact moment to worry about the danger of not having a car seat for her. *Really? I have a few other things on my plate right now.* John slid carefully behind the wheel, cranked the ignition, and reached for the handset.

"Call to base." He winced as the truck bounced through a rabble of potholes. Libby glanced up, looking worried and uncertain.

"Roger base. Go ahead."

"Tina? I have Libby Spenser. We're on route to the Cottage Hospital. Have Chief Nunn meet us there."

"You what? Roger that."

The road smoothed out as John pulled onto Milestone Road. He relaxed, and tested a tentative deep breath. The painful stitch in his right side was subsiding. It only pinched when he put pressure on it. John decided to not do that. He looked down at Libby and he tried to smile. He feared that all she saw was a monstrous grimace. *I'm not sure which one of us looks worse.* "Hang tough, Libby. We're almost home."

She kept silent, studying him over her thumb. The dashboard radio clicked, and Chief Nunn barked, "Detective Jarad? What's your location?"

John ducked his head and glanced through the windshield. "Mile marker 17." He looked up to see a marked SUV racing toward him, red and blue rack lights flashing, in the opposing lane. It was CJ, backing him up, late to the party. CJ flashed by with a rushing wave of sound before pulling a speeding U-turn. Her SUV spun off the pavement. She bullied her way back to the road through the sand. As CJ recovered, her tires threw a cloud of gritty dust into the air. "Detective Allamand has joined me."

"Roger that. We'll notify the Spensers, and radio ahead. Meet you on location."

The radio double clicked. "You found her, John?" CJ asked. "You really found her?"

"Roger that. I've got Libby Spenser. She's fine." John reached over. He smoothed Libby's tousled red hair. Libby smiled up at him, her bright eyes shining with trust. John's heart rolled over. *If this is what it feels like, I'm going to dig being a dad.*

"Nice job, cowboy."

John slowed. He caught the exit lane for the Cottage Hospital, turning right and following the sign to the Emergency entrance. As he screeched to a stop, the double doors opened. Dr. Folger trotted out. She was only the first in a line of initial responders. A stout male nurse and a couple of volunteer aides quickly followed her out the door.

John opened his door as CJ pulled up on his bumper. He limped to the passenger side of the truck. Reaching in, he unbuckled Libby, and he lifted her up. *Bad idea.* The flash of pain buckled his knees. He almost dropped her. "I need some help here."

CJ ran over. She braced his arm. "Let me take her. Let me help."

"No, CJ. I've got this," John snapped. He knew he was being unreasonable, but a small primitive part of his brain didn't trust reality enough to let Libby go. He was afraid that if he put Libby down that he might wake up to find that this was all a fevered fantasy, like his Nazi chase dream. The only thing that seemed authentic was the pain.

The older aide was weeping. She pulled a tissue from her cuff and wiped her eyes. "I can't believe they found her. I can't believe this ended well. It's so not what I expected."

"Let's get her inside, Detective." Dr. Folger carefully transferred Libby into her arms. She noticed the dried blood dribbled on his sleeve. "Is that yours, or hers?"

"Mine. I bit my lip climbing that ladder."

Dr. Folder looked stern. "Is that your definition of 'four weeks of limited activity,' Detective Jarad?" The skin around her eyes crinkled into crow's feet as she smiled. "Let's get you to X-ray and re-check for haemothorax. You're making a visit here a daily occurrence."

A police cruiser squealed into the lot, followed by a lumbering vintage Land Rover. Both vehicles raced straight up to the Emergency entrance. The Land Rover was still moving when the passenger door popped open, and Julia Spenser jumped out. Throwing her arms out, Julia stumbled, and then caught herself on the fly. She began to run across the parking lot, sobbing.

"Libby! My God, baby, I'm here! Libby? Where are you?"

"Mommy!" Libby pushed off Dr. Folger. She struggled to get down. "Mommy! Mommy!"

Julia kicked off her sandals, and ran up barefoot. "Give her to me. I'll take her. Oh, Libby! Baby! Oh, my baby girl." She hugged Libby tight, smothering her in kisses. "I've missed you so, so much!"

Addison caught up with his wife. He threw his arms around Julia and Libby and bowed his head. His shoulders shook as he wept. "Thank God. Oh, thank God. I can't believe this is real."

Chief Nunn was standing quietly to one side. She cocked her head. "Nice work, Detective Jarad. Unorthodox, perhaps, but effective."

"Gus Schlagel kidnapped Libby Spenser." John swayed. He caught himself. "He's locked in their bomb shelter."

"He's secure. Sergeant Parsons has made an arrest."

"I want to know how you found her, Jarad." Mayas jabbed a finger. "How you figured this out. When you get a minute, we need to talk."

"I need to call my wife." John fumbled for his iPhone. His fingers felt numb and unresponsive. He couldn't seem to manage opening the pocket zipper. John suddenly felt so weary that he wanted to drop where he stood. "I don't want Sarah hearing this on the news."

"I'll get that, hero," CJ offered. "You go get taped. If Sarah needs a ride, I'll pick her up."

Dr. Folger grasped John's arm. "Take that suggestion, Detective Jarad. You need medical attention. Now."

John straightened. He studied the cluster of people surrounding him. This was his community, the people he had sworn to protect, and to serve. He had done his very best for them, and given them everything he had to give. Libby Spenser was safely home with her family, where she belonged. Gus was right. Libby was only two. She might not remember too much of this. Pride warmed John's skin. He had done good work for her. He recalled his other recent cases: finding his brother Danny's unmarked grave, and losing his friend Toby Talbot to the sea. Those two events still stung, but not as sharply as before. His life had balanced out. *Sometimes, you can't fix things. Sometimes, you don't get to win. You can only do your best, and then live with what remains.*

CHAPTER THIRTY-ONE

The tape on his ribs itched like a sand flea convention in full swing. John imagined getting to the house, limping straight into the kitchen, and scratching himself into raw bliss using the edge of a metal spatula. *Try explaining that one to Sarah. Honey, I'm home! She'd never use that spatula to cook with again.* The potent paracetamol and codeine combo that Dr. Folger had prescribed thankfully obliterated the pain, but the dosage left John feeling loopy. The big horse pill had also done nothing to fix the aggravating and persistent itch.

He pulled up next to the garage door. In spite of the painkiller, or maybe because of it, John felt like celebrating. *He had rescued Libby Spenser!* It still felt like part of some fantastic dream. John thought about tapping the horn to let Sarah know he was home, but he didn't want to disturb her if she was busily painting. CJ had tried calling Sarah from the emergency room, twice. Both tries had rolled to voicemail. When Sarah was in the thick of inspiration, she muted her cell phone to avoid distraction. John parked, and climbed gingerly out of the truck. He limped for the front door. He hoped that Sarah would drop whatever she was doing, and come celebrate this moment with him. *Sparkling grape juice for everyone!* It had been a rough couple of months, between his demotion, and the new house stresses, and the twins. People were calling him a hero. He wanted to share this special moment with his wife.

The front door swung open at his touch. *That's odd.* "Sarah?"

John looked down. A trail of thick red drips like spaghetti sauce dribbled down the hall. "Sarah?" John ignored the hours of forensic training that whispered *back out now* and he followed the drips into the kitchen.

"Sarah? Answer me, please. Honey?"

John turned the corner and the end of the hallway, and his heart dropped to his knees. Their galley kitchen was a screaming nightmare. One of their rush-bottomed chairs lay tipped over in a rippled crimson puddle of congealed blood. A pink jacket was trapped under the chair, the silk fabric soaked through. *Wasn't that Jackie's?* Sarah's favorite coffee mug lay shattered in ceramic shards on the floor. Her cracked cellphone was next to the coffeemaker and a scattered handful of black plastic zip ties.

"Sarah?" John yelled. "Jackie?"

He raced up the stairs two at a time to check their bedroom. The bedroom was empty, and undisturbed. The attached bathroom door was wide open. The bathroom was empty, too. John didn't know whether to give thanks for the silent emptiness in the house, or to panic. His head felt ready to explode. He stumbled back downstairs, and gasped when he remembered to breathe. *If something was bad wrong with the twins, Sarah would have called me, right? But where would she go without taking her phone?*

John pulled his iPhone out. He speed dialed the Cottage Hospital emergency number. *I was just there. Wouldn't they have told me if Sarah was there and in trouble?*

"Cottage Hospital. How may I help you?"

"Yes." John struggled to keep his voice below a bellow. "This is John Jarad. My wife Sarah is a patient of Dr. Diballa's. She's expecting twins." He swallowed. "Is she there? Has Sarah Jarad been admitted?"

"I'm sorry, sir. HIPPA regulations prohibit me from releasing any information over the phone due to privacy concerns."

John dragged his hand through his hair. He fought to stay rational even as shrieking panic threatened to unseat his mind. "She's my wife!"

"I'm sorry, sir. I can tell you're upset. I will be able to check that for you, if you come to Registration in person, with the proper ID."

"Thank you. Thank you, I knew that." John hung up.

He reached across the counter for Sarah's cellphone to check her recent call log. Frantically, John tried to remember Sarah's password. *HAV2? LUVU? Wasn't that what she had said?* He pushed the commercial zip ties aside, and then stopped and picked one up. *What were they doing here?* His investigative training flicked an answer: *zip ties are used as restraints in place of handcuffs.*

John's legs turned to water. He clutched the counter for support. *Oh, fuck. I've been focused on the wrong things.* John recalled the odd warning phone call Sarah had gotten on their picnic date. *Sarah was right. That fucker Mason is on the island. He's on Nantucket, and he's got Sarah, and Jackie, and the twins.*

He pulled out his iPhone and speed dialed CJ. *Pick up. Pick up. Pick up.*

"Yo, cowboy. How does it feel to be the hometown hero?"

"CJ, I've got big trouble. Sarah's missing. I think Jackie is, too. There's blood on the floor. Sarah left her cell phone here."

"John, hold up. Hold up." She interrupted. "Where are you now?"

"In the kitchen. Our kitchen." His voice cracked as he struggled to maintain control. "Check dispatch. Have we fielded any 911 calls today?"

"Let me check."

CJ put him on hold. The line started playing Beethoven's *Fur Elise*. John cursed the classical soundtrack.

"John? There's nothing on Tina's log." CJ paused. "Have you touched anything out there?"

"I went upstairs." John glanced at Sarah's phone clutched in his right hand. "Her phone. I've touched Sarah's phone."

"Take the phone and back straight out of there. Now. I can be there in eight minutes."

Fear swamped John's brain. "I found zip ties on the counter. CJ, I think Mason took her."

"Sorry? Who's Mason?"

"Sarah's fiancée." John shook his head to clear it. "Her ex. The guy from Pittsburgh. I think he took her."

"John, you sound rattled. You don't know that. Listen to me. Get yourself back outside. I'll notify the team. Eight minutes, John. Let's do this right."

John took her advice. He skirted the terrible red splatter in the hall and stepped outside, breathing in great gulps of fresh air. He couldn't seem to get enough. The breeze cooled his overheated face, and his mind began to clear. *If Mason is on Nantucket, he'd need a place to stay. An in-town hotel or B&B would be too public. Would he use AirBnB? No, same thing. Too many witnesses. He'd find an agent and rent a private house.*

Black dots danced before his eyes. *Oh, shit. Mason was Jackie's new mainland client. Jackie wouldn't have known who Mason was. Sarah was right. Mason's on the island, and he's been playing all of us.*

Hoping against hope, John keyed in Jackie's number. After three rings, his call rolled to voicemail. Keeping his voice steady, John left a message.

"Jackie? It's me. Give me a call when you get this. It's important." He stared at the phone in his hand. John flashed on Jackie's pink jacket, soaked with blood. He fought the soul searing feeling that if his sister was with Mason that she might never return his call.

He checked the time, and stared down the empty road. *CJ said eight minutes. Have I overlooked any options?* John leaned on Logic Tree. *Sarah and Mary Rose are tight. Maybe Mary Rose knows something.* He speed dialed her number next.

"Hey, 'bro. What's up?"

"Mary Rose, have you heard from Sarah, or from Jackie, today?"

"No, not today. What's wrong? You sound funny."

"It looks like there's been an accident at our place. I'm trying to find them."

"What kind of accident?"

John recalled the trailing line of thick bloody droplets. "A bad one."

"Where's Jackie's Jeep? Is it parked there?"

John mentally kicked himself. In his panic, he had overlooked that critical detail. Jackie's red Jeep was missing. They could issue an APB. Someone on the island would see it. It was a solid lead. John swallowed past the lump in his throat.

"No, it's not. Mary Rose, I have to ask you this. Jackie's client, her new client, the mainlander, did Jackie ever say where he was staying?"

"Sure. He's renting the Gantrys' place, in Surfside. John? Why are you asking me that?"

"Because I think Sarah and Jackie might be there."

"Why would they be there? I'm sorry, John. You're not making sense."

John gripped his forehead. He thought his head might split. "I think Jackie's new client is Sarah's ex-fiancée, the guy from Pittsburgh, Mason. I think he took them. I think Surfside is where they went."

"That sounds kind of crazy, John. But what can I do to help?"

He scrambled. "Go to the Cottage Hospital. You'll need to take ID. See if they're there, and then text me."

"Alright. I'm on my way."

"And text me if you hear from either one of them, and I mean anything. Okay?"

"You got it."

John ended the call. He scanned the road. CJ's SUV was still nowhere in sight. *The Gantrys' place was on East Okorwaw Avenue. I've been to lawn parties there. It will take me fifteen minutes.* Now that he had a possible location, John couldn't stand still. *Fuck it. I'll radio CJ to meet me there.*

He ran for the truck. Attaching the magnetic blue flash to the roof, he raced for Milestone Road and reached for the radio to call it in.

"Dispatch. Copy, please."

Tina was on point. "Dispatch. Go."

Now that he had Tina's attention, John wasn't sure what to say. Listening in on police band radio transmissions was an island pastime. John didn't want to broadcast his pursuit to the general public. They'd eagerly join in the hunt. More chaos was the last thing he needed.

"Tina? Patch me through to Unit Four."

"Roger that." There was a quick burst of static like sudden hail on a metal barn roof. "Copy back, Unit Four."

"I'm here," CJ replied, her voice sounding tinny and distant. "Mile marker two. Got stuck behind a goddamned FedEx truck. Sonofabitch wouldn't pull over."

John broke in. "I'm in transit. Meet me at 11 East Okorwaw Avenue. I believe our target is there."

"Pull over in airport lot A-1, and wait for me. You'll need backup."

"Reduce code, and meet me there." John was fine using his flash, but he didn't want CJ roaring up with a siren. If an element of surprise was available, John wanted to use it.

The truck coughed as he accelerated. The pines along the side of the road started to blur as he sped toward town. The truck bounced and his tires squealed as he pulled a too quick left onto Nobadeer Farm Road. As John closed on Ackerman Field, he reconsidered the idea of pulling over and waiting for backup. That was the sensible thing to do. He remembered the blood on the kitchen floor. *Sorry, CJ. It's a good idea but I don't have the time. I still don't know what I'm up against.*

He made a dogleg right onto Old South Road, and then a left on Lovers Lane. Two teenage boys were tossing a lacrosse ball over a golden Lab in the middle of the road. John grappled with the steering wheel and slewed the truck around them. The kids stared in jaw dropping shock as John burned his way back onto the asphalt through the road's shelving shoulder.

The Gantrys' place was just as John remembered it, a weather beaten two-storied shingled house with a row of four double-hung windows on the second floor overlooking the driveway. John killed the flash. His tires crunched as he followed the driveway in. The property was surrounded by a moth-eaten split rail fence and hidden behind a sheltering screen of scrub cedar and pitch pine. John's heart caught in his throat as he cleared the dense green screen. Jackie's red Jeep was carelessly parked out front.

He considered his tactical approach as he slid from the truck. Smoothing the tape on his ribs, John unsnapped his holster and chambered a round in the Glock. There was a festive striped umbrella table and six chairs on the deck, but his eyes caught the drying blood trail that led up the steps to the door. *I've got probable cause.* He pushed the door open, and entered the house.

John paused in the tiled entry, holding the Glock at the ready. A narrow staircase with a wrought iron handrail ran up the left side of the main room to the second floor. The house was strangely silent, except for the rhythmic whirring of the living room's ceiling fan. John checked the small powder room, and the built-in bar on his left. *Clear.* He took two steps into the living room on his right.

Jackie was sprawled on the floor in front of the brick fireplace. John shivered as her dead eyes stared straight through him. Her mouth gaped open, and he half expected her to blink. The blood trail he followed ended in a crimson puddle next to her right elbow. She had a blood-soaked dishtowel tourniquet tied around her arm.

John felt his world collapse into a black hole of sorrow. *Oh, Jackie.* His sister had always put her faith and trust in the wrong people. *All Jackie ever wanted to do was to help other people be happy.* Jackie's death was going to destroy their mother. *This is too high of a price to pay.*

He heard a low, gasping moan coming from upstairs. John turned. He started up the steps. The third wooden step cracked under his weight, and it gave his position away. John continued up. The stairway spilled into a landing with four separate bedrooms. Two on the left, and two more on the right. The groans came from the first bedroom on the right. John shouldered the Glock, and he stepped in.

Sarah's hands were duct-taped to a four-poster bed. She was in obvious distress. Her clothes were stained with sweat, and blood, and even worse. Her dark hair was matted against her forehead. Her exposed belly looked bruised. Sarah was rolling in pain, and panting like an animal. Her heels scrabbled against the mattress as she arched her back against a spasming contraction, and she screamed.

John pointed the Glock at the man calmly sitting next to her in a stout Windsor chair. He looked to be roughly thirty years old, 160 pounds, with a pointed chin, and muscles that bespoke gym conditioning. His medium brown hair was strictly parted on the left side. He held a white ceramic knife loosely in his hands. When he caught sight of John standing in the doorway, he smiled.

"Husband John. I wondered if I was going to meet you."

Mason reached over. He stroked Sarah's tangled hair with his knuckles. She flinched at his touch. "Really, sweetheart? I know I raised the bar, but was he really the best you could do?"

"John?" Sarah turned her face blindly toward the door. "It's too early. My water broke. The twins are coming."

"I think we can all see that, my dear. The truth is self evident."

Sarah screamed. "Jackie is hurt. She's bleeding. John, she needs help."

John stared down the Glock's blue-steeled barrel. "Back away from her. Now."

"No, I really don't think so." Mason pressed the knife against Sarah's jugular vein. "These ceramic knives are surprisingly sharp. Couldn't carry a knife on the plane. Airport security, you know. Had to buy one at a Bait and Tackle shop. Luckily, this island's full of them."

"I'm prepared to shoot on three. One, two …"

"I said, no, I don't think so." Mason pressed the point of the knife against Sarah's throat until a bubble of blood appeared. "Don't you move, Mister Jarad. I'm in control here. One more step and I'll open her up." He moistened his lips. "I know what I want, and I'm not afraid to do what it takes to get there. Are you?"

Black doubt roared in John's ears as he grappled with his darkest fear. *It's Sarah, and the twins. What if I miss? How do I live with that?* John removed his index finger from the trigger as his hand began to imperceptibly shake. "She needs medical attention. Can't you see that?"

"Sarah is busy right now, paying for her sins," Mason said, as Sarah shuddered. "I'll decide what Sarah really needs. As I've said, I'm the one in charge here, not you. It's not your call to make. Sarah never really belonged to you, anyway. She's mine. Isn't that right, sweetheart?"

"John?" Sarah shrieked. "I'm sorry! I'm so, so sorry." Her next scream raised the hair on his arms.

BANG. John flinched as Mason rocked back against the chair. Mason's head bobbled, twice. He spat out a mouthful of blood. The ceramic knife rang off the floor as Mason spread the fingers of his right hand across his chest wound in surprise.

BANG. BANG. BANG. BANG. BANG.

"Stop it, CJ!" John felt deafened. He leapt to her side. "That's enough!"

Pressing his forearm against her stance John forced her weapon down. The bedroom filled with acrid smoke as he shoved CJ against the wall. "Stay there."

Scrabbling across the floor, his fingers closed on the ceramic knife. "Sarah?"

John sawed at the silver duct tape and freed her right hand. "Honey? Stay with me. Breathe, baby. Breathe." He started working on her taped left hand. "I'm getting you out of here. You're going to be alright."

"I need help, John." Sarah whispered. "Something's bad wrong. This isn't going right."

CJ keyed her belt radio. "I'll notify Life Flight. She may need Boston General."

"Hang on, honey." John stroked Sarah's sweat soaked hair. Her eyes were bloodshot and her lids half-closed. She blinked repeatedly, on the edge of unconsciousness. John quickly folded a pillow, and he tucked it beneath her feet. "Help is coming." He covered her with a blanket for warmth, and then added his jacket.

He looked for CJ. She was standing over and studying Mason's corpse. "You didn't need to do that, CJ. I had it covered."

"No, John. I did."

Reaching down, CJ calmly unbuckled and removed her service belt, weaving the slim black leather between her fingers. She wrapped the belt around her holster and settled it, and her detective's badge, on top of the dresser. CJ caressed the silver badge thoughtfully with her thumb. "I know you too well, cowboy. You never would have pulled that trigger." CJ smiled, sadly. "It needed to get done."

CHAPTER THIRTY-TWO

The atmosphere in Moorhaven's library was stately and tranquil, and steadily calm. Jamison had delivered their drinks on a chased silver tray. He had retreated on his silent cat feet, closing the double oak doors behind him as the mantelpiece clock chimed two o'clock.

John stood before the fireplace, leaning his shoulder blades back against the mantle, his hands buried deep in his pockets. He studied the faces of the people gathered in the comfortable room. Howard and Camilla shared the tufted saddle leather sofa. Addison stood by a mullioned window, busily checking his cell phone. Julia was tucked into a brightly upholstered armchair, holding Libby. The sleeping toddler was nestled in her mother's arms. Chief Nunn and Agent Mayas were studying an ancestral portrait by the mahogany china case.

Camilla cleared her throat. "Detective Jarad? I'm curious why we are gathered here. Are you expecting more thanks from us?"

"No," John said. "But there was one question left from my investigation. I wanted to answer it."

Camilla cocked her head. "And what was that?"

"The Alice Spenser ransom money is still missing." John raised a hand and he tapped his lips. "I believe it's still in this house."

Julia looked up brightly. "You think it's in this library?"

"No, but it all started here." John pointed at the colorful spines of the leather books arrayed in their custom oak cases. "When Howard Spenser, Junior hired Karl Schlagel to build these shelves. Everything exceptional in Moorhaven was Karl Schlagel's work. The crown molding, the bannister spindles, the dovetailed drawers in the butler's pantry. I thought the ransom money might be hidden in this library, but I'm wrong. We'll need to go up to the butler's pantry. I think our answer is up there."

John led them up the grand central staircase, past the shrouded wing and down the long carpeted hall. He opened the door to the butler's pantry, and stepped inside. The empty room was cold. It smelled of pine tar and dust. John ran his fingers along a row of lockers. His footsteps echoed as he crossed the empty room.

"When Camilla gave us the tour, she showed us that these lockers and drawers have carved pulls." John pointed to a row of small birds for illustration. "Shells, birds, stars, edelweiss. That tells me that Karl Schlagel was here." John crossed the floor toward a tall linen press. "I wanted to check this locker in particular, because it's the only one that has a carved heart for a pull."

Howard guffawed. "Joke's on you, Detective. That locker's purely decorative. It doesn't open. Never has."

"That's because it's not a locker, or a drawer." John clicked the carved heart to the left, and a horizontal panel popped open. "It's a tray." He slid the tray open on its silent ball bearings.

"Oh, that's marvelous!" Julia handed Libby to Addison. "Is the ransom money there?"

John felt the dusty breath of history as he studied the mint condition, vividly colored, neatly stacked gold certificates. History was alive, and it was playing with his head. Karl Schlagel had been the last person to touch these bills, four generations ago.

Julia tentatively reached out her hand. "Why are the bills red? Is this really the money?"

"Flip it over," John said. "You're looking at the reverse side. That's why they were called gold backs."

Addison cradled Libby against his neck. Rocking her gently, he stared over Julia's slim shoulder. "Does the money still belong to us? To the family, I mean?"

"Yes. The money is still yours. It was always yours, to begin with."

"Damn shame it's worthless," Agent Mayas noted.

"It's not," John said. "Gold certificates were removed from circulation, remember? The Treasury shredded ninety-nine point nine percent of them."

Chief Nunn frowned. "What does that mean, Detective Jarad?"

Julia turned the bill over in her hand. "It's not real money anymore, right?"

"It's not legal currency," John continued, "but each one of those $20 certificates is now a collector's item, since the rest were destroyed. In mint condition, like these are, each one of those bills is worth about $750 to a numismatist."

"I can't do that much math." Addison looked dazed. "What's the total? How much are they worth?"

"With 2,500 bills in the ransom packet, and each bill worth $750, the original fifty grand is now worth approximately two million dollars."

Chief Nunn's eyes went wide. Agent Mayas whistled.

Julia laughed, delighted. She clasped both hands beneath her chin. "Two million dollars? Are you serious?"

"Yes. You might consider donating it to the Cottage Hospital. They're in the middle of a fund raising campaign. It would pay for a nice Spenser wing."

"Not on your life!" Julia snapped. "We're keeping every dime of it. Isn't that right, Addy?"

Addison looked trapped. He studied the floor, and he wouldn't meet John's eyes.

"Sure thing, Jules. Whatever you say."

Julia lifted Libby from Addison's arms. Libby woke up, saw John, and she smiled.

"It's your call," John said. "The money belongs to you. I got my answer."

He turned and led the Chief and Agent Mayas toward the door. They slipped down the shadowy central staircase in silence, and continued along the dim hall. Together, shoulder-to-shoulder, they stepped through the double front door and into the light.

Chief Nunn she slid her sunglasses on. She laughed softly. "There's justice for you. The rich get richer, and the rest of us, well, we soldier on."

"You did solid work on this investigation, Detective Jarad." Mayas resettled his fedora. "Actually, you did solid work on both Spenser investigations. We still have that opening in the Boston Bureau we were holding open for Detective Allamand. She won't be using it. I'd be glad to put in a good word for you if you're interested."

"No, thanks."

John dropped his hands back into his pockets. He felt liberated. Libby Spenser was safe with her family, and Alice Spenser was remembered. He had entered law enforcement to solve Danny's disappearance, and he had solved it. Jackie's death had pushed him out. "I've made other plans." He needed to catch the four o'clock shuttle and get to Boston General, because Sarah, DJ, and little Jennie were waiting.

ABOUT THE AUTHOR

Martha Reed is an award-winning, independently published crime and mystery fiction author. Book one in her Nantucket Mystery series, THE CHOKING GAME, was a 2015 Killer Nashville Silver Falchion nominee for Best Traditional Mystery. Book two, THE NATURE OF THE GRAVE, won an Independent Publisher IPPY Honorable Mention for Mid-Atlantic Best Regional Fiction.

Martha recently completed a four-year term as the National Chapter Liaison for Sisters in Crime, Inc. She loves travel, big jewelry, and simply great coffee. She delights in the never-ending antics of her family, fans, and friends, who she lovingly calls The Mutinous Crew. You can follow Martha online at reedmenow.com or on Twitter @ReedMartha.